RUNNING FROM SOLACE

a novel

Presented to

Barbara Bush Branch Library

By

Barbara Bush Library Friends

**∴ Harris County
   Public Library**
   your pathway to knowledge

NAKIA R. LAUSHAUL

SERENDIPITY BOUND BOOKS
HOUSTON

RUNNING FROM SOLACE

Running from Solace
Copyright © 2011 by Nakia R. Laushaul

ISBN 13 - 978-0-9843682-4-2 ISBN 10 - 0-9843682-4-2
Library of Congress Control Number: 2001012345

Published by Serendipity Bound Books
Houston, TX

Printed in the United States of America
First Edition March 2010

Cover Photography and Design: Kayla Perez
Cover Design & Layout: Elena Covalciuc
Interior Layout: A Reader's Perspective
Editing: Shonell Bacon (CLG Entertainment) & D'edra Y. Armstrong (Speak Write Publications)

For Jazzi.
Fly, Jazzi! The world is waiting
for you. I love you.

RUNNING FROM SOLACE

a novel

They said you will never make it.
Prove them wrong.

CR BO

"You don't have to talk about your mother today. We could talk about something else instead," Dr. Dalton said as I took my seat after my third walk to look out of the scenic office window at the bustling traffic below.

"No. Now is fine."

I shifted in my chair one last time and placed both of my trembling hands, one on top of the other, in my lap. I chose not to lie on the sofa when she offered it to me—not this first time, at least. I would feel too vulnerable lying there, too exposed. I took a deep breath.

Dr. Dalton glanced at the timer ticking away on her expansive mahogany desk, and then looked back at me.

I was about to do one of the hardest things a person could do. *How do you tell a complete stranger that your mother used to beat you?* "I've waited long enough. I, uh—I'm ready. I swallowed a large gulp of nothing—hard. "Let's begin."

PART I
RUNNING FROM THE PAST

Naomi

ONCE, SHE FLUNG a heavy ashtray at my head. Blood spewed onto my new pink dress like red polka dots all because I didn't respond to her calling me, "Naomi! Naomi!" I was trying frantically to reach her special ashtray from underneath the bed. I didn't hear her the first time. By the second call, I could tell she was getting mad, but I almost had the gold colored ashtray in my hand when I heard her say, "If I call you one more time!" That did it for me; I knew I was getting a whooping. I took my time walking back to the living room.

"Don't make me call you again, Naomi," Mama said again as I approached her. I left a small distance between us as I presented her with what she was impatiently waiting for. She went crazy. Mama hit me right on the top of my head over and over again with the glass ashtray.

"You ungrateful little bitch!" she yelled repeatedly in my face. I tried to cover my head with my arms until they grew tired, and I gave up. Fury danced in her eyes and spit sprinkled over me like morning mist. My eyes burned from the tiny flecks of ashes that fell from the ashtray. I tried closing them tightly. Warm blood trickled slowly down my forehead and penetrated my eyelids and cooled the burning sensation.

"Yeah, you must like gettin' hit," Mama screamed so loud I wanted my ears to close. I preferred the deafening sound of peace when she whooped me and she was silent. Out of sheer luck at some point during the beating, I passed out. I usually did. *Thank God.*

When I woke up, I was lying on my bed, which almost never had any sheets on it. I was still wearing what was left of my tattered dress. It was covered in dried blood, more red than pink now. I didn't have the desire to go look in the mirror. I knew already, since this was not the first time. My eyes would be really fat, and this time, one only opened partially. I was able to barely peek out of it. Raised, sweltering, purplish bruises would cover my arms, back and face—the usual damage. My head throbbed. I couldn't lift my arms.

I was afraid to move, afraid to even breathe. I lay there as still as I could. I followed the dingy, white, laced hem of what was once my pretty dress, from my knee to my ankle and across the dirty mattress as it fell off the bed onto the floor where I could see it no more. I wanted to cry, but no tears came. *I must have run out of tears*, I thought as I managed a painful smile that made my head ache from the inside out even more.

"Nobody likes cry baby, bad-assed kids! Shut. The. Fuck Up!"

Mama hated it when I cried; she always said I only wanted people to feel sorry for me. So, if I had run out of tears, that would've made my Mama very happy. I would never have to hear her call me a cry baby anymore, and maybe she would smile at me like she did when I lit her cigarettes on the stove. Well, not like the time when I lit the skinny white one on both ends. I shivered a little when I thought of the whooping I got for doing that. How was I supposed to know when it didn't have the brown paper on one end of it? She'd always taught me to light the white end only.

Ever since that time, I would always ask first, "Which end, Mommy?" I didn't want to disappoint her again or make her mad.

I had an urge to go pee. I was comfortable and warm. I didn't want to move, plus that's when the pain reverberated through me. Of course my head hurt and I had some aches all over my body, but as long as I kept really still it wasn't that bad. It could have been worse, like some of the other times before. Moving was painfully impossible and I knew it, so I didn't

More than the pain, more than anything else, I didn't want Mama to wake up. She was lying right behind me. Her arm was gently positioned around my waist. Her hand rested on my stomach. I was balled in a knot with my back touching against her. I knew she was still asleep. I felt her breath blowing softly on the back of my neck. It felt nice. Every few minutes or so, I could hear her teeth grind against each other or her jaw making a popping sound. The noises terrified me. Still, that was when I loved her the most and felt the safest—when Mama was lying next to me, asleep. I didn't have the nerve to wake her up just to go. So, I just lay there quietly and watched the torn lace through one eye as I listened to her breathe peacefully until I fell asleep again.

Mama nudged me awake with kisses. Her juicy lips left wet marks on my cheeks. I opened my eye slowly. The day had allowed dusk to run its course and only a small amount of natural light filtered through the window.

Mama gasped as I turned toward her. Then she smiled. "Hey, Mama's baby," she cooed.

"Hi, Mama," I said drowsily.

I felt dampness easing up my back. I wondered how long Mama had been up. *Did she know? Did I pee on her?* So many thoughts raced through my mind. I didn't know what to do. I pretended to be terribly exhausted as she kissed me and explained what I needed to do so she wouldn't have to whoop me anymore. I needed to be a good girl and do exactly as she said so she wouldn't have to ever get angry.

"It's not good for little girls to not listen to their mothers," she said with tears in her eyes.

"Yes, Mama," was all I answered over and over again after every statement she made. I wanted her to go away. It hurt too much to nod my head or move my lips, for that matter. "I promise. I will be a good girl, from now on." I only hoped that I looked as sorry as I felt for making Mama angry again. That's what she was waiting for anyway. She wanted me to forgive her so she would be okay—until the next time. I agreed that I was wrong for not hurrying or answering when she called my name.

"I love you, baby," she said as she reached toward me.

I closed my eye and grimaced in anticipation thinking maybe she saw it, felt it. She saw me flinch and then snatched back her hand. I closed my eye quickly in preparation of her smack across my face. Mama hated it when I flinched. The hit took too long to come, so I peeked through my eye again. She was already walking out the door closing it softly behind her.

"I love you, too, Mama," I said to the empty room.

I had to get up and get changed before she came back. I remember willing my aching little body to move. I was tired, but Mama hated when I peed in the little bed we shared. I couldn't let her find out. There were already so many old stains on the smelly mattress and just as many spankings for creating them. No sooner than I raised myself up off of the bed, I heard the door open. I didn't turn around. I stared at the dust around the window sill over the bed. The tattered lace from my dress dangled and tickled my knee as I stood there imagining myself invisible.

"Naomi. Baby, did you pee on yourself?"

She didn't sound mad. I didn't say anything, taking a moment to decide whether I should tell the truth or not.

"MiMi?" she waited.

Okay, she wasn't mad or maybe she was trying to trick me. The only time she ever called me MiMi was when she was in a good mood.

"I…I'm sorry," I stammered. "I peed when I was…when I was sleep." I didn't turn around. I lowered my head and looked for the wet spot on the mattress with my one open eye. My wet underwear suddenly felt colder. The air hitting my damp dress sent a chill over me and I shivered, or maybe it was the impending beating that I knew was coming. I still didn't move, not even when I heard her sigh loudly. The pain all over my body began to come alive and my aches began to scream. I continued to stare at the window sill; the dust seemed so interesting. If I stared really hard I could see shapes. There's an N, like the N in Naomi. She started walking toward me. She put her hand on my shoulder.

"MiMi, you have to learn to wake up," she said. "Big girls don't pee on themselves while they sleep. You are almost six years old."

Just like I thought, no more tears; there were no more to cry. I waited, silently. She moved her hand and my shoulder tingled warm from her touch. I knew this was it; she was going to hit me. I heard her pull the zipper down on the back of my dress. The air brushed against my naked back and made it sting. I felt her hands tugging the dress off my shoulders and down my waist. It fell into a heap at my ankles. We stood like that for a moment. I felt her eyes piercing through me from behind.

"Take those wet panties off," Mama ordered as her heavy footsteps made their way out of the room.

I wasn't sure what was happening. *Was she going to whoop me naked?* I took my time removing my underwear. It hurt my stomach to bend down and I cringed as I pushed my panties down on top of the dress. My panties were so stretched that I was able to step out of them along with my dress at the same time.

I heard bath water running from in the next room. Mama came back in and started shuffling through the laundry hampers where we kept all of our clothes, both clean and dirty. She sniffed a pair of panties, and then pulled out one of her shirts. Finally she turned toward me. She was acting very strangely.

"MiMi, what are you just standing there for?" she asked with a puzzled look on her face. "Go get in the tub, baby."

I walked out of the room, confused. Mama almost never ran my bath. Maybe she was going to whoop me in the tub. I stood on my tiptoes and caught a glimpse of myself in the bathroom mirror as I passed it. I wasn't surprised at what I saw, same damage as usual. My legs didn't hurt that bad, so I lifted them easily over the side of the tub and sat in the really hot water without complaining. It was up to my waist. Mama came in and turned the water off. She sprinkled a white powder in the tub.

"This will make you feel better," she said softly. She sat on the toilet while she bathed me. I ignored the stinging sensation of my bruises as she washed me gently. She hummed the only Christian song I knew, "This Little Light of Mine."

"Lean back." She pushed me down in the water. It almost covered my entire head, but not quite. The warm soapy water stung as she poured it over my matted hair from a red, 7-Eleven cup that she kept on the side of the tub. She never attempted to wash my face. She hummed softly the entire time.

"Are you hungry?" Mama asked as she dried me off and rubbed oil all over my body.

"Yes, Mommy." I felt so much love as she helped me into her shirt. It was big enough to be a dress on me. But, it was hers and I was happy to wear it. I put the beating from that morning out of my head and fell into her arms as she hugged me and told me how much she loved me.

"What do you want to eat?"

"Umm, umm. Cereal," I exclaimed happily. "Captain Crunch Berries!"

Mama brushed my hair gently. "MiMi, you know cereal is for breakfast. Plus, you don't need all that sugar."

My heart sank with disappointment. Maybe I was asking for too much. "But, you can have it for dinner, just this one time," she said as she smiled at me, showing all of her teeth.

Everybody always said I had a pretty Mama and that I looked just like her, only darker. When she smiled, I thought she was pretty, too. Mama showed all of her teeth when she smiled. I didn't. Her teeth were all even and much whiter than mine. Mama said when I grew up I would probably have her pretty teeth, and that pretty teeth ran in her daddy's family. She said that my chipped front tooth would fall out and come back in perfect like hers one day. That's why we didn't get it fixed when she pushed me down the front porch steps and it broke.

Mama finished brushing my damp hair up in a ponytail and I followed her into the kitchen. I sat on the empty milk crate next to the stove and waited patiently as she prepared my cereal. She placed the big, plastic, margarine bowl carefully on my lap and told me to be careful and not to drop it because there was no more left. I held onto the bowl tightly and savored every sweet bite. I kicked my feet with glee because cereal for dinner was a special treat.

The phone rang, and I listened to Mama talk as I ate. She laughed and twisted the telephone cord around her finger. I knew it was a man on the phone. Mama had mostly men friends. I had to call them all uncle so I wouldn't forget their names and get her in trouble.

"Yeah, I'll see you later tonight," I heard her say as she hung up the phone smiling her big smile again.

I already knew what that meant. I was going to bed and Mama was having company. Mama told me that she was putting me to bed early because I needed my rest as though I didn't hear her making plans. She sprinkled the mattress with baby powder and laid a sheet over it from the hamper. She covered me with a thin, ripped blanket and gave me some medicine to help me sleep because I'd had a long day, she had said. I heard a knock on the front door just as she kissed me goodnight.

"Say your prayers. And don't forget to pray for Mama," she told me as she walked out the room. She turned off the light and shut the door behind her.

After a few minutes, I heard my Mama laugh. I could hear the two of them talking and wrangling with each other, causing the raggedy sofa to creak. "Come on, baby. You always teasing me," he said. Then I heard smacking, wet kissing sounds. Not too long after, Mama opened the door to the room we usually shared and whispered my name. I knew not to say anything because she thought I was already asleep.

"Baby, get back in here," he barked at her. He sounded irritated. "Before I give both of y'all some."

"What you was about to say again?" She slammed the door shut and went back to confront him.

"Oh, pretty girl, I was just playing," he said, laughing, trying to lighten the tone of his voice.

I wondered what he had for me. What is *some* and why was Mama upset when he said he wanted to give me something, too? She never got mad at any of the uncles.

I fell asleep listening to him moan loudly, telling my Mama, "That's it. Suck it real good, and Daddy'll give you some of dis."

Naomi

SOMETIMES, I CAN recall in vivid detail those days that changed my life for good. Other times, I don't remember too well. This, I remembered. I had recently turned six years old, but everybody told my Mama that I already acted like an old lady. She said it was because I was always being nosey when she watched her stories on TV, trying to be grown. I didn't like when people said that; it would make Mama so mad at me.

How could I act like the old lady who lived next door to us? All she ever did was smoke cigarettes and stare out of the window all day. She was always nice to me though, but her house still smelled like smoke and bacon all the time. My mama didn't like her. Her name was Mrs. Frances, not Miss Frances; she told me she used to be married and that her husband had died. Even though she was a widow, she still preferred to be called Mrs. Frances, out of respect.

Mrs. Frances used to be an elementary school teacher before she retired so she was always correcting me. She said I was not too young to use the correct pronunciation of my words. It was

Missus, and "you should be able to hear an R in there somewhere when you say it."

When we ran out of stuff, like milk or sugar at our house, Mama always sent me to ask Mrs. Frances because Mrs. Frances always told her "No!" and would slam the door in her face.

Mama quit going and sent me instead. "Go ask that nosey old bat next door for some sugar," she'd say, knowing Mrs. Frances would give me anything I asked for.

If I was out on the little porch our apartments shared, she would call me over to her side and tell me to close my eyes and open my hand. Most of the time, she didn't come all the way out of the house, but hung halfway out the rusty iron doorway. She would place something in my palm and once my fist made a tiny ball I could open my eyes and look. It was always the same thing, a small yellow and red wrapped piece of candy, Bit-O-Honey.

"Don't tell your mama, little suga," she said while smiling at me with her yellow-brown teeth.

Her breath smelled like cigarettes and I cringed every time she kissed me on my forehead leaving that stale smell on my skin. I would immediately run into our house after she closed her door, hide my treat under the mattress, and wash my face.

One time, I showed Mama my treat from Mrs. Frances, she snatched it right out of my hand. "Don't be out there beggin' nobody for shit," she said as she popped it greedily in her mouth. "Uggh! What is this? That's some nasty candy." She took it out of her mouth after she had chewed on it a few times. "Here. You can have this shit back." She offered me the distorted piece of candy.

I took it out of her hand and slipped it in the trash when she wasn't looking so she wouldn't get mad. That's why I began to hide my candy after that. It was our secret, me and Mrs. Frances. We had a lot of secrets that we were not supposed to ever tell my mama about. I trusted Mrs. Frances because she was always nice to me and I never heard her tell Mama about all the secrets.

One day, I was sitting outside on the top step peeling the green paint off of our concrete porch. It fascinated me that there was red underneath, and by scratching it with a little twig, I could make things. I sat outside for a long time and made shapes and letters. Mrs. Frances had helped me learn my ABC's, so I practiced writing them by digging in the paint. I wanted to get every letter just right before I showed Mrs. Frances.

Mama had company that day. Two of my uncles were over at the same time, so Mama told me to go outside and play, but not to leave the porch so she could keep an eye on me. Mama had left the front door open because it was almost summer, and she wanted the breeze to come in to cool off the house. Our electricity didn't work and Mama was trying to get the money together to get it turned back on.

I sat outside until my stomach began to growl and I had to go pee really bad. All the big kids were coming home from school, bouncing down the street eating chips and drinking sodas, making me thirsty. I got up and twisted the handle on the iron screen door. It was locked. I pressed my face against the rusty white holes in the door and tried to peer in with one eye, but I couldn't see anything. The holes were so dusty that they were merely circles of caked-in dirt. I didn't want to knock and disturb Mama because I knew she was in our bedroom with the door closed. The cassette player was playing Mama's favorite song by Prince; she played it so much even I knew the words. *Little red corvette. Little red corvette. You need a love that's gonna lasst. Little red...*

I leaned on the iron door singing and suddenly it swung open. I tripped and fell back on my bottom. Uncle Ray stepped out the door and knelt down on one knee in front of me.

"Hey little mama. You okay?" he asked.

He placed his hand on my shoulder and pulled me up onto my feet. I was so embarrassed that I looked down and stared at the empty holes of my pink and white tennis shoes. "Look, your string is untied. Let Uncle Ray help you." He reached behind me and held up the string to my halter top, the other string dangled in front of me. The flap flipped forward onto my stomach which left my bare chest exposed. I crossed my arms over myself in an attempt to hide my flat chest.

He laughed. "Girl, you ain't got nothing to look at. Not yet, anyway."

He put both of his knees on the ground, still holding my halter string. The screen door creaked as it swayed back and forth in the breeze. Although I didn't look up, I felt him watching me.

"Turn around and let me tie your shirt up for you." His voice was so deep that it clapped in my ears like thunder. He seemed so big and everything about him frightened me.

"No thank you."

He nudged my nose playfully. "Silly, unless you got hands behind your back, you're gonna need a little help." He laughed again. "Turn around."

It was something about his laugh that made me uncomfortable. I didn't like it. His breath was bitter and shot directly into my nose. I wondered why all the grownups smelled like cigarettes. It must have been a grown up thing. When I grew up, I wasn't gonna smoke.

"Turn around," he repeated.

My feet remained planted in place; I was almost never around men alone, only if Mama went to the bathroom or was in the kitchen. Certainly, they never talked to me or acknowledged my presence. He was different. Maybe he was okay. Maybe he was the same uncle that wanted to give me something another time Mama had company. I began to get excited just thinking about getting a piece of candy or some other treat.

"Where's my mama?" I lifted my eyes from the floor, still not looking in his face. I studied the cracked mirror on the wall.

"Oh, yo mama still taking a little nap." He stood and pulled both strings to my halter and began to tie them back together. "Umm, what happened to you?" He started to ask me something, but must have decided against it and was quiet again. Standing up, still gripping my shoulder he pushed me into the living room. He was really tall. "Well, uh. I betta get back to work, lil mama."

I went to go pee and he went into the kitchen. When I came out, I sat in my usual spot on the blue milk crate and watched him move around our tiny kitchen. I thought maybe he was cooking something to eat because flour was getting everywhere, but it didn't smell like anything I'd ever want to eat. Every time he looked at me, I'd look away or I'd count the lines on my hands. We could hear the Prince tape thumping and still playing from the bedroom. Every once in a while he would move and shake to the beat, causing me to giggle a little. I wondered how the radio was still playing.

"How come the radio work without electricity and not the refrigerator?" I'd asked Mama that same question the night before.

All she said was, "Quit asking stupid questions!"

I was happy that Uncle Ray was nice and explained how a radio could work with both batteries and by plugging it into the wall. "Oh," I said, my curiosity satisfied.

"Whatcha cooking?" I asked. I was finally getting comfortable enough to talk to him. I was so hungry, I hoped he'd hurry up and finish whatever he was doing so I could have some of it. Just the sound of the pots opening and closing and the odorless steam rising made my stomach growl.

"Well...I uh...uhhh. I'm not making actual food...I'm—uh"

My stomach started to growl really loud, cutting him off mid-sentence.

"Damn, little girl! You must be really hungry." He opened the refrigerator. "Y'all ain't got shit in here." He stared at the empty shelves in disbelief. "Nothing."

"Mama threw everything away because it got bad. No lights." I shrugged my shoulders.

"Oh, yeah. Well, what did you eat this morning?"

I thought about it for a minute. *Nothing.* The truth was I hadn't eaten since the night before. Earlier that morning, Mama had told me to mix what was left of the powdered milk with a little water and that should hold me for a while.

"Cereal," I lied. "And there ain't no more." I held up both my hands and shrugged my shoulders when I said it.

There was never any, but I was too embarrassed to tell him that. Mama always said she could tell when I was lying. I wondered if he could tell. He looked at me again and I felt embarrassed about our empty cabinets.

"Can I have some of what you cooking?" I asked him once more. I was hungry. He walked toward me and reached for my face. As his long, bony fingers came at me, I closed my eyes and reared back. I covered my face with my hands.

"I'm not gone hurt you." He pushed my hands down to my lap and stooped in front of me. "Who did that to your face?"

I felt uncomfortable when people asked me about my bruises. I had almost forgotten about them. For the most part, the pain was gone, but the bruising and swelling faded slowly. I climbed onto the toilet every morning to get a good look in the mirror just to see.

"Tell me, did your mama do that?"

Mama always told me to tell people that I got the bruises play-ing with Mrs. Frances' cat, unless it was Mrs. Frances who asked. I didn't have to tell her anything. I was supposed to just tell my mama and she would go over there and tell that nosey bat to mind her own damn business if she had any.

"I was playing with the cat next door."

"A cat couldn't do all that. But if you gonna lie about it, Imma just mind my own." He muttered a couple of curse words under his breath about my mama being trifling and turned the slight corner leading toward the bedroom. He tapped lightly on the door with his fist.

"Nola. Eh Nola!" he called my mother's name. "Yo baby out here hongry."

Still no answer. He knocked a little harder, causing the door to rattle the next time as he called Uncle C. They must have been sleeping really hard because nobody answered him.

"Do I look like a fucking babysitter? Shit. I'm out here trying to make this money." He kicked the door and walked away, startling me. I jumped.

Walking back into the kitchen, he saw that he scared me. "Oh, don't worry, lil mama, I ain't gon' do nothing to you. Those fools just wanna lay up all damn day and I'm tryna get paid, you know." He grabbed me by the hand, snatching me up off the crate. "Let's go get you something to eat. You like McDonald's?"

Of course I loved McDonald's, but I wasn't supposed to go past the porch. I tried to snatch my hand away. "I'm not supposed to leave the porch." If my mama woke up and I was gone, I would really get it. I don't think he heard me because he practically dragged me down the three paint-chipped steps. "I'm not supposed to leave the porch!" I repeated. I was excited to be going to McDonalds and nervous because Mama would have a fit if she woke up and found me gone. I only stopped protesting because my stomach was growling and he wouldn't let me go.

It turned out that he was very nice. He let me play on the big yellow Ronald McDonald statue standing outside the doors. I put my tiny feet next to Ronald's big giant red boots. Uncle Ray had a huge stack of money and told me I could have whatever I wanted. I got my first ever happy meal and an ice cream cone. On the way home, I dropped my ice cream. He didn't yell or hit me, and we turned around and went back for another one. He bought two just to be sure because he wasn't going back again, and he let me eat them both.

I had so much fun that I got tired walking home. He pulled me up and carried me like a baby in his arms. Mama never picked me up when I was tired. She would only snatch my arm and jerk it real hard, saying, "Come on, shiiit. I'm tired, too!"

CB & BD

I woke up lying on the living room floor wrapped in a blanket. The little Happy Meal toy was grasped tightly in my hand. I got up to go look for Mama. A light from the street outside the window cast a faint glow into the room which gave just enough brightness for me to make my way through the dark house. I assumed that Uncle Ray must have left already. The kitchen was empty and I was the only one in the living room.

I tiptoed to our bedroom and the door was open. From what I could see, there was no movement and the sound of Mama grinding her teeth filled the room. Mama was a real hard sleeper, so I braved it and went in. I stepped on the clothes that littered the bedroom floor as I walked up to the bed. I put my hand out so I could feel for her body. A hand reached out and grabbed mine.

"Whatchu doin' in here?" Uncle C whispered.

"Oh, I…I am looking for my mama," I whispered too.

"Well, she sleep." He held my hand and pulled me closer toward the bed. Mama kept grinding her teeth. The skin on his hand was rough and scratchy. He had always scared me for sure. Most men did. Chills ran down my arm from his touch.

"Oh, you cold, lil mama?"

I lied and said yes, hoping he would let me go or that Mama would wake up. "Get in the bed with us then." He was still whispering. I tried to pull my hand out of his. I didn't like the sound of his voice. I wanted to get away. He let my hand go. I scampered away as fast as I could back under my little blanket which I rolled myself in tightly.

Something in my heart told me he was gonna follow me. I became aware of every sound. The grasshoppers chirped outside. The blinds fluttered against the open window. I heard his big feet slap the floor. Mama grinding her teeth. The bed creaked as he raised himself out of it. It all sounded like an eerie song from a late night show on Elvira. He was on his way. I didn't know what to do.

"Why you run out like that?" he whispered as he crouched over me. "Don't be scared of me."

I didn't move. I didn't say anything, just watched his shadow through the darkness.

"Hellooo." His heavy voice was right next to my face. "I need you to do something for me. Can you, MiMi?"

"What?" I asked from underneath the blanket.

"Scratch my back for me. Please."

"Umm, my mama will scratch yo back for you."

"Nola still sleep." It seemed like Mama answered with more teeth grinding. "You wanna go wake her up? Go ahead."

If that was all he wanted, then it couldn't be that bad. I wasn't crazy. I was not waking up Mama. I poked my head out. He lay on the floor with his back turned to me as though he knew I would do it. I was still wrapped in the blanket, with only my arms sticking out. I touched his back as gently as I could with my nails.

"Yo mama told me you sometimes scratch her back until she goes to sleep." My nails ran over the bumps on his back. I didn't feel well at all. "Harder. A little lower." He whispered, moaning in appreciation.

Suddenly, he flipped over. His body thudded against the hard floor. The light from the street lamp came through the windows. He only had on a pair of shorts and he wiggled like a fat snake until he had them off.

"Scratch me right here," he said as he grabbed my hand and moved it down between his legs.

I had never seen a naked man before, so of course I was petrified. I wanted my mama to wake up, but she was still mincing her teeth in the next room. He squeezed my wrist harder.

"Touch it!" he ordered.

"I don't want to. I want my mama."

"Really? Well, Nola touch it all the time. Do you want me to go and tell her you out here being bad and not listening to me?" He moved to get up.

"No, no. Please don't," I answered quickly.

There was barely any light in the room to see the anger flash across his face, but I felt it in the grip he had on my wrist. I didn't know what else to do, so I touched it—lightly. He moved his hand from my wrist and covered my hand with one of his big calloused ones, scratching my skin with his. He guided my hand up and down his thing, slowly at first. It expanded in my grip and he started to moan. He moved my hand faster and faster. He made the same sounds I heard all the other uncles make when they came over late at night and I was supposed to be asleep and not eavesdropping with my ear to the bedroom door.

I closed my eyes and imagined that my tears were racing themselves inside my body. I had run out of them long ago, but at that moment I wished I had some to streak my face like rain on a dirty window. As I stood there holding his grimy fat thing in my hand, my mind began to wander. What were tears for anyway? I had cried a million times and had they saved me before?

He moved my hand faster and faster. Jerking wildly back and forth, his face contorted into an evil snarl. He held my hand so forcefully in his grip that my entire body shook as he jerked. Suddenly he stopped moving. His eyes fixated over my shoulder and the look of fear replaced the ecstasy that had just lit his eyes. Morning rushed into the room as light played peek-a-boo between the blinds on the window. Everything was illuminated and I could see him clearly.

"You!" Mama screeched. "Son of a..."

I never had time to turn around before she was standing right next to me. "What?" she yelled as she yanked me up and pushed me out of the way. "AreYouDoingToMyBaby?" She foamed at the mouth as her words ran together.

She pounced on him. She bit and clawed at him like an untamed beast. He attempted to block her blows with his big flabby arms. The shock of what was happening settled in and he finally slapped Mama so hard that she skidded across the living room and landed on the floor. She held her face wailing. I cowered in a ball in a corner near the front door.

"Bitch, don't you ever put yo hands on me! Don't you know who I am?" he said as he stood naked in front of us—shameless.

His thing squirmed limply between his legs. Mama got right back to her feet and rushed him again. Before she could get close enough to him, he extended one of his long arms and grabbed her around the neck as he punched her in the face. The sound of the blows seemed to bounce off of every pore of my body. I felt them all.

"Are you deaf? I ain't yo lil girl, I'll kick yo ass!" he shouted. "You better sit down somewhere."

He held her up off of her feet by her neck and shook her as though she were a tiny rag doll. Blood from her nose ran down and dripped past her lips and chin onto the floor. He didn't let her down on her feet. He threw her down on the floor in a heap and stormed off toward the bedroom. Mama laid there and moaned, holding her nose in her hand. I crawled over to her and caressed her hair and kissed her cheek.

"It's okay, Mama. Don't cry," I said.

"Nola, get yo ass in here and finish me!" He yelled from the bedroom.

The walls trembled under the weight of his anger. Mama didn't move. That was the first time a man ever laid hands on Mama. I knew because I'd always heard her bragging to her friends "I wish a mutha would." She would go on and on about all the things she would do and how she would kill any man that put his hands on her because she was from New Orleans and New Orleans women didn't play that.

"Nola!"

Mama got up and tugged down the hem of her bloody t-shirt. She ran her fingers through her long black hair and walked toward the bedroom.

"Don't go, Mama."

"I'll be right back, Naomi," she said with a little smile. She swiped her forearm across her nose and looked curiously at the blood as though it was the first time she had seen any.

"I'm scared," I pleaded with her. "Please don't leave me."

"I have to, baby. We need him. Nobody else gonna help me with these bills around here?" Mama went in the room. The bedroom door closed shut.

I heard them arguing in hushed tones as I tried to scrub his bitter scent from my hands in the bathroom. I went back to the living room and hid underneath the solace of my warm blanket and tried to sleep the new day away. Later that afternoon, right before the moon replaced the sun, the hum of the refrigerator was back and we had electricity.

CB BO

The next time he came over he didn't even look at me. But, the next time he came for me, Mama didn't stop him. He dropped some little white pebbles in her hand like the ones Uncle Ray made the day we went to McDonald's. Mama held them like a treasure in her fist and scurried into the bedroom. She never looked my way.

"Me and yo mama got a little deal. You understand?" He pulled green Jolly Ranchers candy out of his pocket and when I reached for some, he kissed me right on my mouth. His slimy tongue penetrated my lips and left them wet and sticky. I didn't like Uncle C. He pretended to be nice to me, but he really wanted to hurt me. Mama let him do it. She forced me to sleep in the room with him whenever he came over.

Mama's violence against me increased and the beatings became more frequent, more brutal after she started letting him touch me. She never hit me when he was there, but she hit me more when he took too long to come over. Mama would wait for him outside on the little porch and pace back and forth. If I got in the way, she'd lash out at me. Uncle C walked up as she hit me in the eye once and he slammed her, face down onto the porch.

She yelled as froth formed in the corners of her ashy lips. "I'm gone call the police on you! Mothafucka!"

She had lost one of her pretty front teeth. The blood and foam trickled down onto her shirt. He threw some pebbles at her. Mama scrambled around the ground like a dog to pick them up. After she retrieved her treasure, she retreated to the bedroom.

"I ain't gone neva let nobody hurt you, lil mama," he said, pulling me onto his lap.

I was confused about how I felt about him. He protected me from Mama, but he hurt me at the same time. And my mama—she changed. She didn't comb her hair or dress up in pretty clothes. Mama never laughed much after that. Her friends never came to visit. I never heard Prince playing on the little radio anymore. Our house became dark. Although Uncle C kept the lights on *in* the house, *our* lights refused to shine anymore.

Naomi

I WAS SITTING on the porch having a tea party with our neighbor, Mrs. Frances. It was a little chilly outside, so she made hot chocolate, and she served us from dainty little tea cups that had pink flowers painted along the rim, all the way around. Mama was asleep, so I was really enjoying myself, chatting away. Every few minutes, Mrs. Frances would lean forward in her rocking chair and look up and down the street.

"You looking for somebody, Mrs. Frances?" I asked.

"Are you?" I must have looked confused, because she said, "*Are you looking for someone?* Use complete sentences, Naomi."

"Are you looking for someone, Mrs. Frances?" I asked again.

She opened her mouth to answer when a long van pulled in front of our duplex. Mrs. Frances waved to the driver.

"Do you know that white lady? She coming to see you? She your friend?"

Mrs. Frances shook her head no, and got up and walked in her door, leaving it cracked open. I sat on the porch drinking my hot chocolate and watching the lady in the white van. I wondered why she took so long to get out because I wanted to see where she was going. Maybe she was lost. It was unusual for white people to be in our neighborhood, so that alone piqued my curiosity.

Mrs. Frances returned and sat in her chair with a grunt and rubbed her knees. She glanced back toward the street then said to me, "Come here, baby." Mrs. Frances never called me baby directly. She only said it when speaking about me to my mama: "You better stop hitting on that baby, Nola."

I stood in front of her and waited. She leaned back in her chair and rocked slowly. "You have had such a hard life for someone so young." Tears formed in her eyes. I put my head down and twirled my fingers around the end of my plaits. I didn't want to hear about what a bad person my mama was—not again. There were times when she was nice. "Yeah a hard...hard life."

She pulled my head up by my chin with her finger and looked me in the eyes. It was the first time that I'd noticed how gray her eyes were. "I know the Lord will take care of you. You have been through the worst." Tears streamed down her face. She waited as tears fell onto her healthy chest, then continued, "I promise things will get better, they always do."

She used the hem of her apron to wipe the tears from her eyes. Her other hand opened and exposed a whole handful of Bit O' Honey candies. My eyes grew wide as Mrs. Frances poured the candy into the little front pocket of my red checkered dress. She touched the scar underneath my eye, then pulled me close in an embrace and stroked the messy plaits in my hair.

"Excuse me, I am looking for..." the white lady from the van stood at the base of the steps. Through her thick glasses, she peered at a white piece of paper fastened to a clipboard.

"You in the right place," Mrs. Frances answered before the lady finished asking the question. "This is her," she said looking at me. "You're looking for Naomi."

"Well. Hello, Naomi."

She looked older standing so close in front of us than she did when she was sitting in the van. I put my hands in the front pockets of my dress and toyed with the candy. My head down, I stared at her big black shoes. They seemed too heavy for her little legs.

"Hello, Naomi," she said again.

"Hi." I never looked up.

"Now, she is a little shy, but she's as sweet as a Bit O' Honey. I hope you can find a good place for her. If I could, I would take her in myself."

"We will. Naomi will be well taken care of. Thank you for notifying us. Most people wouldn't do what you've done."

I knew they were talking about me, but I couldn't comprehend exactly what was going on. I tried to pay close attention. They talked as though I wasn't standing there. *A good place for me to do what,* I wondered. Whatever it was, I could feel that it wasn't going to be good. The whole situation seemed strange. I moved to my side of the porch and reached out to open the wrought iron screen door. I just wanted to get inside to be next to my mama. I hoped she was awake. I wished I had never come outside to have a hot chocolate tea party with Mrs. Frances.

Just as the cool handle turned in my hand, the white lady put her wrinkled one on top of mine. "Where you going, suga?"

"To see if my mama woke up."

"That won't be necessary. I'll just knock on the door and you stay right here with me," she said sweetly. She banged on the door with the clipboard and held my hand with her free hand.

My mama took her time coming to the door, and I assumed that she had been asleep. She hated for anyone to wake her up.

"What?" she yelled when she reached the door. "Who the hell is you?" She took one look at the white lady holding my hand from outside the door and immediately began cursing. She pushed the wrought iron screen open, narrowly missing the lady's face with it. "Turn my baby's hand loose." Mama snatched my hand out of the lady's and pushed me behind her as she got up in the lady's face.

"Uh. Uh, Nola. Nola Ba—Ba." Even I could tell that the white lady was deathly intimidated of my mama. Her ghost white face grew even paler until I thought she would disappear into the air around us. Her voice shook and her words carried no weight. Her fear was visible. My mama was the scariest person I knew. She was scarier than Uncle C, so I understood the woman's alarm.

"What!" Mama cut her off. Her voice sounded as sharp as a razor. A uniformed police officer appeared and stood at the edge of the steps with his arms folded. "And what the fuck do *you* want?" Mama cast her eyes in his direction. Nobody said a word. The air was tense, thick. I knew something wasn't right and my stomach began to hurt. Mama held tightly to my hand behind her back and her fingers trembled in mine.

"Go in the house, Naomi."

I didn't move. I was trying to understand what the policeman was doing at our house. What was this lady doing here? Why was everyone acting so weird?

"Stay here, sugar." The woman inhaled and continued in an unsteady voice, "That won't be necessary. We received quite a few complaints regarding a child being abused at this address. Do you want to tell me how Naomi got those bruises on her face?" She pointed at me.

"I don't have to tell you shit. Go in the fucking house, Naomi!" Mama shuffled from one foot to the other. "You can't come up to my house asking me about my damn child!"

Her anger sliced dangerously through her every word. She scratched her arms as she spoke. Her skin was dry and sounded like sandpaper brushing against dry wood. Mama's hair hadn't been combed in days and it was matted with flecks of lint sparkling through it. She fidgeted on one foot then hopped on the other. That was the first time I had paid much attention to my mother. She wasn't pretty anymore. Her white teeth were now decayed and yellowed. She made a sucking sound through her missing tooth.

"I understand your anger, Miss. Barnes, but I have an order to remove Naomi from your home and place her in protective custody." The lady was calm, despite Mama's menacing demeanor.

Mrs. Frances got up from her chair and started to go in her apartment. She was the first to make a move and all of our eyes turned toward her as though we'd been timed perfectly, synchronized with precision.

"You don't understand shit," Mama hissed. She turned her attention to Mrs. Frances. "I know it was you! You old fat cow! Why couldn't you just mind your own damn business?"

Mrs. Frances looked at Mama as though she wanted to rip her head off, her eyes narrowed with an anger that I'd never witnessed in her before. Everyone was angry, for that matter. They all knew what was going on, while all I knew was that it was about me.

"Ms. Barnes, that is not necessary, especially in front of your child." The white lady tried to reason with Mama.

"Why didn't you keep your hands to yourself? You've been treating this baby like a punching bag long enough," Mrs. Frances said. "Don't you think I could hear what was going on through those paper thin walls? I stayed on my knees for this child day and night. How long did you think I would just keep doing nothing? You need help, Nola."

She turned to face me. She blinked to keep the tears from spilling out of her eyes. I wanted to say something, but I just put my head down. I was embarrassed that she'd been hearing everything that had happened to me. She thought my mama was a bad person. I wondered if she heard me scream when Uncle C put his big thing between my legs. I wondered what she thought of me. Did she think I was a nasty little girl like my mama said? I begged Uncle C to stop, but he wouldn't. He put a pillow over my face until I passed out sometimes. Tears ran down my cheeks as I realized that Mrs. Frances knew everything. Tears that I hadn't been able to shed in a real long time rushed out of me.

I was sure that she also knew that my mama had turned into a crackhead. I knew, because that is what my Uncle C had begun to call her. "You ain't shit but a crackhead bitch." He never called her Nola anymore. He tossed crack at her every time he wanted to be alone with me, and she'd go away. "Here, go suck on yo' glass dick!" he'd tell her. Sometimes, Mama wouldn't even leave the room and lit it in front of us.

Just the night before he came over with some of his friends and they all went in the room with Mama. I listened to her scream as she begged for them to stop hurting her. I heard them laughing. I hid under my blanket, afraid that they would come and get me, too. After a long time in the room with the men, they left and Mama went and sat in the bathtub for a long time crying. I went in and offered her some water, but she knocked the glass out of my hand. She slapped me until my nose bled for ruining her life.

Mama was nothing like she used to be. She never wore makeup anymore, or laughed, or combed her long hair in pretty styles. Mama would lie in the bed all day and all night, too, if Uncle C didn't make her get up. If it wasn't for him, I would have had no food to eat because she didn't cook either.

Mrs. Frances knew everything, which was more than I'd ever told her. She looked at my Mama with disgust then turned her attention to me. "Don't worry, Naomi. No matter where you go, you will be safer than right here. Nobody will ever hurt you again as much as you've already been hurt. I'll be praying for you."

She went in her door and closed it gently. We all looked at each other. It was as though we were all waiting for the end of the world to rescue us from the moment. Then, we wouldn't have to do anything. Mrs. Frances turned the deadbolt on her door, it echoed in the silence.

Click. Click.

The policeman coughed to clear his throat. The white lady looked back at him and nodded as though they knew something me and my Mama didn't.

As if someone yelled go, my mother shouted "No!" and pulled me up into her arms. It was then that I became terrified.

"Don't! Don't take my baby away. Please," my mother begged. "I can do better! I promise!" Mama squeezed me so hard I could barely breathe.

I fought the lady, kicking and screaming along with my mother. I wrapped my bony arms tightly around my mother's neck and shoved my feet out to kick the stranger that had invaded my life. The old wrinkly, white lady with peppermint breath tried to physically rip me from my mother's arms.

The lady tried desperately to get me on her side. "This is for your good, suga. Let go, sweetie."

Tears, arms, snot, pleading, legs, vomit, feet, I was in the heat, a knot—the center of a desperate tug-o-war battle. Mama was so frail that I did most of the resisting for the both of us. I didn't want to leave. All I knew was that I belonged with my mama.

Exasperated, the tall policeman, who stood stoically at the base of the steps watching, finally intervened. He plucked me right out of the mayhem with one long arm. He hurled me over his shoulder and stomped down the walkway to the white van. He tossed me in like a rag doll and shoved the door shut. With an air of finality, he crossed his arms over his huge chest and dared anyone to say a word. We stopped fighting it. I was leaving—just like that.

The old lady smoothed out her tousled black skirt and huffed her way into the van. She popped a peppermint in her mouth, started the van and held her chest for a moment.

I watched my mama from the rear window. Her bare fists hammered into the concrete, beating at it until her own vomit splattered up into her face. She sprawled face up in the middle of the street. Her lips moved, but I couldn't hear the sound of her wails over the encompassing roar of the van.

In my mind I've always imagined she was screaming, "Bring me back my baby!" as the van drove away.

"It's for your good, suga. Here, have a peppermint."

She passed a hard candy over her shoulder as though whatever was in the tiny wrapper was supposed to make it all better. I clutched the peppermint in my fist and buried my face in the hard leather seat while she explained what was going to happen to me. She promised that I'd be safe from then on.

"What about my mama?" I asked through my tears.

"She will never be able to hurt you. Ever again."

I never saw my mother after that day. It's hard for me to picture clearly what she looks like.

 C D

"You know what's funny, Dr. Dalton? Mrs. Frances and the social worker were both right. Nobody ever hurt me as much as Nola and Uncle C did ever again. But they should've told me that no one would ever love me either."

"I'm sure that's not true, Naomi. I bet you have wonderful people in your life that love you very much."

PART II
RUNNING FROM THE PRESENT

Naomi

H EY BABE WHAT time are you coming home?" I asked
sweetly—*well almost.*

"I don't know. We've been really busy at the shop."

Jake was lying through his teeth. I could always tell. Actually, we
both were. He didn't want to come home just as much as I didn't
want him to. I was so tired of arguing with him about making
love every single night, and because it was Saturday, he'd really
expect some.

"Well, I miss you, honey, and I cooked your favorite dinner—
smothered pork chops. You know I hate to eat alone." I lied again.
I had already eaten and left his food in the microwave and had
already tidied up our little kitchen. "Love you." I smacked a fake
kiss into my cell and snapped it closed with a smirk.

Jake wasn't coming home anytime soon. "Still at the shop," I
scoffed out loud at his lie.

Did he really think I didn't hear the choir singing in the back-
ground? I knew he was at that church. He spent more time with
those holy fakers than he did with me. After two years of mar-

riage, I was still trying to figure out why I got married in the first place. I actually preferred to be alone. All the pretending was for the birds.

I pulled out my favorite smooth jazz CD and popped it into the multi-disc changer. I had trouble getting it to play. Jake was into the most sophisticated electronic equipment that I couldn't figure out half the time. Our home was straight out of a Best Buy circular. We had every electronic trinket imaginable. There was a remote control for everything, including the lights. I knew how to use, well—none of it. I laughed out loud to myself, *Damn, I guess I do need him for something.* I pressed miscellaneous buttons on the huge remote that operated everything we owned until the music finally blared through the massive speakers and the floor vibrated. I poured myself another glass of Pinot and powered up my laptop to work.

Another evening of peace without my husband trying to climb all over me—*ooh priceless.* I loved my husband just as much as he loved me. It was just that in reality, we wanted different lives. He wanted a big house in the burbs. I was happy living in our condo in the heart of the city. The noise, the traffic, the lights, and all the people moving around downtown Houston excited me. I would sit out on the patio of our sixth floor condo overlooking Texas Avenue for hours on end. I loved to watch as people came and went about their business below. I made up destinations for them and wives waiting for the men at home, even adulterous affairs. It was strange; I never imagined any of them having children. I loved imagining that nobody was truly happy at home—like me.

Not that I was miserable. It was just that Jake and I agreed on next to nothing, most of the time. For instance, Jake wanted a dog. Since I hated pets, I on purpose, picked a condo with a no pet clause. When Jake confronted me about it, I feigned innocence even though he asked me when we signed the lease. Jake wanted a house full of children, somewhere in the arena of about four. I didn't want any. Not one crumb snatcher. I meant it. I told him so on numerous occasions even before we were married.

About a year into our marriage, he confessed that he hadn't given up on his dream to have kids. He held on to the hope that I would change my mind one day, before we got too old. Humph, I don't think he listened closely or maybe he didn't read my lips. No kids, *period.* The real truth of the matter was that I was afraid to have them and doubted if I could anyway. But no was no and I didn't feel like I had to explain everything to him in detail even if he was my husband; it was my personal business.

Jake was a great guy and would be a fantastic dad. I loved seeing him with his nieces and nephews. He was kind and compassionate. He was still a great provider even though he never went to college. He earned more than a few certificates in automotive repair at the local adult school. Actually, that was how we met. I took week-long fundamentals of car care course to learn the importance of preventative maintenance after I'd burned out the engine in my third car since college. Jake was the instructor and the first time he leaned over me as he watched me check the oil, my heart danced in excitement. I literally felt the pounding on the outside. I had always been awkward around men, so after much persistence on his end and from my best friend, I finally agreed to go out with him.

After our first date, we became inseparable. He moved in with me after six months and within our first year of dating, we got married, and that was two years ago. Jake had a huge loving family and wanted a grand wedding with everyone and their mama in attendance. I told him we should save all that money and use it as a down payment on our first place. As usual, I was able to talk him into doing what I wanted. We ran off to the Cayman Islands for a week and had a simple, yet beautiful ceremony on the beach. I dodged having to explain our uneven wedding party. I had no family and very few friends to invite.

Our relationship happened so fast I barely had time to think about what I was doing. I had never been in love before. Come to think of it, I had never had a real boyfriend. Jake was the first man I ever trusted, not completely, but enough. No man deserved complete trust. But, before him, I submerged myself in work and used my studies as an excuse not to date by night. That man came along and convinced me to believe that goodness existed in the world. He pushed me to be successful and applauded my professional progress. He helped me study when I was finishing up my Masters in social work. I then, encouraged him to start his own high-end automotive repair shop.

I thought we complemented each other so well. He showed me that love is a joy and not a burden. When he looked at me, I felt vulnerable. When he wrapped his huge arms around me, I felt protected and loved. Yet, I was alone again just as I had been every night that week. Not that I'd admit it out loud to Jake, but it was my fault.

I was a pitiful sight, sitting there wearing my favorite silk PJ's, sipping Pinot, and picking my marriage to shreds while my husband ran to his church family looking for love. *I was such a coward.* I didn't have the guts to tell him the truth about me and why I was so emotionally distant. Instead, I disconnected from him and the rift dug deeper into our relationship every day. I'd contemplated over and over again how to tell him about my past. I wanted to come right out and say it over breakfast when his mouth was full of toast, when he could only chew and not respond. *Honey, I was molested as a child. My body was so damaged I don't think I'll ever be able to have children. There, now you know so please pass the jelly.*

I wanted to share unabashed honesty with him. He deserved it. If I didn't do something, Jake would leave me. I was sure of it. He had every reason to go. He deserved so much more than a beat up woman like me for a wife. Tears rolled down my cheeks. I threw a few of the overstuffed pillows to the floor partly in frustration and partly to make more room for my long legs on the huge sofa. Maybe I need counseling like my best friend had suggested many times. I let the tears fall as I fell into a restless sleep.

I woke to the sound of the CD scratching. The CD must have rotated and Ro Zimmerman's raspy voice filled the room repeating the same two words over and over again. *Love me. Love me.*

Love me. It took a minute for my eyes to focus in the dark. I rose to my feet and stretched; my foot knocked over the glass of Pinot and hit the metal chair leg. "Shit!" I cursed as I hobbled over to the stereo. The time flashed in bright fluorescent green numbers, 3:40 A.M.

I scurried into the kitchen and flicked on the light. Jake's dirty plate was in the kitchen sink. For some reason, seeing his plate pissed me off. I didn't hear him come in but just knowing he left me asleep on the sofa irritated me. Maybe our marriage was horrible just like I'd imagined. Maybe he didn't even want me next to him in bed anymore. As I cleaned up the spilled wine, I wondered if he was having an affair with some churchy chick. No, not Jake, and I erased the thought from my mind. Jake was a good man. I was the problem.

Jake snored gruffly as I eased into bed next to him and pulled the cool sheets right up to my chin. I adjusted my body to face him and threw my arm around his waist. I watched him sleep. With all my heart, I loved that man. I could see his silhouette slightly in the dark. His hair was cut low and his sideburns connected sexily to his goatee which only accentuated his full masculine lips. Jake visited the barber weekly because he refused to be the stereotypical grimy mechanic people imagined. I watched as his chest rose and fell and the sound of his breathing coupled with the comforting sound of his snoring created a soothing lullaby. Except, every time he exhaled, I caught a whiff of souring alcohol on his breath. Okay, so maybe he *was* doing something.

The ugly thoughts returned and simmered in my mind. Unless Jesus himself was at church last night turning water into wine for their Saturday night service, something was definitely wrong. My heart refused to beat at the thought of Jake not loving me and I held my breath. Maybe I didn't show it all the time or appreciate his overzealous way of demonstrating his love, but I really did love him. I became afraid of losing the only semblance of love that I'd ever known.

I wanted to rewind time. I wanted to go back to the first time Jake said he loved me. I wanted to tell him everything. I just didn't want him to think less of me because I didn't come from a good family like he did or because I lost my virginity when I was six years old. Even after two years of marriage, I continued to harbor feelings of insecurity and worry that the secrets of my past would reach into my future and take Jake away from me.

Jake began to move around in our king-sized bed and finally came to rest with his arm wrapped around me. I moved my body in closer to his, my heart even closer to him. I could hear his heartbeat echoing in my own. Tomorrow will be different. *I will tell him tomorrow and we could go from there.* I began to relax in my husband's embrace; it felt really good to be held for a change. Tomorrow I'd forget about him leaving me asleep on the sofa alone and not pick a fight. I needed to make a real effort to be satisfied with his love. *Satisfied,* yeah that's what I was going to be. My decision helped me drift into a peaceful sleep, safe in my husband's arms.

CΆ ℬϽ

"What's that smell?" Jake asked as soon as I opened my eyes.

He stared at me through the full-length mirror in our bedroom. He was already up and almost ready for church and I had just settled into my sleep good. It sure didn't look like he was going to ask me to go with him today like he usually did. I pulled the cover over my head to hide the disappointment in my eyes. Jake was an eye reader. A tone reader. And a mind reader. He held the trophy for deciphering my intentions just by looking and listening to me. Jake had three older sisters, which put me at a serious disadvantage, and I couldn't get anything past him.

"Huh?" I yawned. "Oh that. It's eucalyptus. They put some in vases around the office at work, and I thought it smelled divine." I pretended again. *Didn't I make an agreement with myself to be open and honest last night?* "So, I bought some. Do you like it?" *Please*

ask me. Just this last time and I'll get up and be ready in five minutes.
I wanted nothing more than to spend the day with my man, especially today when I had something very important to tell him. If
he walked out the door without me, I knew I would lose the will
to do it—again.

"Yeah. It's different, but it's still nice," he said sitting on the
edge of the bed.

I snatched the cover back down from over my head and watched
him put on his socks and shoes. He always put on his clothes in
the same order—pants, socks and shoes before his shirt because
that was the way his daddy did it. Daddy's boy. I smiled.

"Maybe I should get some for the shop," he said.

"What you should get is some lotion for your ashy heels." I
giggled as I tried to sound playful despite the trepidation in my
heart. "Look, you just snagged your stockings," I chided.

He looked down at his foot with a handsome boyish grin on his
face and saw the hole on his heel. I got out of the bed and walked
across the cool hardwood floor to the mahogany dresser on his
side of the bed and dug around for another pair of gray dress
socks and tossed them over to him.

I was mildly irritated. If he didn't hurry up and ask me to go
with him, I was going to lose my mind. I walked into the bathroom and began to brush my teeth as I rummaged under the
bathroom cabinet in search of the lotion.

"Wait honey, lotion first," I said to him with the toothbrush
dangling out from between my lips. I walked back into the bathroom. "And I bought too much eucalyptus. You can take the rest
for the shop."

Here we were, with all these problems in our marriage, namely
me. And I was talking about eucalyptus and ashy feet! Skirting the
issue was the normal way for me to deal with my marriage. *Okay,
Naomi, just get yourself dressed, surprise him and go, he's not gonna ask,*
I coached myself. I plugged up the curlers then turned on the
shower and stepped in.

I wondered how much time I had. I rush scrubbed my body. I didn't think he'd eaten breakfast, so that would buy me a few minutes. I could grab a cereal bar on the way out, I plotted. If I pinned my hair up instead of wearing it down that'd save lots of time. Especially since I forgot to put on my shower cap and the steam for sure would be a nightmare on my hair. I'd need another half an hour to pull that together.

I watched him brush his hair through the foggy shower door. He looked like a shadow. Disappearing and reappearing from focus right before my eyes. With my important parts clean, I quickly hopped out of the shower before I realized that I was in all my naked splendor. Jake was closest to the towels, so I bashfully asked him to hand me one. He examined me so intensely with his eyes that I clammed up and snatched the towel from his hand. A feeling of shame blanketed me as he ogled my body. I felt like taking another shower.

"Baby, why do you always do that? You're perfect." I rolled my eyes at him. The moment was ruined. He walked out of the bathroom saying, "I wish you could see it, too."

Whatever, I was gonna ignore that little episode. Bottom line, I was going to church with my husband. *Period.* I rubbed my body down with baby oil and went into the walk in closet that was right off the bathroom. I pulled out my no fuss, black wrap dress and grabbed a simple pair of black shoes.

Gospel music streamed through our condo and Jake sang along with the music as he rattled pots and pans in the kitchen. I'm ashamed to say, but I didn't know the words to any gospel songs, and my husband knew them all. The local gospel station was programmed on his radio and when I used his truck I was stuck listening to the gospel morning show on my way to work instead of NPR. I had to admit, I did like listening to those funny Bishop skits. He pretty much summed up how I saw those fake, tithes preaching men of the cloth. Well, Jake's pastor was okay, considering they were boys. I actually loved and respected Paul.

I stood in the bathroom mirror putting the finishing touches on my hair and makeup when Jake slid his arms around my waist and pulled me into him from behind. In my mind, I thanked God that I put on a short robe just seconds before he walked in. I didn't like for him to see me with no clothes and once was enough for today. If I was moving around, I didn't mind so much. It was when I was still that I felt so overexposed, like all of his attention was on my imperfections—my scars. It unnerved me feeling so vulnerable and powerless under the scrutiny of his eyes. The first time we made love, I wore my nightie the entire time. I still did when he let me. Not that we did it very often.

"Where you going today, beautiful?" he kissed me on the neck.

Jake smelled so good that I wanted to melt. If nothing else, he still had the same effect on me as the day we met. I leaned back into his affection, adjusting my body to fit perfectly inside his man groove.

"Umm. That's nice. What did you say again?" I asked coyly as I stalled for time.

"Where?" He kissed me between each word. "Are you going?" he asked with my earlobe tucked between his teeth.

He watched my reaction in the bathroom mirror the entire time. I pushed further into him. His manhood rapped anxiously at my back. I put the mascara in my hand down on the counter and turned to face him. I wanted to look up into his eyes while we kissed. He turned me back around to face the mirror.

"No. Watch." He demanded.

He kissed my neck and played with my nipples through the thin material until they were at full attention.

"You are so beautiful. I want you to see yourself." He untied my robe and held it together. My heart raced, no longer from his kisses, but from apprehension. I didn't want to see myself. He knew that. I didn't understand what had gotten into Jake. Why did he want to push me? I held my breath and tried to relax anyway because I didn't want an argument. *Let go.*

Carefully, he opened my robe just as an artist unveils a prized masterpiece. Our eyes met in the mirror. My heart raced. *Relax self.* This was crazy. I didn't need him trying to prove a point to me. *Relax self.* I mean I've seen my body a thousand times. Hell, it was my body. *Relax self.* I was the good wife and the bad wife on my own shoulders.

I counted backwards in my head to take my mind away from the moment as a relaxation technique. *Ten. Nine.* I pretended he wasn't there. *Eight.* My robe was wide open and my breasts were fully exposed. *Seven.* Chill bumps popped up on my arms. He kissed my shoulder, never taking his eyes off of me in the mirror. *Six.* Damn I was uncomfortable. I looked in the mirror and beads of sweat had gathered on my top lip. My robe hit the floor and I focused on the scar that ran up my inner thigh to my vagina.

Five. Four. He put one hand on the triangle between my legs. His body twined into mine from behind and it felt nice...but. Okay, counting worked...kind of. *Three.* I heard that counting would relieve my anxiety, but that was a lie. *Two.* His hand cupped my breast. He watched me. Loving me with his eyes. Feasting on the image of my body in the mirror. I became more self-conscious than ever.

I tried to manipulate my body around to face him. He pushed my legs into the counter and held me firmly from behind with his body. He pushed me forward until my legs were wedged between him and the counter. He held me pinned with his solid rock of a body behind me. I couldn't move. One more number to go. I should have started from twenty because I needed more time to count down. I was so anxious, anticipating his every touch. It's not that my body wasn't enjoying the foreplay. His hands were ... it was me.

My mind raced from the current moment to those long past. If I went with the flow, maybe I'd forget. Forget I was naked. Forget that my husband was taking advantage of me. No wait, he was my husband and couldn't take anything from me that I wasn't supposed to give. Oh, damn. I wanted to disconnect the lights and sirens roaring in my brain. I closed my eyes. I didn't need to see me. I knew I looked damaged.

My stomach twisted and turned. I heard the ceiling fan in the bedroom as it whirred, making me dizzy. The track lighting mounted over the mirror in the bathroom cast a bright spotlight on my torture. Jake was never so dominant; I don't know what got into him. My palms were sweaty. I was trapped inside of my mind. My body wanted him terribly, but my mind wouldn't let me accept the good feeling escalating and yearning between my legs. His tongue ran up and down my spine. Again, my self-consciousness won. He knew it when he placed his eager fingers between my legs. Dry as the desert on the hottest day of summer, a tumbleweed's paradise.

"Baby, please just relax," he pleaded with me "just this one time." He twirled me around to face him, gripped my shoulders in his strong hands.

"I'm trying," I said weakly.

And I was. *Wasn't I?* I don't think I was sure myself of what kept happening. I'd think I was getting better and then I'd get worse.

"Let's take this to the bedroom?" I asked hopefully. *So I could hide under the sheets.*

I didn't want him to stop. I really wanted him. I just couldn't do it like that. Not with the lights and mirrors. Especially not with Jake eyeballing me like that. At least in the bedroom I could hide my scars by wrapping up in a sheet and only expose the parts of myself that were fit to be seen.

We'd been married for a couple years, and yeah I did find it strange that he never looked at my body and said, What's this? Or that? Or what happened to you? Or worse, who did this to you? Damn scars, I hated them. They were the permanent tattoo left over from my horrible childhood. I couldn't take a shower without thinking of them. Jake always made me feel so accepting of myself that they shouldn't have mattered. But with all his talk of kids, they began to matter again, so much so they seemed to grow.

"Nah. I'm gonna be late for church." He glanced at his watch.

I knew he was thanking God for a way out again. I knew he didn't really want to make love to me, Naomi the molested and raped little girl. I immediately picked up my robe and covered myself up, but I still felt naked.

"Must be the Lord's way of telling me to get going. We have a new associate pastor and I want to be there early in case she needs anything." He moved over to the double sink and washed his hands and smoothed his goatee. He picked up my favorite aftershave and rubbed it on his face.

She. My ears perked up at the way he said it. In case *she* needs anything. *She.* My woman siren screamed, alert—intruder. Why was he thinking about what another woman needed right at this second when I needed him? Okay, I was going too far again. I had to get myself into some type of counseling—and fast. I was seriously losing it.

"Well, I'll see you later, honey." His voice was flat and distant, in sync with the perfunctory kiss on the cheek. But hell, what did I expect? I knew I was hard to deal with, but I was trying. I wish I could show him that.

I stood there for what seemed like an eternity staring at myself in the mirror until I heard first the radio shut off, then the front door close. *Not even a second thought.* My dress laughed at me from the hook on the bathroom door. I grabbed it and threw it in a ball on the closet floor. I can't believe he walked out the door without me. All my good intentions had evaporated faster than the steam from my shower—into nothing, in a matter of minutes. *What the hell happened?*

We were supposed to be riding along together, arguing over which radio station to listen to. Of course I couldn't blame it all on Jake; I never went to church anyway. It was another one of those things he thought he could change about me. I guess he finally got comfortable with the fact that I was a heathen, that's what church folks called people like me. Still, he used to *always* at least ask. For some reason, I needed to go today. I really needed to be with him so that I could explain some things, the kid thing especially.

It wasn't lost on me that our gap had grown since he started thinking about kids—and that was a problem. If he only knew what kind of childhood I had and what kind of mother I would be. I saw it every day at work, like mother, like daughter. My mind drifted back to my lack of one. I thought of my parents, namely my mother; I never knew my father. I often wondered where she was. If her course stayed the same as the last time I saw her thirty years ago, she was probably six feet deep by now. That, I was sure of.

I'd combed local cemeteries for years. I never found Nola. Right before Jake and I got married, he crept up on me while I searched the Internet looking for her. I almost disintegrated into thin air when he read the name aloud over my shoulder, "Who is Nola—?"

"Umm, nobody. Mr. Nosey," I said, cutting him off and I logged off the computer.

Although I'd rehearsed my lines perfectly, I was so caught off guard I didn't remember which lie I used. In any case the search came up empty. She was a ghost. Yesterday's illusion captured by my imagination. Nola didn't exist anymore and the sooner I got over my past the better for my life. For my marriage.

Naomi

S O, CHECK THIS out!" Dae said excitedly, arms dancing in the air as she spoke. "Last Friday night he took me to that restaurant downtown that spins around. It was beautiful, the stars, the moon, everything was perfect. I'm in love."

No sooner than I got out of my car, my best friend pounced on me with the details of her fabulous weekend. She had shimmering stars twinkling in her eyes. I was a little jealous because Dae was living such a fabulous single life and I was very married and very miserable.

Dae and I met as undergrads at the University of Houston several years ago. As freshmen we were roommates. The next year, we got an apartment together and remained roommates until after we graduated. Both of us were very serious about school so we never had any problems other than the normal, *that's my lipstick* drama. We shared the same major, and since cash was tight for both of us we saved money by sharing books, causing us to be roomies slash study buddies and most importantly to me, best friends for life.

Dae was the only person that knew everything about me. She knew about the bogeyman that hid in my closet and threatened to take all my joy away at a moment's notice. Dae was first generation American born and the first to go to college in her cash-strapped family. Growing up immersed in American culture caused a lot of conflict with her parents who wanted a traditional Asian daughter, meek, mild tempered—and married. Dae, however, lived as though everyday was the Fourth of July, ready to explode with a myriad of emotions all at once. She wasn't worried about marriage. And, she stood up to anyone at any time which made it hard for her to meet the Mr. Right of her parents' dreams.

I loved her spunk from our very first encounter. Dae schooled me on the correct pronunciation of her name almost immediately "My name is Dae Kim. That's Dae, like day of the week. It means greatness." And while we're on the subject, I'm not Chinese or Japanese. I am Korean. My parents were immigrants, but I am a born and raised American citizen."

That explained why her English was flawless. No broken syllables or choppy sentences, I just assumed she'd lived in America awhile. But she was born in Texas, not that I cared anyway.

"Ohh, there's a difference?" I asked. "Aren't you all Orientals or something like that?" I asked snidely.

"I'm about as Oriental as a rug on the floor." She looked at me like I didn't know anything. Maybe I didn't, but she was still getting on my nerves acting like she was straight out of the hood with all the eye rolling. If that was her impression of black people, she had me pegged completely wrong. "People can't be Oriental. It's not even a race, it's a rug," she said impatiently.

Dae sucked her tongue and rolled her neck in an annoying stereotypical and flamboyant interpretation of a black woman. "Yes. There is a difference. My family is from Korea, a country *in* Asia." She smacked her lips. Her manicured hands were placed defiantly on her hips. I was willing to bet my last five that Dae's family owned a nail salon somewhere in the hood. She was taking the mad black woman thing a little too far; she'd had some contact.

"Do all black people live in the ghetto and have a bunch of baby daddies?"

Yeah, a little too much. All the neck rolling was excessive. I wondered if there was still time to snag another roommate because this was not going to work. All I wanted was a little peace while I pursued my education. This was too much drama on day one.

"No!" I had an attitude then. Dae giggled. "You see something funny?"

My arms crossed each other over my chest. I was a good three inches taller than the little lab rat laughing in my face as though I was the joke. I sized her up and figured I'd be cool if I tried to tie her little ass in a bow, that's if she didn't know karate. Then, she might be able to take me.

"Yes." She was in a fit of laughter now and could barely get her words out. She didn't seem a bit fazed by my demeanor which was quite intimidating, even for a passive person like me. I hated violence. "I just thought we'd get all the stereotypes out the way early." She was still laughing at her antics.

"The what?" I was hot.

"Ok, I already have preconceived notions about black people." Dae spoke more intelligently. "I know you have an image of what an Asian person is in your head as well. If we are going to share this tiny drab room for an entire year, I'd like for us to be friends. I want to know you for you. I don't care what color you are." She paused to give her words the space they needed for me to adjust to her quick change in thoughts.

This chick was going straight We Are the World on me. And it was working. I really understood where she was coming from. In all honesty, I was a little worried about race when I found out she was going to be Oriental ... I mean Asian.

I cocked my head to the side. "Go ahead."

"So if I promise not to push off what I've seen of black people, mostly from videos and the news, on you, will you do the same? Can I just be me with Naomi? Just Dae?"

Dae held up her tiny hand in a fist and held out her pinky. I thought she was kidding at first, but she held it out and waited.

"So does that mean you *don't* know karate?" I asked in the most serious voice I could muster without cracking a smile.

"What?" I caught her completely off guard just after her love thy neighbor speech. "No, I don't know karate!" Her face flushed red with anger.

It was my turn to laugh. I held out my pinky finger. "So no nail salon either, huh? Okay. Okay. I'm just kidding. I pinky swear. No stereotypes."

We became inseparable after that. I learned so much about her culture. The intimate details reserved for people who share a common race. I even shared with her why some black women wore weaves and permed their hair, and a few other secrets of the black society. We pretty much figured out that as women, taking into account the difference in color, we were more alike than we thought.

Dae had an amazing family that welcomed me into their home for holidays and school breaks since I didn't have a family of my own to go back to. Once you aged out of the foster care system that was it for you. Once the checks stopped, you were on your own and left out in the cold.

Dae became my family, and if she caught me sulking or withdrawing, she would snap me out of it Dae style. I had never met anyone as straight to the point as her. She introduced me to friendship and family. She was the first woman I ever trusted. The only woman I trust today. If it wasn't for Dae, I would have never gone out with Jake in the first place, she practically forced me. So, when I had a really bad day dealing with my marriage, like today. I blamed Dae for it.

"Uh. Good morning to you," I said obviously in a bad mood.

"Damn, what bit you on the arse?" The excitement over her weekend deflated instantly. Nonetheless, Dae was still interested in what happened to me. That's what I loved about her. "Talk to me, sister."

"Great. Now, it's raining," I said as the first raindrop fell on my cheek and I became even further annoyed because my hands were full.

I had my overstuffed laptop bag, oversized purse, and bulky lunch sack. Dae quickly put her hand in my purse and grabbed my umbrella, propping it over our heads as though it were second nature to her. I smiled because she knew how conscious I was about my hair getting wet. We huddled close, walking quickly through the parking lot to the building where we worked. Houston had a way with rain. It never started with a light sprinkle. There was no warning. It's as though the sky opened and someone turned the faucet to full blast.

"Dae, I did it again. I froze." I was almost glad it was raining so she couldn't see my tears. "I wanted to tell him this weekend why I keep doing it. But I can't. Now it seems that we're getting worse. Sometimes, I feel as if he has already left, and only a shell of what we had remains. And the worst ever thing is that I think he is seeing someone else."

Dae stopped walking for a second. "You do? Who?"

"I don't know. I'm not even sure. It's just a thought right now. I don't have any real proof yet."

Dae fell into step with me again. "Jake is a good man, Naomi. I don't think he'd do something like that to you. Like I told you before, you need to consider counseling. It would help if you..."

"I don't want to pour my heart out to some stranger, Dae. That's what I have you for." She put one comforting arm around my shoulder. "I already know what they'd say. Naomi, you have abandonment issues. Self-esteem issues. Intimacy issues. You are one damaged lady. Damaged goods. Take two of these a day to relieve the stress and anxiety. Pay your co-pay at the desk. See you next week." I pretended to check my flaws off on an invisible list in the rain.

Dae giggled at my last statement. She laughed just to keep from letting her honest opinion slip out and calling shots in the conversation. I always teased her that she'd talk right through the listening parts of any discussion. I saw that she was making a real effort to work on those important flaws. Especially with me, because boy, with all my problems, I need both of her ears at my full attention.

As usual, the rain stopped just as we approached the awning and jumped over the last muddy pothole in the parking lot. Crazy Houston weather, you never knew what to expect. Even if you lived here your entire life, you never get used to the coming and going of the sudden rain. The sun even had the nerve to peek around the corner of the clouds just to be sure it was safe to come out. We were in for another hot and humid day.

"You need a lunch buddy today?" Dae offered with a smile.

We stepped inside the aging building, which made our No Personal Business Zone pact go into effect. We pinky swore on that, too. Gossip spread around the mostly women occupied employee government office building faster than a wild fire racing up a rolling California hill.

"Maybe. Let's see what we have in store for us today. You know Mondays can be brutal around here."

We both worked for Child Protective Services. Dae had just received a promotion and was now my supervisor. I would have been jealous, but her mouth kept her into trouble with the parents who thought they could push her around because she was Asian. So the less exposure she had to those fools the better.

"Yeah, all those crazies out there had two days to come up with new ways to terrorize their children," Dae said. "Not to mention it rained most of the weekend, leaving those poor kids locked inside with no place to go."

We rode the elevator up in uneasy silence, both of us trying not to put a real face on a child that may have suffered over the weekend as we went about our own lives. We got off the elevator on the ninth floor. I turned to Dae. "To the bat cave," I said, saluting.

Dae went left to her new office and I went right into cubicle land. My tiny cubicle might as well have been a cave. The state stuffed as many of us as possible into a sardine can of an office because most of our work was done out in the field anyway.

Out of habit, I glanced at the phone to see if the red light would blink impatiently at me as usual. I dumped all my belongings onto the tiny cluttered desk and locked my purse in the bottom drawer. I listened to the office chatter as it invaded my space for a brief minute. The gossip-enthused conversations went from weekend happenings, personal marital problems, and vent fests about overloaded case loads. A few colleagues walked past my cave and tossed in hurried hellos, fewer waited for a response.

I sat in my uncomfortable leather chair and stared at the psyche ward gray carpet on the cubicle divider in front of me. One of the wheels on my chair was broken, so it wobbled. I spent a lot of time trying to balance it with my feet just to keep it still. I chuckled inwardly because I spent just as much time trying to keep my thoughts balanced with everything going on around me. My walls had so many holes and rips from pushing pins through it to tack up this memo and that memorandum with the appropriate attached addendum that it looked more like a gray bowl of shredded wheat.

On the wall behind me, I pinned all the multi-colored pictures my kids drew for me, along with their photos. Whenever I felt like grabbing my things and walking out because of government politics, I'd turn around and absorb the positive energy contained in all the scribbled love you notes. Sometimes, I went home so overwhelmed by my day at work that Jake begged for me to quit. He said I could work at the shop with him. But I just couldn't leave. I couldn't tear myself away and abandon my kids.

Like every other day for the last six years, I reached for the phone first. It was something about that blazing red light that made me want to quiet it by checking my messages immediately. I heard my PDA vibrating restlessly in my purse. I thought it better to filter through voicemails first as I checked my email. I had twelve messages and twice that in emails. What a hectic Monday it would be. I took out my pen and notebook and pushed the message button. As the complaints droned on forever, I flipped through my planner and checked for appointments and court dates.

I listened intently as Mrs. Fildhurst, a foster parent, rattled off one complaint after another on my voicemail. She had so much to say, that she'd hung up and called back to finish her message. She wanted me to remove a seven-year-old I had recently placed in her home a week prior because the child wanted his mother. That woman was never satisfied; she complained when we didn't place any children with her, then threatened to return them like an unwanted gift the day after Christmas if the check was a few days late. When was she going to get her money was really what she wanted to discuss. That woman was always my last resort. Good foster parents were in short supply, especially black ones. *What a shame*, I thought as I dialed her number by heart.

"Praise the Lord. This is Mrs. Fildhurst." I cringed at the sound of her crackling voice. She always sounded as though she needed a good cough to clear her throat. It was so gross.

"Good morning, Mrs. Fildhurst. I am returning your call from Friday evening." I paused, in an attempt to rid myself of the loathing feeling creeping up my vocal chords from the sour pit of my stomach. Man, that woman did it for me. "I understand you would like for us to remove Jordan from your home and find other placement?" I didn't care too much for the woman. "I'm sorry it's not working out." I lied. If I were to be sorry for anyone, it was for Jordan.

"Oh, well you know an old woman like me is on a tight, fixed income."

She got right to the point. I knew her kind. The long messages she left on my voicemail was just so I would call her back immediately.

"I have been feeding this child for the last week off of my own money, which isn't much. I don't mind sharing, but this is a job for me. Taking in these kids when their own parents don't want them is my income."

The thin wispy hairs on the back of my neck stood on end and a chill ran down my spine as though it were running from the evil posing as concern in her voice. The woman was absolutely heartless. My fingers moved to pull on a stray lock of hair and I twirled it repeatedly between my fingers.

"Mrs. Fildhurst, Jordan has only been with you since Wednesday. It takes a couple of weeks for the funds to move through the accounting department." I tried desperately to hide my frustration. I decided not to entertain the conversation for too much longer. "Would you like for me to call the accounting department to pin down a date you can expect to receive the check?"

"Oh no, baby. I don't want to put you through any—"

"It's no trouble, please hold."

I pushed the hold button while she was still speaking. I really wanted to hang up in her face. I had no intention of calling accounting. I checked my email for a few minutes before I released the hold button. I could hear her humming "This Little Light of Mine." She was such a hypocrite, like all the other church folks I knew. I don't think I'd ever understand how my husband spent so much time with those kinds of people.

"Mrs. Fildhurst?"

"I'm still here, sweetheart."

"Did you get the emergency food and clothing stipend? It was mailed out on Friday." I asked, already knowing the answer. It was only Monday morning.

I don't know why foster parents always thought the state was trying to do them in. Mrs. Fildhurst had been a foster parent for over twenty years. She could manipulate the system inside and out, much better than me for that matter. She knew what to expect and how to work it to her advantage.

"The mailman hasn't come by today yet, honey," she said it as though I wasn't able to figure that out on my own, it was only nine in the morning.

"Well, I have already begun looking for another foster home for Jordan. I really hate that he has been of so much trouble to you. I think I may be able to have him moved by—"

I decided to make her suffer for calling, harassing me first thing on a Monday morning. Jordan's mother had recently relinquished her rights for good and Mrs. Fildhurst was worried about a couple of dollars.

"Oh, wait a minute, sweetheart," she interjected. "I never said I wanted y'all to pick up him up."

I barely believed what I was hearing because those were her exact words. I listened as she rambled out excuses for the message she had left over the weekend. I let her talk while I continued to update my planner with future meetings and trainings. I kicked off my shoes underneath my desk and propped my bare feet up on the plush, matted cubicle wall in front of me. Of course, I planned to leave Jordan right where he was at. Not so much for Mrs. Fildhurst's benefit, but because there was no other home to put him in.

Jordan was only seven years old but on his third round in the foster care system. His mother was college educated and actually provided a very good home for him. He had many luxuries at home that some of the other kids never had. Jordan's mother was not the problem at all, but it was still her fault that her child had become a ward of the court and that he moved in and out of the system, again and again.

She was pathetic, just like most of the other mothers. They never put the welfare of their children ahead of their own gratification. Jordan was born when his mother was a senior in high school. His maternal grandmother raised him until the time of her death at which time his mother had finished college and had gotten married. Jordan moved in with his mother and her new husband. The stepfather didn't like the idea of sharing his wife or middle class life with her bastard son. The abuse began immediately. Every time she left Jordan at home alone with her husband, she would come back to find him with a new contusion.

When Jordan was about five years old, he fled the home and ran out into the street running from a beating. A car almost hit him. The driver called the police because he suspected abuse after he watched the stepfather drag Jordan back across the lawn and into the house by his arm. CPS was called and Jordan became a ward of the state. Jordan's mother finally signed documents relinquishing all rights to her son after Jordan went to school with a busted lip and the authorities were notified for the third time. Her husband was not willing to go to family counseling, nor wanted Jordan back in his home. She neatly packed all of Jordan's designer clothing and expensive gaming systems in designer luggage and dropped it all off at my office just as painless as if she were donating to charity. She didn't even have the decency to turn off the motor when she popped the trunk to get his things out of her luxurious Mercedes.

I asked if she wanted to tell Jordan goodbye or reconsider. He had been asking to see her.

"No, that won't be necessary. I think this way is best for the entire family," she said fingering the half-moon of a diamond ring resting on her finger.

"Best for whose family?" I'd asked.

I was blown away by her candidness and teetered on the verge of stepping over my professional boundaries. I hated her so much. She was weak. Women like her came a dime a dozen, always looked for a man to validate their entire existence at any cost. My throat tightened and threatened not to swallow the ball of rage growing in it. I forced back my own tears. I wanted her to take her words back.

"I don't want Jordan," she had said. "I can't do it anymore. I'm done trying. It's too hard."

Just like that. As easy as if she had said I don't like pickles and don't put them on my hamburger. The words fell from her lips of her own free will. She meant them. She held her head high and straightened her back as if challenging me. She stared right into my eyes, unblinking as though we were discussing what we wanted for lunch. Cold. Direct. There was no sorrow. There was nothing. There was no life behind her hardened hazel eyes. They were like two cold stone pebbles that would accidentally wash across your feet at the seashore.

"Isn't Jordan your family? What about what's best for him?" I attempted to slide a little reasoning and compassion through the closed door to her heart. I tapped the trunk of her shiny, black car with my fist for emphasis.

I really wanted her to think about what she was doing. What she was saying. She didn't respond. She used two fingers and massaged her temple as though the sound of my voice caused a throbbing pain in her head. She turned and slid behind the wheel of her sixty thousand dollar car and drove away. Jordan's mother chose to trade her son, her only child for an upper middle class life. She preferred the empty echo of a six bedroom home and the love of a man that didn't give a damn about her over her own child. By the time she realized how prized the possession she was giving up, it would be too late.

Jordan, at seven years, old had become nothing more than a stray, an uncomfortable accessory. It was highly probable that he would be in the system for the rest of his life. Mrs. Fildhurst knew all of that. That hag still called to complain about a lousy couple hundred dollars anyway. I wanted to drive over to her house and pop the hell out of her.

"So, are you saying you would like to keep Jordan?" I asked, interrupting Mrs. Fildhurst in the midst of her ramblings about the problems she was having with her blood pressure. I was becoming extremely agitated. I was not her friend and refused to get wrapped up in her trivial life.

"Oh, yes of course. I can't turn that poor child away. You know he don't have nobody else. Didn't you say, his mother signed over parental rights?"

Her tone suggested I'd accused her of doing something ridiculous like threatening to give him back. The change of concern once the financial issue was resolved simply amazed me. I rushed her through the rest of the call and hung up the phone and scratched *move Jordan Walker* off my long to-do list.

My cell buzzed in the drawer again.

"Ok. Ok," I said aloud to myself, wondering what's next.

My job didn't allow me the luxury of planning in an attempt to be proactive. Oh no, it was always one thing, one crisis after another. By the time I located my phone at the bottom of my bag, the buzzing had stopped. It was Jake. I bet he was calling to apologize for not spending time with me yesterday.

I glanced up at my email again and had a message from Dae; she'd forwarded a message from Statewide Intake. I hurriedly slipped my shoes back on under my desk as I scribbled down the details. I began throwing my things back into my bag, preparing to leave. A local middle school had reported a case of suspected child abuse. There were two children involved. One of the kids was being held in the office at the school and he was allegedly in pretty bad shape. I exhaled deeply. I hoped this was a false alarm. I had no place for the children already on my caseload. How was I going to find a place for two siblings? And of course, they'd want to be together.

I peeked over into the cubicle behind mine just in time to see Maria pick her nose and flick the contents on the cubicle wall. My stomach turned. Reason number one thousand and one why we needed private offices. I knew whose dish I would never eat at the potluck again! *Yuck.*

"Hey, Maria. I got a new call. I'll most likely be out the rest of the day." She shook her head knowingly, holding the phone to her ear.

"Oh, one more thing. Just in case, if you have a lead on placement for a family of two, send me a message with the information." She gave me a familiar are you kidding look and waved me off with her nasty hand.

I stood waiting for the elevator, nervously twirling my hair around my fingers. My heart was beating so frantically that it became hard to breathe. It always happened every time I received a new call. I thought about her. I thought just maybe this was it, the time we'd come face to face again. That's only if she was still alive, which I seriously doubted. I knew deep down inside that the crack era most likely killed her.

"Stop doing that." Dae walked past me and plucked my hair out of my hand. She didn't even stop. She was like a drive-by bad habit blocker.

Naomi

BY THE TIME I made it to the school, a marked police car was already parked directly in front of the office doors. I guess the school called them as well. I pulled behind the cruiser and grabbed my cell phone out of the ashtray and fit it snugly into the holster on my waist as I got out of the car.

I knocked on the window of the police car and nodded for the officer to follow me into the school. The police didn't have to be directly involved, so this must have been serious for the school to have called them as well.

I stepped into the extremely cool foyer of the middle school and immediately wrapped my cardigan tighter around me as I entered the office. I showed my badge and asked to speak to the principal. The officer took a seat in one of the hard chairs and leaned his head against the wall and closed his eyes.

The stout elderly woman at the desk shook her graying, curly head and tsk'd her tongue sympathetically. She knew why I was there. She pressed the antiquated intercom on her desk which buzzed her voice into another room.

"CPS is here to see you, Mr. Jones," southern charm oozing from every syllable. "Mr. Jones?"

Without waiting for a response, she quickly rose from her desk with more energy than I anticipated for someone her age, which I guessed to be about sixty. "Follow me, hun-ney," she said as she led me down a long hallway through worn corridors.

We stopped in front of a door that was slightly open and I could see the back of a young boy staring out the window at the playground. The secretary nodded in the boy's direction and touched my arm lightly.

"I hope y'all finally do something about that woman. Take care of him, he's a good boy. He's so sweet," she whispered before pushing the door completely open. She quickly headed back in the direction we came from.

"Well, well, Naomi, I'd like to say it's nice to see you; however, I find it difficult to be excited to see you under the same circumstances again," the principal said as he cupped both of my hands in his massive ones. "This here is Xavier," he waved in the young boy's direction before leaving the conference room.

"Hello, Xavier, I'm Naomi." I gathered my spiel in my head, ready to go into textbook mode. I wanted to make Xavier feel comfortable before we got started on the reason I had been called.

"I want to leave. I can't stay with *her* anymore." Xavier got straight to the point first.

I was a little taken aback at first. It was the first time I'd seen an alleged victim jump right in like that. He still had his back to me, so I couldn't see his face.

"I'm tired of her hitting me—well us. I don't think I can't protect them anymore." His voice was undergoing the change of puberty and cracked as he spoke. "She. My mother is evil. Nothing I do makes her happy. I'm tired of everything."

Xavier stuffed his hands in his pockets and inhaled and exhaled deeply, as though this was the first time he was breathing on his own. "This kid in my class is in a foster home because his mother is bipolar and she wigs out sometimes."

That's when I knew where the conversation was going. I was so stunned that I forgot *my* lines. I still hadn't seen Xavier's face, but I was under a spell from the sound of his voice. I knew it took a lot of maturity and strength for him say what he was about to say. But then again, most victims of abuse had no choice but to be overly adult. Since I didn't have to draw him out with small talk, I just listened.

"I think my mother is bipolar, I looked it up on the Internet." Xavier blurted out. "Can you take me and my brother and sister to a foster home?" Xavier turned to finally face me. "Please." He voice wasn't changing. He was crying. "Help us," he pleaded.

He was one of the most beautiful kids that I'd ever seen, even with the bruising around his left eye. Someone had given him a really good thrashing. I shoved my hand out to touch his face, but lowered it to handshake level. *What is wrong with me?* He stared at my hand until I brought it back down to settle on my waist.

His stunning large brown eyes held a river of tears that he was unable to keep contained. He had eyelashes women paid top dollars for wrapped around his eyelids. His skin was smooth and I resisted the urge to wipe the tears that splashed onto his bruised face. I wanted to grab him into my arms and love his pain away. I felt like I already knew him. I winced at every tear that fell from his eyes. No matter how many cases of child abuse I'd investigated, every new one stung as though it was my first time seeing the horror of it. I stood there with my notepad in my hand and my heart in his hands trying to maintain protocol. You know, keep my cool, as the seasoned social workers always reminded us.

"Well, Xavier, it's not as easy as you think." I could barely get the words out; my voice was so backed up with emotion. I had never felt such an immediate connection with any of my other cases. I walked over to the massive table that was centered in the middle of room and pulled out two chairs. I had to keep moving to keep from pulling the boy in my arms.

"What's not easy? My mother has a mind altering disease, like Tommy's mom." Xavier was quoting directly from the Internet.

I pointed to the chair across from mine as a signal for Xavier to sit. He practically dragged himself across the room and grimaced as he settled in the chair. There was definitely some physical pain in existence. I made a mental note to myself to ask him about that as well.

"Tell me more about your mom?" I decided to forego small talk and jumped in with both feet. Xavier was ready. "You stated that she tried to kill you."

"No, I *said*, if I stay, she would end up killing me. She always said she wished I was dead." Xavier's demeanor changed slightly. I felt his attitude shift toward defensiveness.

"Who's us? I asked with my pen poised over my notepad.

"My sister and brother, Genesis and Sean."

"How old are they?"

Xavier and I talked through the horrific details that to him, was everyday life. I noted the bruises on his neck and arms. Xavier unsuccessfully attempted to place one hand over the other to hide some of the welts as he sang like a bird. He was more than ready to get away from his mother. His mind was set and he'd tell me whatever I needed to know in order to make it happen.

After Xavier ran out of words, I stretched my arms over my head and glanced at my watch. It had been three hours. I had pages of notes and enough information to launch a full investigation. And enough to remove the children from the home—immediately. Xavier's mother was definitely unfit. The way she treated her children unsettled me. It appeared that he had it the hardest in their home. She was mean to the other children, but exceptionally cruel to Xavier. The kid had it hard and he was only thirteen.

"What time is it?"

"A quarter past three," I yawned. "Oh, excuse me."

Xavier jumped out of his chair. "School's almost out. I have to go meet Genesis."

As if on cue, the school bell rang. The sound of rambunctious youth filled the halls. You could practically feel the vibration of the lockers slamming open and closed.

"Where is she?" I asked.

"She's supposed to wait by her locker so we can walk home together. Are you gonna take us to a foster home or not?" Xavier demanded. "Because if you can't do nothing…Imma have to go." His eyes pleaded with me while his voice held a false sense of authority.

With what Xavier told me, I knew that I couldn't send them back to the home without a full investigation. Whether his mother was bipolar or not was up to the psychologist that she really needed to see. But she was definitely disturbed in my book.

"I need to step out for a minute and make a few telephone calls," I rose from my chair.

"What about me?"

I walked closer to the door and paused with it slightly open and my hand on the knob. "You probably won't be going home tonight. I'll let Mr. Jones know to bring your sister to the office," I said.

I stepped out of the room with a heavy heart. Mr. Jones must've read my mind because he was standing directly outside the door with a girl that somewhat resembled Xavier minus the large brown eyes. She didn't pay any attention to me but brushed past and shot through the door. She stopped in Xavier's face.

"Xavier," she shouted, "what's up? Tell me! What did you do?"

Xavier had already told me that his sister had no knowledge of what he'd planned to do that day. He was afraid that Genesis would tell their mother out of fear to stop him. Apparently, Genesis didn't receive very many beatings from their mother. From his account, he took the blunt of the abuse and allowed himself to be blamed for any wrongdoings that took place in the home.

"We're leaving. Mom is bipolar, and it's not a safe environment for us." Xavier remained calm as he spoke. "Miss…" he paused not sure of the correct salutation for my name.

"Naomi is fine."

"Naomi is going to make sure that she can't hurt me—or us, anymore."

Xavier's strength amazed me. It was obvious that he command-ed respect from his older sister because she stopped shouting at him and plopped heavily onto the bench next to the window, sob-bing. She pulled her feet up against her chest and rocked back and forth. Her sandy brown hair fell forward and hid her face.

"Do you know what she is gonna do when she finds out?" Genesis asked through her tears. "Do you? OMG, you are in so much trouble."

"I know what she'll do, Sissy." Xavier looked at me. "But, we're not going back."

Xavier sat next to his sister and put his arm around her. I glanced at Mr. Jones and pulled the door closed, leaving them alone in the room. He shook his head sympathetically and headed back down the hall.

"I knew this was going to happen, it was just a matter of time. That's one crazy woman," while he was still within earshot, he added, "You'll see."

I leaned heavily against the closed door. I could still hear Gen-esis crying inside and the muffled sound of Xavier's voice as he attempted to provide solace for her. I pulled my phone out of its holster and called Dae first to let her know that this was a serious situation, and we'd need a court order. I called the unit clerk so that she could begin looking for temporary placement for all the children and hopefully together. It was already late in the after-noon and looking like a long night. I made a mental checklist of the things that needed to be done as I held the phone while the clerk searched the database. I really needed Genesis' account of their home situation, including more information on the young-est sibling at home. Then, I prayed to Jake's God that I wouldn't have to take them to a group home.

We, *oh no*...I almost forgot the police officer waiting outside in the lobby. I rushed out into the lobby and he was sitting in the same spot—fast asleep.

"Excuse me." I nudged him with my free hand and hoped that I wouldn't lose my weak signal in the old building while I waited on hold. "Excuse me," I peeked at the name on his badge, "Uh. Officer Shaw."

The officer stirred awake. "Well? What's the deal?" He stood and stretched his stubby arms above his head. I was shocked that he could sleep with all the after school racket going on around him.

"These kids are in a bad circumstance here. We can't allow them to go home. They are very afraid of what the mother would do to them." I quickly explained the situation. "There are three minor children in the home. Two attend this school and they are in the back waiting. We still have to obtain custody of the youngest minor child who is home with the mother."

"Should we take them to the station and have her meet us there?" he asked.

"From what the eldest has told me, she is not very rational. If the kids don't come home from school, she might get suspicious. She probably won't show. Let's go to the home." I heard a distant hello on the other end of the phone.

"Uh, hello. Yes." I held up one finger to excuse myself. "You have a place? Great! With whom? I smiled for the first time all day, only because the kids would have a home to go to—together. "No, I don't need the address, I know where it is. Thanks." I flipped the phone shut. "Well, we have a home. Dae is working on the court order. We should be all set in a few."

"Oh yeah." The officer smirked. "I'm glad you think so. Planning is a whole lot easier than actually *taking* a woman's baby from her. Let's go."

Xavier

NO ONE SAID a word the five minute drive to our house. Genesis sat next to me and stared out the window the entire time. She wasn't crying anymore, but every once in a while she sighed loudly. Naomi drove us while the police officer followed close behind. I wanted to say a prayer but couldn't think of what to say to God. That wasn't entirely true. I wanted to pray that the earth opened up and swallowed me. I wanted to vanish from the spot that I sat in. Mostly, I wanted Mona, my mother, to drop dead before we got there. I knew it was a mean thought to have about my own mother. But, it was true. I didn't love her at all—not anymore.

I had finally decided that I hated her. I hated her more than I hated the kids at school asking me, *what happened to your hands?* Sometimes I went to school with a black eye, a knot on my temple, those I could easily lie about. It was the burn marks on my knuckles that were the worst. The burns embarrassed me the most. When the scabs healed and fell off, the skin underneath remained white, hard and crusty. For that reason, I kept my hands in my pockets most of the time. My mom, which I hoped to never see again after today, had burned almost every last one of my knuckles. Genesis must have felt what I was thinking because she reached over and pulled my hands loose from the ball I'd formed in my lap. She always did that, touched my hands. That time, I thought it was her way of letting me know that she understood. That she trusted what I'd done. I smiled a little, because to tell the truth, I was scared. *What had I done?*

"Which building is yours?" Naomi asked, slowing the car. Her phone rang and she spoke quietly. I heard her mention something about a court order. Genesis and I looked at each other.

I seemed to have lost my voice because I couldn't respond. I sat there with fear lodged in my throat. We were actually right in front of our townhouse. Naomi looked over the seat at me and waited for an answer. Genesis squeezed and rubbed my hand, a signal for me to answer. I couldn't talk. My stomach suddenly came alive and squirmed at the thought of seeing Mona's face. Although Naomi had already told me that I—we wouldn't have to actually face her. I was frozen as panic detonated in my belly. I knew it was coming and I couldn't stop it. I threw up in my lap.

"Oh my God," Naomi screamed. She shoved the car in park, causing it to jerk forward.

More vomit flew from between my lips and stuck like silly putty to the back of the tan upholstery of the seat in front of me. Sweat began to rain down from my forehead and it dripped into the lumpy pool of throw up on my lap. It was all over Genesis' hand as well as she still held mine. The car door opened and Naomi wiped my face with a paper napkin. I closed my eyes, unable to lift a finger to help clean myself. I felt so weak. I was tired—of everything and especially, life.

"Give me some?" I heard Genesis ask Naomi for a few of the paper towels. As Naomi wiped my face clean, Genesis did the same for my lap and hands.

"What's going on here?" I heard the officer's voice ask gruffly.

I opened my eyes and he stood right outside of the car door.

Naomi was bent over my lap as she cleaned up the mess I'd made; I had a clear view of him. His hand was positioned over his sparkling gun. In my mind, I imagined myself pushing Naomi out of the way as I snatched the gun from his belt. I blinked again to the vision of pulling the trigger with the gun lodged in Mona's mouth. I shuddered from the thought.

"It's okay, just a little accident," Naomi responded to the officer. She rubbed her hand gently across my cheek. "Everything will be all right." She ran her hand across my other cheek and held it there. "Don't cry, Xavier."

I hadn't realized that I was crying. It was the first time I'd cried all day—actual tears because, I usually cried hate. *Men don't cry*, I told myself as Naomi's hand warmed my face. I squeezed my lips together, hard and pressed my head back into the seat. Genesis continued to wring my hand and never said a word.

"I think that's it over there," the police officer said, pointing in the direction of my house. "You need to get your car out of the street. Oh yeah, the natives are getting ready for the show."

A police car wasn't very common in our quiet, apartment complex, so it meant get ready for some action. I wondered if Mona was looking out of the window. What was she was thinking?

I pushed my head deeper into the cushion. There was no turning back. I'd told Ms. Naomi everything. Well, not everything. There were some things that I'd never repeat. Not even to God. Every time I closed my eyes, last weekend replayed in my head. I could still feel her like she was right in front of me…her face in mine, screaming, and her fists pounding on me.

C3 & 80

"Boy, if you don't get the belt. I'm tired of talking to you. Candice, I'll call you back tomorrow. These damn kids are going to make me kill 'em. And I need to head out for work anyway." She raised her eyebrows as if to say to me—I'm waiting. "Okay, I'll talk to you later, girl," she said into the phone and hung it up.

I stomped up the raggedy, wooden stairs while Mona finished talking to her friend on the phone. My eyes filled to the brim with tears. My bottom lip quivered. I knew I wasn't gonna be able to fight it. I tried to hold them at bay by telling myself that boys didn't cry—and I was practically a man. I wasn't scared of the whooping I was about to get. I was used to that. I was tired of her hitting me for no damn reason.

I liked how the word damn sounded as I toyed with the word in my head. My friends and I had been experimenting with cursing. I didn't say any of the really bad words. Mona said so many of them that I never needed to hear or say a four letter word again in my life. I never wanted to be anything like her. *Ever.* I ran my hand up along the wooden banister, and wiped the dust on my jeans when I got to the top of the stairs where my little brother Sean was waiting for me with his thumb in his mouth.

"Waz wrong?" he asked. He'd heard our mother yelling from downstairs. "I tole you she was gone get mad. You shoulda left her alone," he said between sucking on a mouthful of his thumb.

"Look, Sean, what was I supposed to do? Starve? You know she wasn't going to cook. I was making us a bologna sandwich when…" I tried to calm down. It didn't make sense to yell at him. He was only four. What did he know?

"Xavier, get your ass down here and you better have the belt! Genesis! You get your ass down here, too, and clean up this kitchen!" Mona yelled at the top of her lungs; her voice rode the stillness of the house up the stairs and pinched at the nerves on my butt. "You think because I'm tired, I'm not gonna kick yo ass. Look at this mayonnaise on the damn floor! A whole jar of mayonnaise. Gone. Look. Just look at this damn kitchen," she went on and on, ranting to no one in particular.

The thing about Mona was this; the more Mona screamed, the madder she got. Her voice began to split wide open with fury and held everyone in the house hostage. She was about to blow and if I didn't hurry up and get down there, we'd all be in trouble.

"What did you do now?" Genesis asked, busting into the room I shared with my little brother without knocking. I knew the door was open, but still. She whispered so Mona wouldn't hear us talking. Mona always thought that we were plotting against her or something, especially when she was pissed.

"Leave me alone, Sissy," I shooed my sister out of my room with my hands. "We were hungry and I was making sandwiches. The mayonnaise slipped outta my hand. We haven't eaten anything all day. Mona been downstairs talking on the phone and watching TV."

As weird as it was, Mona didn't like for us to call her Mama, Mom, or any other word that resembled it. She felt like she was too young and beautiful to be somebody's—anybody's Mama. We all called her Mona. We always had.

I reached into the closet and pulled out Mona's favorite whooping belt. After every beating, Mona hung the belt up in my closet as a reminder of what would happen to me if we got out of hand again. It was my constant reminder. It still had tiny traces of my dried blood on it.

"Oh, okay then. But, you still gone get it. You know she been in a bad mood ever since Sean's father left." Genesis turned to go downstairs. She didn't want to walk down the stairs the same time as me because there was no telling how Mona would release her wrath. Everybody was a target when she gave her beatings.

I could hear Mona downstairs slamming pots and pans around in the kitchen. Cabinets opened, drawers slammed closed causing the air to vibrate with tension. She was pissed. The sound of her slippers slid across the tiled floor of the kitchen and into the living room. It was time for me to go down. I knew she was waiting at the base of the stairs, her foot tapped against the bottom stair. Her every move echoed loudly in my mind.

"Get down here now. Don't make me come up there!" Mona screeched with anger.

I could just see the pulse in her temple jumping out of her forehead. Her brown eyes, black with rage.

My little brother Sean gave me a hug around both of my knees. I headed down the stairs. If I kept Mona waiting, it would only serve to make it worse. I took each heavy step down the stairs, slowly. The thick brown leather belt dangled loosely at my side and slapped eagerly at my legs in anticipation. Mona had slapped me yesterday and beat me the day before that with her fists. The welts from those beatings pulsated with a well-knowing dread.

"You look just like your no good ass father," Mona spit out as soon as I came nearer to the bottom step. "I hate him and I'm not too fond of your ass either."

You see, my father left before I was born. Mona said he'd told her that he couldn't be with someone that he'd never marry. Especially if she was just gonna sit around smoking weed and having babies. Besides, he never thought we were his kids anyway. Well, Genesis he knew was his. It was me that he wasn't so sure about. Sean had a different father, altogether. All I knew about my father was that he'd married some white lady and moved to California before I was ever born. Mona always blamed it on me. I don't know how many times I heard her say, "Before you came, we were doing just fine."

The more Mona thought about my father, the more pissed off she got. I watched from the stairs as her anger elevated itself. Before I even reached the bottom step, she reached out and snatched the belt out of my hand and slapped me across the face with it. The buckle scraped across my cheek. *Ding.* Her wrath had arrived to the penthouse level.

"Wait, Mama. I was only...I was only." Not able to hold them back any longer, tears gushed from my eyes. I tried to explain to her how it came about that I broke the mayonnaise.

"What did you call me?" She put her hand on her hips and stared through me as if I were a foreign species and not her son.

"I told you not to call me, Mama. My mother. Named me Mona!" Mona was in her zone. It was no sense explaining nothing. Mona didn't believe in accidents or sorry. I closed my eyes, held my breath, and waited for the beating to be unleashed. She snatched me off the last step and shoved me down to the floor. She put her foot on my back. "You better not move." She threatened. "I don't have all day to kick your ass. I have to put food on the table."

She hit me again—and again—and again. Each strike was nastier—harder than its predecessor. I screamed out loud every time the belt smacked across my back and legs, but I didn't move. She told me to be quiet or it would be worse. The belt made a swishing sound in the air and it coupled with the taps to my back, creating a sinister beat. *Smack. Swish.*

I could see Genesis as I lay on the floor. She clutched a soapy glass in her trembling hands. She stared as Mona beat me lost in her rage.

I stopped screaming when the belt connected with the back of my head for the second time. *That's enough!* She had gone too far. It was more than I could bear. Mona pressed her foot deeper into my back until I felt the pressure in my empty stomach. She had already hit me countless times and didn't seem in the least bit tired. I remember once she beat me all night. She stopped only to smoke a cigarette and to catch her breath. It seemed like I was about to relive one of those times, but something in me knew that I had to stop her.

"Don't nobody want a woman with bad ass kids. You hear me. You gonna learn to respect me." She enunciated each syllable as she hit me. *Smack.* She hit me again for the third time on the back of my head. *Smack.*

In one motion, before I realized what I was doing, I rolled over on the floor, making eye contact with Genesis. She shook her head as if to say, don't do it. Mona lost her balance and started to fall backwards when I grabbed the belt from her hand with so much intensity she fell forward onto the floor almost on top of me. She still held on to her end of the thick brown leather belt.

"You motha…" she started to say.

Her eyes bulged as I pulled myself out of the tangled heap we ended up in on the floor. I stood to my feet, taking the belt with me. I stood there for a moment looking down at her unsure of what to do next. Better yet, unsure of what Mona was going to do next. I didn't mean for that to happen. I only wanted her to stop hitting me in the back of my head with the belt buckle. I was so shocked at myself that I let the belt drop from my hand onto the floor. Mona stared at it, mesmerized, as the buckle clanged against the floor. The belt landed in a snakelike heap near my foot.

Mona pulled herself up from the floor slowly along with the belt. She held it out for me. I didn't move my hand to take it back. I didn't want to touch it. My heart pounded heavily in my ears. And there was something else there pounding in my heart. Something else materialized within me that I had never felt so strongly in all of my life.

"Take it," she commanded, still holding the belt toward me.

I shook my head no, very slowly in response while the strange feeling grew larger and bolder within me. My chest began to heave as I breathed deeply—in and out. Heat rose deep inside me as beads of nervous sweat broke out over my face.

She walked closer to me and locked eyes with me. "Take. The. Damn. Belt." Her words were slow to form and filled with contempt. "Here. I thought you wanted it." She touched my hand with it and attempted to gently nudge my closed fists open. The corners of her lips turned up into a sick smile. "You all puffed up like a jellyfish. Whatchu gonna do? Huh, Xavier? Hit me? Do you want to hit me, Xavier? You do, don't you?"

I didn't answer her. I opened my hand and stretched my fingers, open. Then I closed them tightly again. The unidentified darkness pounded inside me. It continued to rise as steadily as my chest and breathing.

"Take the belt, boy! You bad! Take it. You know why I want you to have it?" She sneered as she forced the belt into my hand.

I whispered a barely audible, "No."

"Because I don't need no damn belt to kick your ass! Not as long as I got these."

Mona reached her arm back and punched me dead center in

my left eye as hard as she could. It was so unexpected that I stumbled, but my pride didn't let me fall. I straightened myself up and stood in place. I didn't attempt to cover my eye even though a sharp pain seared through it and white flashes of light blinded it.

"Oh, you gone stand there, huh? I get it. You tough now? You think you grown, right?" Mona pointed her long finger in my face and touched the tip of my nose with her fingertip. I jerked away from her. She grabbed me around my throat with her free hand.

"Boy, you ain't gone never get too big for me to kick your ass. I gave birth to you…not the other way around. The next time you want to huff up at me, you can get the fuck out. You gotta little height on you and you wanna start smelling yourself. Right?" Mona asked questions she expected no answer for.

"Shiiit, I never wanted your trifling ass anyway. I wish. Ooh, I wish I had listened to my mother and never had you," she said through clenched teeth.

I didn't move away from her grip. I didn't blink. I stared at her. Her words sunk deep inside me, but this time I didn't feel anything. I also wished she never had me. Mona used to hit me with her hands, a belt, a shoe, or burned me with cigarettes on my fingers and I'd turn into a whimpering baby. I would cry because that was what she wanted. Because I wanted her to love me.

Crying was the only thing that made her shut up. This time was different. I stood there facing her with a mass of hatred churning inside me. Hate. I hated Mona more than I loved anything in my life. I hated her so much that if I had to choose between being alive or being dead, I'd choose death just to get away from her. Every day, I thought about leaving for school and never coming back. But, leaving Sean and Genesis with her, without me, caused me to come back every single time.

My head ached. My core filled with dark intentions. I wanted to take the belt that I was holding in my hand and wrap it neatly around her neck. I wanted to pull on the slack until it cut off all the blood circulating to her head. I wanted to fix it so that I would never hear her irritating voice again. I wanted to watch her lifeless body drop to the floor and never move again. Those thoughts kept me from crying. No matter what she did to me, I was never going to cry again.

I think she saw it. In my eyes, I think Mona could see the thoughts that played themselves out like a movie in my head. The image of Mona quiet for an eternity brought a smile to my face even though she continued to hold a firm grip on my throat.

"Go to your room before I hurt you," she said, removing her hand from my throat and shoving me backwards.

"Yes, Mona," I said, my voice thick with hatred.

Mona turned away and stomped off toward the kitchen. I stood there for a moment reliving what had just happened. I couldn't believe that I stood up to Mona the monster. I wasn't quite sure whether I'd won the battle or not. But I did feel some sort of victory for standing up to her the way that I did. I quickly tried to imagine all the things that might happen as a result of what I'd done. Thinking about that made me a little nervous. I pushed the thoughts aside to celebrate my tiny victory to myself. I turned to head up the stairs to my room. The feeling of hate began to quiet itself inside my stomach.

Smack! "What the fuck are you looking at?" Mona screeched.

I turned back just in time to see Genesis pull her hands up over her face, causing her to drop the soapy glass in her hand. Mona turned to look back at me.

"Clean this shit up," Mona hissed at Sissy. She watched me as she spoke to her. Mona made sure to lock our eyes together. She smirked, grabbed her bag and keys off of the counter and walked out the back door, slamming it behind her.

The hate churned once again inside me. I knew what I had to do. I had to get us away from her for good. All of us.

Mona

"BUT CANDICE, YOU should've seen his face. If looks could kill…" I shuddered to myself just thinking about it. "I'd be in a pine box right this second. That boy wanted to kill me."

I pulled my youngest child, Sean close to me and played with the dark ringlets of curly hair piled on his head. No matter what I said or how I tried to explain it to Candice, who by the way, only recently had her first child, she wouldn't understand.

"Girl, he snatched the belt out of my hand and held his chest out like he wanted to fight me." I let go of a lock of Sean's hair to pull the blunt away from my lips, sucking in air as I did so.

"Not Xavier!" Candice cried in disbelief. "Genesis has a little fire in her, but Xavier is as sweet as sugar. To be totally honest with you, Mona…" She paused and tilted her head to the side. "Xavier is getting kinda big for you to be beating on him like you do."

"*Beating?*" I raised one eyebrow. "What do you mean by that, Candice?" My eyes dared her to say it again.

"You know what I mean, girl." Candice kicked off her shoes

and pulled both feet underneath her on the sofa. With a little hesitation in her voice, she continued. "I know it's none of my business, but that boy is almost as tall as you are now. You can't go on using your fists on him forever. I mean really, Mona, he is a good kid."

I passed Candice the blunt just to shut her up and focused my eyes on the television next to her. Sean snored lightly on my lap and instinctively I put one hand back in his curly hair. Candice smoked and continued to run her mouth. I barely heard a word she said. I blocked her out. It amazed me how folks smoked a lil weed and all of a sudden became the most philosophical people you ever met in your life.

Candice had one kid and a great husband to take care of her at home. She didn't even have to work. She had no clue what it was like to be me—always wanting and needing and never receiving any love or appreciation. Even from the kids you pushed out yourself. It seemed as though everyone was waiting in line to attack me. The whole world was against me, crushing the life out of me.

"I saw Xavier on his way to school this morning, and his eye was a mess. You better be careful treating those kids like that. You probably should have kept him home today. You know the school is already watching you and ya just never know." Candice exhaled a puff of white smoke.

I didn't know how much longer I was willing to stand her coming at me about my personal business like she was Miss Perfect or something. Wait until her baby grew up, she would spank her kid, too. I just didn't get up in folks' business like that. I was getting pretty irritated with her real fast. These were my kids. Mine. I wish somebody would come up in here and try to snatch something I gave birth to from me. I loved my kids and I didn't give a damn who didn't believe it. All the anger management I needed was in my hand rolled up in a chocolate-flavored Swisher Sweet.

"You know what, Candice? You're right. It's none of your damn business!" My anger crept through my lips before I could stop it.

"I'm sick of all of you goody two-shoes motha fuckas always trying to tell me what to do like you are better than me or something. What? You don't think I love my kids?"

"Mona. That's not what I'm saying at all." Candice was clearly shocked by my outburst and softened her tone. "I just want what's best for you *and* the kids, that's all."

"Well, what's best is if you mind your own and let me handle me and mine," I said.

"Why are you getting so mad? I'm just trying to be a friend. I've wanted to tell you this for a long time but didn't know how. Really Mona, what could Xavier have done that was so bad that you gave him a black eye?" Candice put what was left of the blunt in the ashtray and leaned in toward me, waiting for an answer.

"Are you fucking questioning me?" I yelled.

"Yes. Mona, I want to know. What did he do?" She yelled back with a look of total repulsion plastered on her face. "What? He didn't take out the trash again?" Candice sneered.

I was a little shocked because she was usually more reserved. I had never seen her so confrontational before, which made me a little embarrassed. On a real note, I didn't even know *what* to say that wouldn't come out sounding stupid. He broke a jar of mayonnaise. That was it wasn't it. What started it all? Xavier broke a jar of mayonnaise and I spanked him. No, I beat him. But he deserved it, right?

Maybe I did beat him for something stupid. But I damn sure didn't have to answer to Candice in my own house about it. It was bad enough that I felt sorry for hurting him. The last thing I needed was somebody up in here smoking up my weed and trying to make me feel even worse than I already did, asking stupid questions. Those were my kids and I could do what I damn well pleased with them.

Hell, I even tried to apologize to Xavier after I got off of work later that night. I went into his room and I could tell that he was awake, but pretending to be asleep. When I climbed into the bed next to him—he flinched when I touched him. I laid there next to him for a few minutes and played with his wavy hair like I used to do when he was little. I smiled, thinking about how much he used to love when I did that. Then, I whispered into his ear that I was really sorry and I'd never hit him like that again, he didn't move or respond. He continued to breathe heavily and pretended to be asleep. So screw it—what was I supposed to do? Beg him to forgive me—again? Bottom line was that Xavier was gonna have to learn to listen to me and do what I say. Stay in a child's place.

Now, the black eye was another thing. *I gave him a black eye?* Damn. Nervousness seized my stomach and unsettled me. That morning I waited until Xavier and Genesis had left for school before I came out of my room because I couldn't face him. This was the first I'd heard of Xavier going to school with a black eye. Had I known, I would have made him stay home.

I know that it was easy for me to lose my temper. I'd promised my kids so many times that I would stop hitting them. Maybe I do need some kinda psychological help. I looked up and Candice was still staring at me with that disgusted look on her face, waiting for an answer. I felt like a science experiment, squirming around in a petri dish under the hot lens of a microscope. I moved Sean off of my lap and placed his head gently on a pillow at the opposite end of the sofa and put my face in my hands.

I am a monster. I am everything that I had always hated and feared that I would become. *My mother.* How could I make Candice understand? The last thing I ever wanted to do was hurt my babies.

"Answer the question," Candice said slowly, her eyes narrowing into angry slits. "You can't answer it, can you? Do you know why I always get up and leave when it even looks like you are going to be mad at your kids? Have you ever noticed that I only come over when they are at school now? It's because you go too far. You never know when to stop and I don't want to be here while you treat your own kids like garbage. You better get your shit together, or CPS is gonna be knocking at your door. Or worse, those kids are gonna hate you forever."

Candice was the only real friend I thought I had. She was the first person in the neighborhood to speak to me when I moved in. We got close real fast; she was like the sister that I never had but, always wanted. But right now, I didn't feel like she was being a good friend, but being my judge.

"I think it's time for you to go," I said. I needed to think.

Candice got up and walked toward the door then turned around and came back. I thought she was gonna apologize and I perked up. Like I said before, I didn't have any other friends and I didn't want to lose her. Not over something silly like me spanking my kids, at least.

"You know, my father beat my mother and me when I was a kid," she continued. "We used to lock ourselves in the bathroom until he passed out drunk. I promised myself that I would never be with a man like him. When I saw your son this morning, it brought those memories back to me. Going to school hiding my bruises, getting teased by the other kids. I remember helping my mom pack on make-up to cover up her bruises so she could go to work. Everybody knew and nobody helped us. They said that my father had a good job and my mother would be crazy to leave. So we stayed." Candice swiped at the tears on her cheeks.

Any other day, Candice could've told me that story and it would have been waterworks up in the piece. Not today. This bitch was all up in my house comparing me to her abusive ass father. What in the hell? I leaned back on the sofa and half listened to her words as I focused on the TV. I wanted her to take the hint and leave.

"Today, I decided that I refuse to have a friend like you. You are just as evil as my father. A sorry excuse for a woman and especially for a mother." Candice spat out her words as if blowing out all the contempt she could ever feel for one person on me. I felt like shit.

"Girl, this ain't no damn soap opera. I said get the fuck out!" I raised my voice, even the sleeping Sean jerked awake under the weight of it.

"I'm leaving…I'm leaving," Candice said, holding up both of her hands.

Just as soon as she slammed the door behind her, tears that I didn't know I had found their way down my face.

"What's the matter, Mommy?" Sean said, climbing onto my lap.

"Nothing, baby. Want Mommy to take a nap with you?"

"Yes," he said, rubbing his eyes with both fists.

"You love Mommy?"

"Uh huh."

I adjusted his little body so that both of ours could be positioned on the couch with me behind him. He was so warm and lovable. I wrapped him in my arms and did what I always did. I quietly cried myself to sleep thinking about how Candice was right. I was a sorry excuse of a mother.

It felt like I was only asleep for a few minutes. I raised my head just a little to make sure that I heard it the first time and someone wasn't beating me on my head in a dream.

Bam. Bam. Bam.

Yes, someone was surely knocking on the door. I glanced at the clock over the TV and it read 4:45 P.M. I wondered if Genesis and Xavier had made it home already. If so, I didn't hear them come in. Well, it's not like they would disturb me when I was asleep. They knew better. I moved Sean back away from the edge of the sofa as I got up. The only person that visited me was Candice, but she never knocked. But after the fight we had earlier—*maybe*. I would bet anything that she wanted to make up with me. I all but skipped with glee to the door.

Bam. Bam. Bam.

I gladly snatched the door open, hoping to see Candice standing there.

"It's okay, girl. You don't have to— apologize," I said, grinning from ear to ear before I looked to see who it actually was.

My smile did an immediate turn straight down. A uniformed police officer stood in front of me. Next to him, was a small-framed woman with a yellow pad in her hand. She looked familiar for some reason. Maybe I'd seen her at the kids' school. Briefly, thoughts of Genesis and Xavier flashed through my mind, but I was almost certain that my kids were upstairs.

"Mrs. Mona Thomas?" the officer said, sounding like this was some serious official business.

"Yeah, I'm Mona. Mrs. Thomas is my mother." I don't know why I said that. I once heard someone say it on television before and I always wanted to use that line. Plus, I was nervous.

The butterflies in my stomach moved around. Until he said my name, I had hoped that he had the wrong house. I was more concerned about all the marijuana I'd left lying on the kitchen table. This was a totally unexpected visit. My mind wandered in so many directions at one time as the butterflies in my stomach flitted their way up to my brain. I felt lightheaded. Opening your door and seeing the police standing there if you didn't call them, could only mean one thing—*trouble*.

Xavier

SISSY AND I watched as the door opened and my mother stepped out onto the porch. I felt sick to my stomach again. Sissy squeezed my hand some more. I don't know if it was because she was scared or because she knew that I was. *It's really about to happen* was all I could think over and over again. At that point there was no turning back. I would never be able to undo telling the principal the truth about Mona.

"I wonder if they'll let us get some of our clothes," Genesis asked.

"Nah, I already asked that. Naomi said these things sometimes don't go well. And it may be that all we have are the clothes on our backs." I sighed loudly, wanting the whole thing to hurry up and be over.

I could only see Naomi's side profile as she pulled a badge out of her pocket and showed it to Mona. I wished I could hear what they were saying because Mona took a step back and put her hand over her chest. The police officer spoke to Mona and then he walked away from the door and stood off to the side playing with his cell phone while Mona and Naomi talked.

"Oh no, my books. What about my snake books?" Sissy exclaimed. "Do you think I can go in and get my books?"

"You can get new books, Sissy," I said.

I really wanted to tell her to shut up. But I knew that she was just scared and that's why she kept talking about stupid stuff. I didn't care if I never got any of my old stuff back. I only wanted to be away from Mona. I didn't say it though because I knew that Sissy didn't understand how much I hated Mona.

"What about the teddy bear my daddy gave me?" Sissy added.

"That's enough, Sissy! All you are worried about is your *stuff*," I said with more irritation in my voice than I intended.

"And all you are worried about is yourself," she countered.

"Oh really. Look at *my* eye. Look at *my* hands," I said. I pulled them away from hers and waved my scorched fists in her face.

"Well, if you hadn't of stood up to her, she wouldn't have socked you in the eye."

"Did you forget that she slapped you, too? For nothing."

"Well, only after *you* made her so mad!" Genesis crossed her arms over her chest and turned away from me. She stared out the window into an empty field.

"Are you mad at me because I told?" I asked.

"Yes," Genesis said, never taking her eyes off of the empty lot. "I can't believe you told on Mona. She's our mother. You don't know what's gonna happen to us now. Or to her. What if she goes to jail?"

"Don't be scared, Sissy. I promise I'll take care of you and Sean, and I won't let anything bad happen to you guys."

"You couldn't stop Mona from hitting you all the time, could you? Or me and Sean. How do you think you are gonna protect us?" Genesis retorted.

"I could have stopped her if I wanted to!" I leaned to one side and pulled a Swiss army knife out of my back pocket and flashed it in front of Sissy's face before returning it to its safety nest in my jeans.

"Where did you get that from? I'm telling!" She demanded to know. Her eyes opened wide in shock at my weapon.

"Tell who?" I laughed nervously. "I got it from Tommy at school. His mother was crazy, too and—"

"Mona is not crazy!" Sissy cut me off. "She just hates you because you remind her of our daddy!"

"Same thing, right? It's stupid for her to be mad at me because of a man that I don't even know. That's not crazy to you?"

"She's just going through a lot of changes right now. Sean's daddy just left and her hours got cut at work. We are all she—"

"You sound just like her," I said, cutting Sissy off. "If we are all she has, then why does she treat us like shit?"

"You don't understand."

"No! You don't understand," I said.

I was pissed that Sissy always defended Mona and took her side and not mine. I was the one sitting there with a black eye. I didn't know why I expected Sissy to understand; she always made excuses for Mona, no matter what she did. I decided to just keep my mouth closed. I stared at the side of Sissy's head and realized how much *she* looked like Mona, sitting there with her face twisted in anger. Her pretty features immediately creased and wrinkled— like Mona's.

I directed my attention back out the window of the car just in time to see Mona craning her neck around Naomi to get a look into the police car. I think she thought we were in it. I was grateful that Naomi drove a normal car with no markings on it.

I slumped down in my seat anyway. Sissy saw her looking, too, and she raised her hand and waved it furiously at Mona like she was happy to see her or something. I couldn't believe Sissy just did that. And right in my face. I began to question whether we were in this thing together.

Naomi

"YOU AIN'T TAKING my kids!"

"I'm going to need you to calm down," I raised my voice just a little to get her attention. I'd never understand how a woman that beat and scorched the skin off of her own children could be so attached to them. I felt like I was doing her a favor by taking them off of her miserable hands.

"Who called you? It was Candice, wasn't it? I know you don't believe her. She was at my house this morning and we had a fight. That bitch is just trying to get even with me because I put her fake ass outta my house."

"Mona, look. Don't you think it would be better if we took this inside?" I tried to reason with her; this situation had the makings of a huge dramatic scene. "Your neighbors are all watching." I nodded in the direction of the growing pool of people forming, waiting for some drama to jump off.

"Let them watch! Do you think I care?" she screamed. "Where's Xavier and Genesis? Where are my damn kids?"

"Okay. Okay," I said. "Your children are safe and are under the protection of the state. Like I said before, we are now here for Sean. They are all going to be together. You will have the opportunity to state your side at a court hearing which will be held within the next 48 hours."

"You're not taking my kids!" She put both of her hands on her narrow hips defiantly.

I almost laughed out loud in her face instead of in my head. We already had two of the children in our custody. I don't know why *these* people always think that by the time the state is called in, they still have a choice in these matters. Bottom line, we weren't leaving without Sean. I always tried to reason with these women to get them to give the children over to me peacefully. It always ended up the same. I found it ironic that we had to take them in the same manner the parents treated the children—*by force*. It's the only language abusive parents understood. If they knew another way of doing things, I wouldn't have a job.

"Miss. I mean Mona, we already have your children. Can we go inside so that I can talk to you in private for a minute?"

"Hell no! You ain't coming in my house." She squinted her eyes and stretched her neck around in an attempt to look over my shoulder into the police car that was parked across the street in hopes of seeing her kids.

I stepped over just a little to block her view of the cars. Then I nodded in the officer's direction as both a signal to her that he was there and for him to call for backup. I wasn't sure if she saw the kids or not, but it was time to wrap this sordid scene up. I didn't want to be out all night and I still had to drop the children off to their temporary placement location before it got too late.

"There has to be a mistake somewhere," Mona kept repeating. "A big misunderstanding. Candice is trying to get me in trouble by calling you," She explained.

Talk about somebody in denial. I was standing at her door, telling her that she had lost legal custody of the children that she birthed and all she really wanted to know was who snitched on her. It was too much. Wait until she found out that her own son was tired of being treated like an ashtray. And I meant that literally.

"Either you go inside and get Sean or the officer here will have to do it for you," I said running out of patience.

She reached behind her and pulled her front door closed completely as she stepped out onto the porch. "Do what you need to do." The faint woodsy scent of marijuana emanated from her lips.

Drugs were definitely involved. Xavier didn't tell me that part. I had a feeling that things were going to get real ugly. Her demeanor was typical of abusers. I looked over helplessly at Officer Shaw for support and shrugged my shoulders. He grinned and peered at his shoes. I decided to attempt reasoning one more time before she got a chance to see up close the back seat of the police car for obstructing justice.

She wasn't that big of a woman, actually she was kinda small. If I weren't repulsed by people like her so much, I would have, under different circumstances, thought she was pretty. She had dark curly rings of shoulder length hair framing her petite face. Her skin was smooth but told the tender tale of teenage acne from long ago. Genesis looked a lot like her sans the snarled upper lip which hid a perfect set of white teeth. Xavier was taller and much bigger than Mona already.

Had I walked past her on the street, I would've never guessed that this woman had not one, but two teenage children and a toddler. Either she aged very well or she was very young. My bet was on the latter. Teenage parents were more likely than any other parental group to become abusers. The stress of rearing children and losing out on their own childhood did something terrible to their mental state. Kids were not emotionally ready to raise children.

"You don't want to do this, Mona," I issued a warning.

Out of the corner of my eye, I saw another police cruiser pull up. Officer Shaw walked off to meet and brief the arriving officer. Some of her neighbors were sitting outside on lawn chairs.

The word fight, fight, fight echoed from their silent lips. They wanted to see some action. It was clear that Mona was feeding off of their interest in the matter and was getting high off their adrenaline.

"Look at you, Miss high and mighty," she hissed. "Rolling up in here like you better than somebody else. You ain't shit but a simple minded government employee. I pay my taxes. I pay *you*."

Okay so we're at the part where the insults got hurled. Blows were never far away. I'd heard it all before. My palms began to sweat. Not that I was afraid, but I hated violence. I chose this job to help innocent children, not to verbally fight with parents and especially not physically. This part of my job sucked, but hey it came with the territory. I planned on getting the last insult when I drove off with this demon's kids. I smiled at her verbal abuse.

"You think you can just come up in here and snatch somebody's kids from them. You got another thing coming."

"Like I said before, Mona, we had a report of child abuse. You will have a court date very soon and you can state your case. If the court finds that you haven't done any wrongdoings, then—"

"Then what? I can get my kids back?" she interjected.

For a brief second, I thought I heard desperation in her voice. She relaxed her stance and allowed her guard to drop. Hmm. It was going to be easier than I thought. Maybe I was underestimating this woman. I decided to run with it and get the job done.

"Yes, you *may* be able to take your kids home. You will *have* to show up," I said, lying through my teeth. She was clearly more unfit than a pair of size too little jeans. After what Xavier said about her, she would have better luck joining the circus as a dancing tightrope act than she would getting her kids back in a couple of days. It was apparent that she had no clue of the depth this investigation had already gone. Xavier had given me an earful. It was too late. Her abusive tendencies had allowed the system to come in.

She turned her back to us and put her hand on the door. A female police officer had arrived and stood off to the side laughing with Officer Shaw. Mona, with much hesitation, pushed the door open. There was a commotion in the crowd and someone hollered, "Hey Candice, you better go check on your girl. CPS is here!"

"She's not my girl," a woman replied.

I sucked in my breath, hoping Mona didn't hear it or would ignore it. It was too late. She whipped around and darted off in the direction of the small crowd and stopped in front of a young woman holding a toddler by the hand.

"It's like that, Candice?" Mona pushed the girl with both hands.

"Like what? You brought this on yourself," the girl named Candice replied.

"Snitch!"

Both of the police officers followed the confusion, breaking into the crowd forming around the two women. This was turning into a ghetto nightmare and a typical one at that. I planned to get Sean and get going. I turned my attention back to the door which Mona had so conveniently left open and seriously contemplated entering. It went against all kinds of state policies for us to enter a home without being asked inside.

I peeked my head inside the door. The apartment was dimly lit, but from what I could see, very clean and tastefully furnished. I looked over my shoulder to see if the confrontation was still going on, knowing I didn't have much time. The female officer was talking to Mona who had begun to cry. Officer Shaw attempted to disperse the onlookers. I was nervous because I was a by-the-book type of government employee. I seemed to be in a world of my own, knowingly breaking the law was a lonely feeling and it made me uneasy.

"Sean. Sean," I called out first before entering.

I placed both hands on the doorway and leered in more.

"Sean. Are you in there?" I yelled a little louder that time.

I was about to take that critical criminal step inside when the most adorable little boy appeared before me, rubbing his eyes with one hand and pulling a dingy teddy bear by the leg with the other. He looked a lot like Genesis. I could tell that he had been asleep because he had strategic indents on his face which could have only come from snoozing on a textured pillow or sofa.

"Is your name Sean?" I asked just to be on the safe side. I didn't want to do a snatch and run with a neighbor's kid.

"Where's my mama?" the little boy asked.

"Oh, she's talking to your neighbor," I replied with what was only a half lie.

"Wanna tell me your name?" I took his hand in mine.

"I want my mama." He began to cry.

"Do you know Genesis and Xavier?"

"Yes," he said. I finally had his attention.

"Well, I have them with me. I'm just looking for their little brother Sean, so everyone can be together. Now, I just need for you to tell me your name."

"Sean. I'm Sean," he said, perking up. "I want my Sissy! Take me to my Sissy, please."

"Well, let's go, Sean," I said in my cheeriest voice.

Bingo. It would have been nice if Mona would have let me take some of the children's things. Oh well. I quickly pulled Sean in the direction of my car parked across the street. The crowd had doubled in such a short time. Those that weren't interested in watching another young woman lose her children to the system were for sure interested in a girl fight. Talk about priorities in this neighborhood. I thought it would be best if I signaled the police officers after I was in the safety of my car with Sean. From the size of the crowd, they would be out there a while trying to calm things down.

"Always make sure you look both ways before crossing the street," I said to Sean as I looked left and right.

My goal was to make him comfortable with me. I could see Genesis in the window. I wondered where Xavier had gone. Sean and I were halfway across the street when I saw Xavier's head pop up in the window. It looked like he was excited to see his brother and he waved frantically at us. I smiled and waved back at him as if to say, *got him*.

"Where the fuck you think you going?" Mona's winded voice came out of nowhere.

Before I turned to face her, she shoved me as hard as she could. I almost lost my balance because of my heels. I stumbled a few steps and quickly regained my composure, still maintaining my grip on Sean's hand. No matter what, I was not letting him go.

"Where you going with my son?" she asked again, this time getting into a fighting stance.

"Look, Mona, we already discussed this. I don't want any problems," I replied.

Mona was ready for a confrontation. She was like an angry lioness and was out to protect what she considered hers. I didn't want her to know that Genesis and Xavier were in the car directly behind me. This needed to end fast.

"Oh you want some problems, lady," she said heatedly. "You seriously think I'm just gonna let you take my kids and walk away like it ain't nothing."

I looked up to see where the police officers were and why they didn't have Mona. I saw Officer Shaw look in my direction and head my way. I held on to Sean's hand as he buried his face in my legs. It was no use reasoning with her. It would be best to just let them handle Mona.

"Genesis! Baby, get over here."

Genesis? I looked over my shoulder and Genesis was walking toward Mona. What in the hell was going on here? I looked back and didn't see Xavier.

"I'm staying with my Mom!" Genesis proclaimed.

"Get back in the car, Genesis," I said sternly.

"Don't tell my daughter what to do! Get over here, girl. Where's your brother?"

"In the car. He told them, Mama. He told them everything. He told on you. He said—" Genesis began to cry.

"Just shut up and get over here." Mona yelled at her. "Come here, Sean."

"Genesis. Get back in the car and wait!" I ordered. I had a tight grip on Sean's hand, so I was less worried about him.

Mona lunged at me. She grabbed my hair so fast that I had little time to protect myself. All those self defense techniques I learned from the classes the state made us take went right out the window when I needed them most.

"I told you that I wasn't playing with you, you fucking bitch!" Mona screeched.

Somehow Mona had me around the neck and was blocking my airways. I tried to writhe free, clawing at her arm around my neck. I was forced to let go of Sean's hand. Out of the corner of my eye, I saw Genesis grab him. Sean was screaming for help. I was gasping for air.

"What you gone do now? You tough enough to come up in my house, but I got yo' ass now."

Her voice. That voice was so familiar and evil. Years of abuse came flooding back to me and I was a six year old victim again and Nola had her hands around my throat. Officer Shaw struggled to pull us apart. He pushed Mona with so much force she hit the ground and toppled over. I fell to my knees, holding my throat.

Xavier was suddenly by my side with something shiny in his hand asking me if I was okay. Genesis was crouching near the car with Sean in tow. It all got out of control so fast. Everything was a tumultuous haze as I struggled to regain my breath.

She put her hands on me. I began to seethe in shades of crimson and the whole scene became a blur. Anger singed my blood and blinded my sense of reason. I had never wanted to hurt someone more than I wanted to hurt Mona in all of my life. It had been years since someone—anyone physically put their hands on me. I hadn't been touched by evil since I was taken from Nola. Mona was pure evil like the rest of those unfit mothers out there. I pulled myself up from my knees to my feet with Xavier's help.

"Oh so you gone help that bitch get up, Xavier, and not your own mother!" Mona yelled.

Xavier didn't answer. He looked helplessly to the ground with a guilty face.

Her voice annoyed me. If she knew any better, she would stop talking. *Now.*

"I know what you did," she continued her rant. "When I come for Genesis and Sean, I don't want your trifling ass back. I'm gonna let the state keep you!" She laughed at the look of hurt that crossed Xavier's face.

That did it.

I casually walked over to where Officer Shaw was putting handcuffs on Mona and spit squarely in her face, right between her eyebrows. I'd had enough of her. And before my spit had time to submerge into her pores good, I raised my right hand and slapped her with the back of it. Spittle flew out of the side of her mouth.

Mona was so stunned that her eyes did all the talking for her and that wasn't saying much. I know she felt it. All the hate bottled up within me was put into that one blow. Her cheek quickly reconstructed my handprint as though it were a work of art. If hate could be a brand, I left it on her face to remember me.

I don't know what came over me. I felt vindicated for Xavier, temporarily at least. The crowd cheered and some laughed, including the girl Candice who put two fingers in her mouth and whistled loudly. I knew I would pay later for what I did to Mona. I decided to worry about how I was gonna talk myself out of the trouble that I was in later on that evening. Hell, my best friend was my supervisor, remember.

I looked over at Xavier as he tried to hide a little smile and I winked at him. Point one for the good guys. For the first time in my life, I lived in the right now. Even if I must say so myself, that brief, quiet moment that I may regret later was—priceless.

Mona

THEY TOOK MY kids. *Just took them away from me.* I didn't know what to do with myself but think about ways to die. I had never been without them. I had Genesis when I was fifteen years old and Xavier quickly followed. That was more than half of my life right there. I'd spent my entire adult life raising them all by myself. Now they were all gone and I didn't have a clue where or with whom. I'd been sitting in the same spot, unmoving for hours trying to figure out where everything in my life went so wrong.

Their father and I had so many plans for a great future. He went to the military right after he graduated from high school and was supposed to come and get me so we could begin a new life together, somewhere far away from the south side of Houston, Texas, after boot camp. He came all right. He came and got me pregnant with Xavier when he was home on leave and promised that we'd get married when he got settled in California. That day never came and I had to hear that he was married from someone in the neighborhood.

"Hey Mona, so your baby daddy got married?" they'd joked. "And she's white."

I was the laughingstock of the neighborhood and everybody either joked about me behind my back or felt sorry for me in my face. He got married and left me with two kids. Then he told everybody that they weren't even his, well, that Xavier wasn't his. But if he wasn't gonna claim Xavier, he damn sure wasn't gonna be in Genesis' life either. He sent Genesis one lousy teddy bear for her fifth birthday. That was the last I ever heard from him.

I don't quite know which part hurt the most. That he left me or that he disowned our children. The fact that he married a white girl really didn't bother me. Hell, she could've been purple for all I cared. He was the first man that I ever loved and that I thought genuinely loved me. He snatched all of my dreams of a happy family right from underneath my feet. Even when he knew the truth about what I was dealing with at home, he left me worse off than he'd found me.

"I'll never hurt you, Mona." He promised me—repeatedly.

I had to quit regular school when I had those kids. I gave up everything to raise them. Every time I watched the Olympics on television, I got mad at myself. Had it not been for my own stupidity that could have been me competing for gold medals. Back in high school, nobody could run faster than me. I may have been short, but I was as fast as a bolt of lightning. If I could turn back the hands of time, I would. I wouldn't have believed anything that lying dog had to say. I would have never skipped track practice to be with him.

"You're not gonna get pregnant, baby. Especially your first time," he'd said to me. "And if you do, I got you."

Humph. Why in the hell did I trust him? Because as sure as my name was Mona, I got pregnant the first time *we* had sex. Cheated on for the first time and finally dumped for the first time. It took me years to get over his ass. I could just scream at all of the mistakes that I'd made. My problems all started with men and ended with—kids.

I don't even want to start thinking about little Sean's daddy. Actually, if I'm honest with myself, he was a good man. He really tried to help. I wished I would have taken his advice and went to counseling. He wanted to marry me, even though I already had two kids with another man. He was willing to accept that added responsibility. We only fought over one thing—me spanking the kids, Xavier mostly.

"You better not ever put your hands on my son like that," he threatened me once.

I didn't know why he thought I would hurt his son. I loved Sean. He was my baby. But that's what finally broke us up. He walked in one day on me holding a Swisher to Xavier's knuckles and he went ballistic. It was the first and last time that he ever hit me. He packed his things and told me that it was over because I was crazy and needed help. I helped him get his shit together by tossing it down the stairs. He must have thought I was gonna be a fool to lay up with a man after he put his hands on me.

That was a few weeks ago, and last Saturday I received a summons to appear before the family court. He had the nerve to file for sole custody of Sean. Any man that hit a woman was worthless. I was gonna tell the court about what really happened, too. I was glad that I took pictures of my lip as proof. He was not getting my son. Over my dead body would I let my baby go live with that woman beater. Screw him.

And screw Xavier because my present circumstance was all his fault. Seriously, I'd devoted half of my life to being their mother and this is how he repaid me. By telling those people that I abused him. At first I thought it was Candice, but when Genesis said that it was Xavier, it solidified my hatred for him. Then he ran to the side of that damn social worker woman with a knife in his hand like he was gonna do something to *me*. His mother! Did he actually think she gave a damn about him? He was just like his daddy. No damn good because that whole thing was a bunch of bull.

Just as soon as I get out of here, I'm going to—.

"Mona. Mona Thomas?" A police officer yelled into my cell, his voice echoed off the dirty concrete walls.

All the other women started looking around, wishing it was their name being called. I just about raced to the opening doors.

"That's me!" I yelped excitedly.

"Someone has posted bond for you. Follow me."

The sound of the closing iron bars behind me clanged loudly in my ears. I didn't even look back. I was so ready to get out of that cramped, funky cell I could've kissed the police officer. Mind you, it had only been about five or six hours, but still. I had never been in jail and this trip sealed the deal that I'd never and I mean never go back. I was so tight on the officer's heels that I almost tripped him. I slowed my gait when he gave me the evil eye. The last thing I wanted was to make him angry and end up having to spend the whole night in that pissy, funky hole with a bunch of hookers.

I already knew who had posted my bond. I was pissed that it took her so long to get it done. The officer walked me to the front desk and pushed several papers in my face that required my signature. I didn't read one word. I didn't care what those pages said. I wanted to go home and at the moment I'd give my first born to make that happen. I take that back, the state already had my first born and my second. They could keep him. Shit on Xavier. He was dead to me.

"You can go now. Remember your court date," the officer said with his back to me as if I were an invisible wretch.

"So, I see you found some more trouble to get into, eh?" my mother said.

I looked around the counter in the direction of her voice.

"No, trouble found me this time," I replied.

She stood and made her way to the exit door. I followed behind her trying to explain my new dilemma.

"You know that damn Xavier—" I began.

She looked down her nose to shush me. Well, barely. She was only a hair taller than I was. But it still felt like she was looking down at me, which is what she usually did.

"Wait until we get in the car," she never turned to look at me.

I trailed quietly behind and all the while got my side of what had taken place together in my head. My mother had the ability to pick a story apart in search for *her* version of the truth. She was a master at forcing her ideals on you. Once we got inside the confines of her car, she let her fury unfurl. I scooted as close to the passenger side door as I could.

"What did I tell you, Mona? I told you to stop hitting those kids like that. I told you this very morning exactly what was going to happen. And just look at you. Sitting in some prison like a common criminal."

"It wasn't prison. It was a precinct jail," I tried to explain.

She poked me in the forehead with her long manicured fingernail. I decided to just be quiet.

"What! You really are pathetic, you know that? Do you think it really makes a difference whether it was prison or a precinct cell that you were sitting in?" She fumed as I sunk further down in the creamy leather of the passenger seat.

"I had to…We had to put our house up to get you out of there. And in the middle of the night no less. And all you care to say is that it was a precinct jail and *not a prison*," she said, mimicking me.

Don't say another word Mona. I stared out of the window as she drove me home. I didn't believe that she had to put her house up. It was no use attempting to rationalize with my mother. She was always right and was always going to be right. Nothing I ever did made her happy. I only lived about half an hour from the station; hopefully, I could make it without this scene blowing up in my face, too. That's all I needed to go along without the other bombs going off in my life was for Mother to trip out.

"I know that I raised you better than all of this," she continued, waving her hand erratically around the car for added emphasis.

No you didn't, I thought.

"Your little friend Candice had to be the one to call me to tell me what happened today. Do you know how embarrassed I was? I was in a very important meeting with your father that is about to change our lives forever. And then this. You go and get yourself arrested for striking a state employee *and* abusing your children all in the same day." She stopped to take a breath before finishing. "Have you lost your God-fearing mind?"

Fear God. No. The only person I fear is you.

"I just can't believe how you treat those kids, like...like dogs."

Those kids? Those kids are your grandchildren that you never visit. I said nothing and just rolled my eyes out of the window. I only wanted to get home in peace.

"I don't know what has gotten in to you, Mona, but they are for sure better off in a foster home. You are not fit to be anybody's mother. You disgust me. I wish I never had you. Especially if this is how you are going to treat another human being."

Funny, I've been wishing the same thing.

"We didn't treat you like this when you were a child. I don't know where you went wrong. Probably from laying up with those no good ghetto birds all day."

Wrong again. You must have forgotten the things you and Daddy did to me growing up before you got all saved and sanctified. Her extreme case of selective amnesia annoyed me.

"I need for you to understand that we can't take anymore foolishness from you. You are too unpredictable and volatile. Your behavior is going to ruin *my* life," she said before going quiet the rest of the drive to my place.

My life. Did she just say that I was going to ruin "her" life? Everything has always been only about her and Daddy.

We pulled in front of my building. I was glad it was late at night, so no one would see me come in without my children. I just wanted to get as far away from my mother as I could. I wanted to rush inside, climb in my bed, and never wake up again.

She yanked on my arm so that I would face her. I couldn't, so instead I focused on her diamond studded pearl earrings as she spoke her final parting words. Her salt and pepper hair was in the neatest and most tight bun I'd ever seen in my life. I grinned to think that it was because her hair was pulled so tight that she lost some of her brain functions, like her ability to be rational. She smiled back at me, warmly, as though we were on the same side.

"Don't worry about those kids, Mona. Let the state keep them. Look at all that they have put you through. Those kids don't appreciate you, baby. Take this opportunity to get your life back together while you still have time. Look at you, you're still a pretty girl and the entire world can be your oyster." She smiled brighter, leaving a streak of bright red lipstick across her teeth.

"Thanks for coming to get me, Mother," I said, getting out of the car. Leaning into the open door, I added, "Don't worry, I'll make my court date. I hate to put you and Daddy out like this." I tried to sound as sincere as possible.

She started her car then shut it off again and quickly ran around to my side before I headed up the walkway.

"Wait. Wait," she said cupping both of my hands in hers.

"We didn't pray, baby. Mother is gonna take care of everything, okay. Don't worry or you'll wrinkle up your pretty face. Now, bow your head, honey."

And they think that I'm the crazy one.

"Dear Heavenly Father, we come to you as humbly we know how, asking you once again—"

I didn't listen. I couldn't. She was such a hypocrite. I couldn't stand her most of the time. Her prayers fell on deaf ears. If there was anyone that I wanted praying for me, it sure as hell wasn't Lenora Thomas.

Naomi

I TOSSED AND turned in the bed so furiously that Jake gave me an ultimatum—go sleep on the couch or he would. I grabbed my robe and went with no complaints, especially since he was already in bed asleep when I got home. I grabbed a glass of wine to take the edge off of my nerves and sat on the patio and watched the stars. I half expected him to still be at church. Yes, church. Jake spent every waking second over there. It was his home away from work, not home. He only came here to sleep and eat and not much of that either. In any case, Jake being asleep worked out in my favor because I had a lot on my mind. I was not in the mood to answer a bunch of questions about my day or suffer through any of his fondling.

In my line of work, I fully expected to have twists and turns, most days. After all the years I've had on my job, today was extremely bizarre. Something about the family that I encountered today shook me. I regretted not being able to spend much time making sure the kids were comfortable with Mrs. Fildhurst before I left. I wondered how they were doing.

When I left, Sean was crying non-stop. Xavier and Genesis seemed to have experienced some sort of rift between them and they weren't talking at all. These things were usually really hard on kids. Still, going into placement was best for them, that I was sure of.

"Are you okay, honey?" Jake said, interrupting my thoughts.

"Yes. I'm fine. Why are you up?" I flashed a phony smile his way. I didn't want to explain my thoughts.

"I felt guilty for kicking you out of the bed, that's all. And I came to check on you. See if you're ready to come back and be still. I'm not used to sleeping without you."

"Really? Well I'm used to sleeping without you," I said before I had time to think about my choice of words.

"What's that supposed to mean?" He sat down in the chair next to mine and waited for an answer.

I didn't feel like arguing with Jake. Not tonight especially with everything else I had to worry about. I was already worrying about this new case. I still had Dae to deal with. I was so happy she didn't answer her cell when I called to give her my side of what happened personally before she had a chance to read the report later. I left a brief message and decided it would be better to just deal with it tomorrow. That's how I usually dealt with big things—by putting them off.

Jake pulled my feet onto his lap and began to massage them gently. "I don't want to fight with you tonight."

"I know. Neither do I. I'm sorry for saying that. I just have a lot on my mind right now," I said. I leaned my head back and searched the sky for stars. His hands felt so good. Most of the time, he knew the right things to do.

"Do you want to talk about it?"

"No, it's work stuff," I said. "Just keep doing what you're doing right now."

"You know, you never talk about your job."

"Well, most of the aspects of my job are confidential. Plus, I wouldn't want to bore you."

"What you do is far from boring," he said, working his hands to my ankles. "You are out there making a difference every day."

"Oh, you think so," I said, chuckling. "Try telling that to some deranged mother when I tell her that she's unfit to retain custody of her children."

"I'm sure all the mothers aren't that bad. Some people just need a little help, that's all. And a little Jesus wouldn't hurt."

Okay, I was waiting for his Jesus speech to start. Jake seemed to think that his invisible God could solve any problem with a wave of his mighty hand. I wished he could've met Xavier today or spent a little time with Jordan. Where's Jake's God in this world full of psychotics? Where was he when I needed him? Instead of starting up with Jake again, I just nodded my head as though I agreed.

"That feels good, honey," I said.

"I know you're trying to change the subject." He knew me all too well.

"No I'm not." I laughed. "You don't know these women like I do. The horrible physical and mental trauma they put these poor kids through. Even Jesus himself couldn't save them."

"Have you ever thought that maybe they are hurting, too? Hurting people hurt others. And nobody is beyond God's reach," Jake said, waving his hands toward the sky.

"I was," I mumbled under my breath.

"What did you say?"

"Nothing." I removed my feet from his hands and slid them back into my slippers. "Want a glass of wine?"

"How about a beer?"

I walked into the kitchen hoping that by the time I rejoined my husband, I would have the courage to talk to him. If there was ever a time to go ahead and tell Jake about my childhood, this was it. We were both in an easy mood, even considering the day I'd had. Jake usually had that effect on me. He had the most soothing aura; it was one of the things that had attracted me to him in the first place. He always told me that it was the God in him.

Since we were both wide awake, I decided to fix us a small snack of grapes, cheese, and crackers. I had been too busy, not to mention, too flustered to eat dinner. I had a lot to say and we were going to be up for a while. It was nice just chatting with him like we used to do, before our lives got so complicated. I really missed our alone time.

I heard his cell phone ring from in the bedroom and instinctively looked at the time. It was almost one in the morning. I wondered who was calling my husband in the middle of the night. I didn't think he heard it so I raced into the bedroom and answered before looking at the Caller ID screen.

"Hello," I said impatiently.

"Uh. Uh. Brother Jake?" A woman's voice asked hesitantly.

"No, this is his *wife*, Naomi." Damn church people again.

"His wife?" she asked as though shocked.

"Yes, his wife," I shot back defensively.

"Oh, I'm sorry, sweetheart. I don't think we've met before. I'm the new associate pastor of The Redeeming Tree of Life Church. I had a meeting with Jake tonight and had to run out unexpectedly for a family emergency. I left my briefcase at the church and I wanted to know when a good time would be to pick it up tomorrow. Is he available?"

"Yes, hold on a second," I said, letting my guards down. She sounded harmless enough, so I walked the phone outside to the patio to Jake. I rubbed him on his head and gave him a quick peck on the cheek before I went back inside to grab the tray which contained our midnight snack.

I knew all those women at that church were feeling my husband. I only attended a few times. I mostly went for special occasions or when Jake was angry with me. Mentioning the word Jesus usually got my husband out of a bad mood. Every time I went, those women always ran up to me as though we already knew each other. Telling me what a lucky woman I was to have snagged Jacob Mitchell right from under their noses. Jake had belonged to the same church for many years. Everyone there acted like they had some special claim to him because of it. You gotta watch those women, always on the prowl for somebody else's man.

Jake was very active in his church. From what he'd been telling me lately, it was a growing ministry since the original pastor had died and his young son, Paul, had taken over. He was bringing in new people and changing the church to keep up with the times. Jake was his right hand man, they'd grown up together. Paul was single, so women were running in droves from all over the city looking to nab the young pastor. That's where my concern started, my husband was married and I wasn't too keen on women calling neither my house, nor his cell all times of the night.

I stepped back out on the patio, struggling to balance the tray with the wine, beer and snacks on it and close the door at the same time. Jake reached over to offer assistance although he was still on the telephone. He took the tray from me and placed it on the table. I pulled the citronella candles from under the patio table and lit them to ward off Houston's notorious king-sized mosquitoes before I set up our snack.

I leaned back in my chair while Jake never stopped chattering on the phone. I watched his thick lips move as he spoke. The candles cast a faint, yellowed glow on his skin. My husband was gorgeous. Those women had a right to be miffed at me.

"Yes, we are excited to have you with us, Sister...I mean, Pastor Thomas." He chuckled into his cell. "Okay. Okay. Lenora."

Hmm, she wanted him to call her by her first name. A twinge of envy crossed over me briefly. Although it was a right humid evening, I pulled the throw over my feet just to have something to do. I didn't want it to seem like I was eavesdropping on his conversation. Jake pulled my feet back onto his lap and continued to talk on the phone. He was too smart. I smiled inwardly as he blew a silent kiss my way.

"No, don't worry about the time. My beautiful wife understands the work I do for the Lord's kingdom." He glanced up at me as if to say, *satisfied?* "I can't wait for you meet her. She will be at the ceremony."

I raised one eyebrow. I had no clue what he was talking about. Whatever it was, I made a mental note to myself that I needed to be there. They were on the phone entirely too long, and I needed to see who this sister was.

"God bless you, too. Give my regards to Brother Thomas and I hope everything works out for your family. You are in my prayers," he continued. "I'll see you around noon tomorrow. Goodnight."

Okay so she was married, too. My ho radar inched from 100 to 70—slowly. I could tell the call was nearing the end, so I popped open Jake's beer and set it in front of him. I poured myself another glass of wine. No sooner than I popped a grape in my mouth, Jake snapped his phone closed and directed his attention to me.

"Come here," he said, patting his lap. "Where were we before we were rudely interrupted?" He put one finger on his chin as though he were in deep thought. "Ah, ha! You, my beautiful wife, were telling me about your day." He let the recliner back and pulled me into his chest.

"Well...it all started when my husband left for work and didn't tell me goodbye," I chided. "I knew it was going to be a bad day."

"What kind of husband would do such a thing to the most beautiful woman in the world?"

Jake's phone rang again. He reached for it as though he was going to answer it, checked the Caller ID, and powered it down until it shut completely off. Now, *that* bothered me. I wondered who was on the phone that time. I needed to pay more attention. Especially where my husband was concerned. I'd been pretty distant lately and I wondered if I was putting myself in a position to lose Jake.

"Who was that?" I asked, unable to contain my curiosity.

"Just someone from the church. I'm on duty for the prayer line this evening."

"They call you this late?" I quizzed.

"We don't like for people to. It's usually the middle of the night when people realize how much they are hurting. When it gets quiet, and there's no one to talk to but themselves—and God."

"And you," I added.

I went ahead and decided to be satisfied with his answer—for now. He sounded sincere enough, so I let it go even though he didn't answer the call.

I passed him his beer and put my head on his chest. I listened to the sound of the liquid as it made its way from his throat to his stomach. Jake was so normal. I secretly wished that I could be like him. Easy going and free. I thought about his words and how true they were. I stayed up many nights trying to piece together the unstableness of my mind to no avail. I was destined to be ruined forever. My thoughts turned to Nola and I shivered.

Jake put both of his arms around me and rubbed my exposed arm. "Something is bothering you. I can feel it," he said.

"I'm okay," I lied.

"I can't help if you don't talk to me. I'm your husband, Naomi, and you can tell me anything."

Bet I can't, I thought.

"I was just thinking about the way that woman looked at her son today. She looked at him with so much hatred that it sent chills up my spine. I'm worried about him—all of them, the next to oldest one, mostly."

"Okay, you went from nothing to something, huh." Jake continued to rub my arms.

"It's just that I can't get them out of my mind. And the mother, she was so familiar to me. Just plain cruel."

"Maybe you've worked with this family before," Jake offered an answer and yawned.

"No, I would've remembered them. When I get to the office tomorrow, I'll be able to look them up. I hope I can find someone in the family that is willing to take them in. I don't think they will do well in foster care." I sighed before continuing, "I'm worried about that family. If evil had a name, her name was Mona. She was calculating. It was as though she was playing some sick mental game with her children."

I decided to go for it—my turn to tell the truth. "You know what? She actually reminded me of…of my mother." I paused to see what Jake was going to say. I took his silence as a cue to go on. I inhaled deeply, "Did I ever tell you that I was raised in a foster home? I haven't seen my mother since I was six years old. And I never—"

Jake let out a snore and interrupted me. My heart sank. He hadn't heard a word I said. Maybe it wasn't time. A lump held securely fastened to the inside of my throat and I had to swallow hard to get rid of it. I untangled myself from Jake's arms and put the tray in the kitchen. I returned to the patio and shook him gently until his eyes were able to focus on me.

"Huh, whatcha say, baby?" he asked sleepily, letting out a small growl as he stretched to his feet and pulled me into his arms.

"Nothing, baby. Let's go to bed." I said as I took his hand and led him to our bedroom.

Jake never missed a snore and was fast asleep as soon as his body hit the bed. I had to hoist him over just to squeeze my body into the arc of his protection. Even while sleep he was affectionate and threw his huge arms over me. I lay there, counting his heartbeats until I fell into a restless sleep.

"Did you tell that old lady next door about what we do?" he asked. He slowly peeled the wrapper from around a shiny blow pop.

"No," I said, watching his hands. I licked my lips in anticipation of receiving a treat.

"Good, that's our business. You a real good girl, Naomi. You know I love you, right?

"Yes," I said.

"And what are you supposed to say?"

"Umm…I love you, too, Uncle C." I would've said anything for that blow pop. I could smell the aroma of the watermelon flavor, my favorite, drifting in the air, intoxicating me. I never took my eyes off of his hands as he revealed more and more of the round, bright red treat.

"You know what makes Uncle C happy, right?" He finally removed

the entire wrapper, leaving the shiny sucker totally exposed.

"Yes," I said, lowering my eyes. I didn't want the candy anymore. I knew what he wanted. He wanted to hurt me again, like all the other times.

It all started when Uncle C came in that night. He was in a good mood. He sent Nola out to turn a few tricks. I didn't remember it being Halloween. No laughing kids knocked on our door yelling, "Trick o' Treat, smell my feet gimme something good to eat." I smiled just thinking about the funny rhyme the kids would say outside our door

"Oh, you like candy, don't you, baby?" Uncle C thought that I was smiling at the unwrapped sucker.

Earlier, I'd asked him what kind of treats was Nola bringing back, he laughed and said the crispy, green, kind if she knew what was good for her. I was confused but decided not to ask any more questions. Grownups had a way of confusing me. I went back to watching the old beat up TV. Then Uncle C flashed a small brown paper bag full of candy in my face.

"If you go run me some bath water, I'll give you all of this," he said, smiling. "Don't forget the bubbles. You know how I like it."

I was so excited at the mere thought of eating all of that candy that I almost poured the entire bottle of dish soap in the tub. Bubbles were brimming over, falling to the floor, bouncing like clear balls when Uncle C walked into the bathroom with no clothes on.

"Oh, you made it real romantic for us, didn't you, baby?" he smiled. He had a sucker in one hand and the entire bag of candy in the other. "Take yo' clothes off and get in with me. I want you to wash my back."

"That's it?" I asked.

"Yes, sweetheart. Uncle C is tired. Come wash my back and you can have this here piece of candy.

I believed him. I wasn't ashamed to be naked in front of him anymore because he made me and Mama walk around the house naked all the time. He got in the tub first, carefully holding up the sucker like a prize I could have for doing good. More bubbles spilled out onto the floor and some floated in the air. I quickly snatched my clothes off and joined him in the tub. I reached for the sucker.

"Not so fast."

I leaned back in the tub. I knew what he wanted me to do for it. I know Uncle C said that he loved me, still, I didn't want to. Both of his legs were stretched out wide and I sat facing him. My legs were cemented together between his open ones. I was happy that I couldn't see the bottom of the tub because of the bubbles. The soapy water was very warm, almost too warm for me. It still didn't stop the cold fear from whipping around my shoulders. Uncle C noticed and pulled me closer to him.

"You cold, baby?" He stuck his tongue in my ear.

"Nooo," I said, trying to pull myself away from his firm grip.

"Do you want this candy?"

"Yes," I whimpered.

"Well, kiss your Uncle C then," he demanded and quickly covered my cries with his mouth.

I tried to resist and attempted to pull myself away from him. He searched inside my mouth for my tongue and pulled on it with his teeth until I screamed out in pain.

"No!"

"Naomi! Baby. Baby."

I felt Jake trying to shake me awake. I was trapped. Lost in a nightmare somewhere between today and the past. I could hear Jake's voice calling out to me in my dream.

"Naomi. Naomi. Wake up, baby!"

I opened my eyes and yes, Jake was right there. I needed to touch him. He was my constant and if I could only put my hands on him I could tear away from the terrible images creeping into my dreams. He got up to leave and I grabbed on to him.

"No, don't leave me," I shouted.

"I'm not going anywhere. Let me get you a towel. You are dripping wet."

"No," I yelled again. "Don't leave me. Just stay with me, Jake. I'm so scared. Please." The tremble in my body was evident in my shaking voice.

Jake came right back to my side. He took off the t-shirt he

was wearing and dabbled at my sweat-drenched face with it. The entire time he kept repeating, "It's okay, baby. I'm here. Shhhh."

My heart raced and dread glued itself to the humid air making it heavy like another skin. I was terrified, the dream seemed real. It had been years since I'd had a nightmare about Uncle C and Nola. Now, it seemed as though they were etched to the insides of my eyelids. I was afraid to close my eyes, fearing they would be right there, waiting for me—again. I felt like I had vanished into some sort of psychotic movie where it was okay to hurt children. I held onto Jake's arm until my knuckles turned white and my fingers cramped up. I licked my dry lips with my even drier tongue and I could taste the smell of Uncle C's lips on mine. I dry heaved into Jake's shirt as he held on to me.

I was sweating so profusely that my hair stuck to the sides of my face. Perspiration dripped from the tip of my nose. Jake rose to leave again. I held on to him once more. "No." I begged, too feeble to put up a real fight. "Stay."

Jake left my side, but only long enough to grab a glass of water from the bathroom faucet. He put the rim of the glass up to my quivering lips. More water ran down my chin than what actually went down my throat. Even that small amount was enough to cause me to vomit again. I felt a chill resonating in my bones and my teeth chattered creating an eerie beat.

Jake had never seen me like this. When I lived in a foster home, the nightmares were a frequent occurrence. Many times, I had to sleep in the bed with my foster mother. When I had too many nightmares, I was prone to severe bouts of depression and spontaneous anxiety attacks. None of which I'd experienced since I'd been with Jake. I knew that Jake's love for me was the only thing protecting me from the nightmares.

Dae knew, however. I was so young when we met. I couldn't keep my past contained within the frail prison of my mind. Sharing a one-room dorm, it was hard to keep my little secret from escaping the confines of my dreams and I called out many nights for Dae to hold me until I fell asleep. Dae would sing soothing songs in her native Korean language. I didn't know the words, but the melodies were so serene that they calmed my spirit as her voice ushered me back to reality. Back to the truth, that Nola and Uncle C were long gone from my life.

"What is wrong with you, Naomi?" Jake asked, covering my shaking body with the chenille throw from the foot of the bed. He wiped what I assumed to be the remnants of bile or sweat from my quivering lips.

"I don't know. Just hold me."

"You were having a really bad dream. You were screaming and begging for someone named Uncle C to stop. You said that he was hurting you. What was that all about? Who is this Uncle C? I didn't know you had an uncle. Do you?"

"I don't," I said barely above a whisper.

Jake fired off so many questions, I began to feel dizzy. I just wanted him to be quiet and let me think. *How many years had it been since I'd had an episode? Six. No, it had to be more. I think ten years at best. Let's see, I met Jake in two thousand—*

"Naomi!" Jake's voice interrupted my mindless calculations. "You! You just peed in the bed!"

The look on his face was a mixture of shock and sympathy. I didn't know what to say. I had to keep my mind busy, so I continued to calculate how many years it had been since I'd lost my mind—the last time. I wondered why it happened and why today. I went to work. I came home. I only had one glass of wine.

I hit myself pathetically in the head with one balled fist to jar my memory. "Come on, self. Think," I looked up at Jake who stood by helplessly, as he stared at me drawing numbers and writing notes to myself in the air. Not to mention thump myself in the head.

"I need you to get up, Naomi, so I can clean you up." He walked back into the bathroom.

"No. I think I have it almost figured out, Jake," I replied calmly. At that moment, I felt a cold, wet feeling come over my midsection. "Honey, I'm wet," I said, simply and went back to counting the years since I'd succumbed to the evil spirits in my mind.

As I tried to square everything together, Jake picked my limp body up from the bed and cupped me in his arms. I didn't hear the bath water running until I was sitting on the toilet. I looked over and the white foam was forming into big delicious bubbles under the pouring hot water. Jake had his massive hands on me, underneath my chin unbuttoning the green satin nightshirt that I was wearing. The peachy aroma of the suds emanated from the frothy pool and filled my nostrils with its sweetness.

"I don't want a lollipop," I began to scream repeatedly, swatting Jake's hands away from me. "No! Don't touch me! Don't touch me, Uncle C!"

My eyes were open, yet my imagination ran wild, wreaking havoc on my consciousness. Uncle C wanted to take a bath with me again—to rape me. I couldn't let that happen—not anymore.

No, it was my husband Jake trying to bathe me. I threw up more of the empty contents of my stomach and urinated again at the same time. I begged Jake to help me. My mind played devious games with me until Jake grabbed me up in a huge bear hug. He pinned my arms behind me until I couldn't fight any more.

"Look at me, Naomi. Baby. It's me. I won't let anything happen to you. I promise. You hear me. Nobody will ever hurt you. I got you, baby. Naomi. Come back to me. Look at me. I love you, baby. I need you with me."

The exasperation in Jake's voice reached that seldom seen place inside my heart. "Please. Come on, Naomi, come back to me. Please." His voice choked on the tears caught in his throat.

"Lord, I plead the blood of Jesus on the demons that threaten to set up a stronghold against my wife," Jake prayed for me as he held one hand on my forehead and the other on my arms to keep my hands pinned behind my back.

His words began to take effect on me. Or maybe it was the sound of a grown man, crying. I don't know. I felt myself snapping out of hysteria. I looked down and my nightshirt was hanging halfway off of my body, the scars on my stomach totally exposed. Jake had sunk down to his knees deep in prayer with his head on my thighs. My legs were wet with his tears. I fell to the floor with him and he continued to pray for me.

After what seemed like hours, I woke up and found myself sprawled out on the bathroom floor with Jake beside me. We were hanging on to each other as though our lives depended on it. Scenes of the night before replayed in vivid detail in my mind. I could still hear Jake praying for the Lord to save me. I heard him pray for a deeper connection with his wife—with me. He told God that he was prepared to finally know me. That he wanted to be the man that God called him to be, so that he could help me. Jake even remembered to pray for the unborn children that I was so worried about having.

It all seemed unreal, but my fragile heart did feel a little different. I couldn't quite place my finger on it, but some alteration had definitely taken place inside of me.

Xavier

I CAN'T BELIEVE Naomi dumped us here and walked away like that. Maybe Sissy was right and I shouldn't trust her. I looked around at the old fashioned furniture in the bedroom and cringed. The yellow paint was scraped off parts of the wall, leaving the pale white underneath exposed. If I moved more than an inch, my nose was for sure gonna touch the low ceiling. The tiny light in the room barely gave enough light to see my hand in front of me, especially way up here. What was worse, the old bed was so rickety I was afraid to move because it might tip over. My room at home looked a whole lot better than this.

Sean tossed and turned periodically underneath me on the bottom bunk. It was crazy how fast he went into a deep sleep. I lay in the bed with him for a long time before climbing up to the top bunk. Our new foster mother had come in just minutes before he went to sleep and found us in the bed together and frowned at me.

"Get up and get in your own bed," she'd said to me. "That's nasty, two boys sleeping together."

I didn't see what was so nasty about it. Sean was my little brother and he was scared. It was my job to take care of him. I decided to do what she said just to make it easy. Naomi promised that we would be safe here, and I had no choice at the moment but to believe her. It was too late to try to go back on everything that had happened and go back to Mona. I tried to make the best of it and decided not to complain. As long as Mrs. Fildhurst wasn't as mean as Mona, I was good.

Sissy was in another room somewhere else in the old house that smelled like stale fried chicken. She was still not talking to me for choosing to protect Naomi and not Mona. She didn't understand, I know how crazy Mona can be and I didn't want to see Naomi hurt because of us. Plus, I hated Mona with everything in me. I hated her because I had to sleep in a tiny bed with a mattress so thin I felt the springs protrude through the material and pierce my back. I hated Mona because Sean cried for hours for her. I hated Mona because now my sister, who'd always been my best friend, hated me.

A small alarm clock sat on a desk near the door. The fire engine red neon light flashed 1:22 A.M. and lit up the black room. I couldn't sleep at all. I had so many unanswered questions. Some things I knew to expect because Tommy had already told me how foster care worked. But, I still had lots of questions, like were we going to school tomorrow and where. I was too afraid to go to our old school. If I closed my eyes, I could just imagine Mona sitting in my first period class waiting for me, ready to burn the skin off of my fingers, or worse. I flexed them under the itchy blanket. I touched the rough patches where new skin refused to grow back. I hated my hands.

"Xavier. Are you still awake?" I heard Sissy whisper softly in my ear. I was finally almost asleep.

"Yeah," I whispered, glancing at the time on the little clock. 3:47 A.M.

"I can't stay here. I can't sleep in a house with strangers. It's creepy. They might do something to us?"

"What are you going to do?" I asked as my eyes tried to adjust in the darkness and focus on Genesis. The flashing alarm clock cast a red glow on Sissy and I could tell that she was fully dressed.

"I'm going home," she said with authority. "I don't know this lady. I already hate it here. I want my stuff, my bed, and my mother."

"No, Sissy…you can't," I pleaded. "Just wait until tomorrow and let's see what happens. Maybe Naomi can take us somewhere else."

"Somewhere else? Boy, are you crazy?" Sissy hissed. "It's your fault we're here right now." Her voice began to rise with anger. "I'm going home. Right now!"

"Shhh. You don't want her to come in here. "

"I don't care. I don't know her and I *don't* have to do what she says. If you would've just kept your big mouth shut, we wouldn't be in this mess right now."

"Okay. Okay. So how are you going to get home?" There was no sense trying to reason with her once she got angry.

"I don't know. I was hoping you and Sean were gonna come with me."

Sissy didn't even have a plan. She was leaving and that was that. I knew she was determined. Whatever she was going to do, I just wanted her to go do it. The red glow of the alarm eerily lit up Sissy's face every few seconds. Looking at the angry Sissy—was like looking at Mona, something I didn't feel like doing. I wanted her out of my face. She felt like she had a home to go to, not me.

I didn't like the old lady Mrs. Fildhurst either, but I bet she wasn't near as bad as Mona. I decided that I was gonna take my chances right where I was at. If I went with Sissy and ended up with Mona, I was as good as dead.

"Well?" Sissy asked impatiently.

"I'm staying here. Sean too," I said. "I really don't think you should go either. One, you don't know *where* you're going. Two, it's the middle of the night and you don't know what could happen to you out there."

"You always wanna act like you somebody's daddy."

Sissy turned around and headed for the door. She came back and leaned down and placed a kiss on Sean's cheek. She knew not to even ask about taking him. Sean was always *my* responsibility. Sissy closed the door softly behind her. After how Sissy treated me today, I decided not to worry about her and let her do whatever she wanted.

I could hear the old floors speaking in creaks under Sissy's footsteps. Then silence. I smiled to myself thinking that maybe she decided to just go back to bed like I suggested. I moved around the bed, attempting to avoid the escaped spring with my body and closed my eyes.

4:12 A.M.

I was awakened from my light sleep again by a shrill scream. No, a siren and a bright flashing light crept in underneath the bedroom door. My first thought went to Sissy, thinking she had made it out and something had already happened to her outside the front door and those were police sirens that I heard. *Dumb girl.*

I jumped off the top bunk, peeked at Sean, who never moved. I ran out into the hallway where the sound got louder and the flashing light grew brighter. I looked up and I was standing directly underneath the light. I heard Mrs. Fildhurst yelling over the roaring siren. With all the commotion I wasn't sure which way to go, especially since I didn't know the house too well. I finally made my way to the loud voices.

Mrs. Fildhurst had Sissy by the arm with one hand and was turning off the security system with the other. Just like that, the lights and the sirens stopped.

"What happened?" I asked.

"None of yo' business," Mrs. Fildhurst hissed at me. "Go back to bed."

She turned her attention back to Sissy, and snatched her by the arm and shoved her into the nearest chair which was covered with thick, hard plastic. I didn't go back to my room, but I did move out of sight a little. It was my job to see what was going on with my sister. I didn't like how Mrs. Fildhurst pulled on her arm like that. She wasn't our mother.

"You one of those types of kids, huh? A runaway. I done seen y'all come and go. Come and go. And you know what happens to kids like you?" She paused for Sissy to answer, and then continued when she figured out that Sissy wasn't gonna say anything. "You end up dead or in jail. Once you get in the system, there is no way out unless you do what you are told."

What system? Nothing was going to happen to my sister.

"How old are you again?" she asked, taking a seat in the matching flowery chair directly opposite Sissy.

"Almost fourteen," Sissy said, holding her head up. She was mad that she got caught, and I could see Mona's thumb print all over her. "Look lady. I don't want to be here anymore than you want us here. I don't care about no system, jail, or nothing else. I just want to go home to my mother, where I belong."

"If you belonged with your mother, you would be there, not here," Mrs. Fildhurst shot back. "If something wasn't wrong, the state would've never taken y'all. So don't come up in here getting all huffy with me, little girl. I done had thirty-seven children move through this house since I started taking in kids twenty years ago. Thirty-seven. I've seen all kinds and I already know what kind you are." She glared at Sissy.

"What kind am I, then?" Sissy asked sarcastically.

Mrs. Fildhurst stood up from her chair and straightened her house robe. "The kind an ole lady like me don't feel like being bothered with no more. You try running away again and you won't have to run. I'll tell them social workers to come get ya. If you plan to be a handful, you gonna need to do that somewhere else. I done already raised my kids and a bunch more. I'm trying to help—"

Sissy stood up, too. "Do I look like I need your help, old lady? I have a mother who loves me. This is all Xavier's fault for being a snitch."

My fault? I felt like a rock hit me in the stomach. Sissy watched Mona torment me for years. She watched me cry so many nights. She helped me put Band Aids and Neosporin on more bruises than I could count. She kissed my hands once and told me that they didn't look that bad and that Mona was wrong for doing all of that to me. Here we are and all she had to say was this was *all my fault*. I was done with her, I couldn't trust her anymore. If she wanted to be on Mona's side—let her.

Sissy continued, "I don't need to be here. My mother loves me. She wants me."

Funny how Sissy kept referring to Mona as *her mother* all of a sudden. We weren't even allowed to call her that. To us, she had always been known as Mona. I felt my body sinking to the floor, but I held myself up. I tried to erase Sissy's voice from my head. Mona did love her and Sean more. Yeah, she whooped them too but never as bad as she did me. Maybe I *was* wrong for doing this to them. I didn't know. I headed back to bed on uncertain legs and wanted to just drop dead right then and there. As I entered the bedroom that I shared with Sean, I could still hear Mrs. Fildhurst talking.

"If she loved you all so much, why are you here?"

Sissy didn't respond.

"Go to bed, little girl. If you try that again, you're out of here."

"Whatever. My mother is going to come get me anyway."

"Oh yeah?" Mrs. Fildhurst laughed. "That's what they all say."

I closed the door to my room. I'd heard enough. I climbed up to the top bunk and found Sean laying there. I didn't feel like moving him back down so I gently pushed him closer to the wall to make room for myself. He turned over and sniffled in his sleep. I didn't have any more trouble falling asleep. My eyelids were heavier than my heart.

Naomi

I LAY IN bed as Jake bustled around in the kitchen. The aroma of fresh brewed coffee filled our apartment. I was almost tempted to run into the kitchen for a cup, but I really wanted Jake to leave before I got out of bed. Last night was too much and I really didn't know how to face him, not just yet. Like, what was I gonna say?

My episode last night wasn't exactly how I wanted my story to come out. I was more than a little embarrassed and wondered what Jake thought of me now. He didn't know the whole story, but Jake was a smart man and I'm sure he filled in some of the blanks on his own.

Before Jake left for work, he quietly came back into our bedroom. I felt his hands on me, praying for me again. I pretended to be asleep. I didn't want to take the pleasure of praying for his wife away from him. But I wanted to laugh at the thought of God hearing a prayer with my name attached to it. Just mention the name Naomi and God's ears closed instantly. If Jake felt better believing, he could go right ahead. I pretended to be in a deep sleep until he said his final amen.

I exhaled as soon as I heard the front door slam closed. I rolled over with my head down in my pillow and screamed into it. "Lord, if you do exist, fix me. Please. Amen." If my life got any worse, I was seriously going to consider jumping off our patio onto Texas Avenue during rush hour.

I hopped out of bed and gave myself a big girl talk while I made a cup of coffee. I pulled out a pad and pencil, sat down at the kitchen table, and wrote a list of things that I needed to take care of. It always helped when I wrote my thoughts out on paper. It took three cups of coffee before I had it all straight—or as close to making sense as I could get at the moment.

First things first, I had to deal with Dae at work. I know slapping Mona was wrong. I was willing to face the music. I wrote down all the possible excuses that I could have for doing something like that. None of them made sense.

A smile crept upon my lips when I thought about my handprint on her cheek. Whatever was gonna happen in that case, I was willing to deal with it like a soldier. *Another smile.* Damn, before I met with Dae, I better figure out how to keep the smile off of my face, for sure that wouldn't go over well with her, as my manager or my friend.

I also had to make some phone calls for the kids. Xavier told me that his and Genesis' father lived in another state. He said Sean's father left a few weeks ago and hadn't been back to see his son since. *Deadbeat.* As much as I hated to, I was going to have to call all of the fathers for first dibs at custody and notify them of the pending court date.

Last on my to do list was to talk to Jake. I needed to get it all out before my husband started to think that I was crazy. Yes, I was a little disturbed by my life's situation. And yes, it was time that I took control of it. Hopefully, that would be something I could do while keeping my marriage, and most importantly, my sanity intact.

I was almost dressed when my work cell phone rang. It was Dae. A walnut sized lump lodged itself in my throat.

"Hey, Dae," I said, trying not to sound too cheery. I was supposed to be distressed over what happened.

"Hi, Naomi." Her voice was dry. "I'm at the airport right now so I can't talk very long."

"The airport?"

"Yes, the airport. Remember I have that training in Vegas the rest of this week. I reminded you yesterday."

"Oh yeah." I didn't remember.

"Anyway, I'm going to get right to it." She put her super professional voice on. *I was so in trouble.* "I heard about what happened yesterday. Officer Shaw left me a voicemail last night on my phone. I'm not even going to ask why you didn't tell me first. You know what has to be done now, don't you?" She paused.

"No, nothing like this has ever happened to me. I don't know what came over me. I'm sorry, Dae, that I put you in this position." I stopped explaining as real tears welled up in my eyes. My best friend was pretty angry at me.

"You should be sorry," Dae's voice was cold. "Well, lucky for you, Officer Shaw has decided not to file his report just yet. He did say that she attacked you first and it's understandable that you reacted. But she *was* subdued when you slapped her, Naomi. And you *spit* on her? That was the worst. Naomi, you *spit* on another human being." Her last statement humiliated me.

"You need to keep in mind that we are supposed to be the good guys. We must set the standard for how to settle disputes. Your behavior was totally unacceptable. I'll be back next Monday, and I expect to have your report on my desk." She sighed as though a heavy weight sat on her thoughts. "You could be looking at suspension, or worse—termination. Next week we'll see how this thing plays out. For now, don't take on any new cases. Work with what you have and stay away from Ms. Thomas and her children. Do a handover with Maria."

Without saying another word, Dae hung up the phone. That was rude, but I dealt with it. The victory that I felt earlier was surmounted by Dae's disappointment in me. Maybe spitting on her was a little excessive. The smile that I'd had a hard time containing earlier went as far south as a flock of geese fleeing from an icy winter. My right eye started to twitch; it usually happened only when I felt extreme levels of stress.

I understood Dae's anger, but on the other hand, how much was I, a social worker, looking out for the benefit and well-being of children, supposed to take? Dae had spent enough time in the field to know what went on. Everybody had a breaking point and Mona hit mine. I did find a little gratification that I wouldn't have to even think about what I'd done until next week. From the looks of things, this was something else that I'd have to share with Jake. I raised my eyes in the direction of Jake's God. "Well Lord, you let him pick a real winner, didn't you?"

The long walk from the employee parking lot to the office building felt empty without Dae by my side. We usually talked on the phone our entire way to work and waited for each other to arrive to finish the conversation. It was our girlfriend gossip and counseling session time. Dae was a real social butterfly, so she had lots of activities outside of work, which left little time for me outside of work, unless I tagged along to one of her many social events.

I hoped our friendship wouldn't suffer too much over the thing with Mona. Just the thought of her name made me think evil thoughts. It was all because of her. I had never physically hit another human being in my life. I wanted to, but I never did. I walked briskly past the smoking section of our building and my ears immediately began to burn. All eyes were on me and my senses let me know they knew something. I kept my head up high and walked right past them. One of the ladies, Maria, put her half-smoked cigarette out and raced to my side to get on the elevator with me.

"How are you today?" she asked politely.

"I'm great, Maria. How are you?"

"Well, you know everybody is talking 'bout you hit a parent yesterday." I remained quiet and listened. "I told them. No! Not Naomi, I know her and she wouldn't do something like that."

Maria's accent was thick. In the last couple of years, the state began to hire Spanish speaking workers at lightning speed. She had been sitting behind me for the better part of a year and I hadn't realized how broken her English was because I barely ever heard her speak it.

"Well, Maria, you know how gossip is. Just as long as you don't believe or repeat everything you hear."

"I'm here if you...you need to talk."

The doors opened and I walked off the elevator and went straight for my desk. Heads bobbed up and down over the cubicle walls and hushed whispers announced my arrival. Their voices followed me like soulless ghosts all the way to my cave. I put it all out of my mind and went about my daily ritual. They could gossip all day if they wanted to, but the reality was that over 3 million reports of child abuse were made every year. And every day our lives were put in danger to save them. I didn't see anyone gossiping about that.

Of course there was a call from Mrs. Fildhurst. It just wouldn't be right if she didn't call with a laundry list of complaints. She was a bitter lemon to the palate, but she was dependable, something those kids needed in their lives. Hmm, this time her call was valid. Genesis attempted to run away last night. I knew that girl was going to be trouble. She was innocent at first sight, but as stubborn as all get out. With the right accelerant, I could see her getting into a lot of trouble. I already planned to check on them one last time, so I didn't rush to return Mrs. Fildhurst's telephone call.

I set the case up for a court hearing. By law, a parent has the right to state their side and since Mona was so irrational last night, it had to be done soon. For now, the state had temporary guardianship over the children, but I was sure that we would have just cause to make it a little more permanent. Mona had no business raising kids. She was one of those people that shouldn't have been allowed to have children. I would never understand why people had to jump through hoops to adopt a dog from the shelter, but a crazy woman can push out as many babies as her body would allow in a nine-month conception rotation. Just ridiculous.

One of my co-workers liked to chide, "If they don't keep having babies to fill up the system, then we would all be out of a job." Actually she would be out of a job. I would have found something more useful to do with my life.

I tried to focus on work and began to check my email. Soon, I was interrupted by a pounding headache. My mind kept replaying the second I stooped to Mona's level and acted out of violence. My fifth foster parent used to say that I couldn't win for losing—she was right.

My predicament began to close in on me and I felt like I was beginning to suffocate. I felt like a stranger in my own life. I had no clue how to get to know my real self. I'd been living a lie ever since I could remember and it was about to come to a head.

"God, if you are there, now is another one of those good times." I closed my eyes and leaned back in my rollaway chair. I massaged my temples and took a few deep breaths in an attempt to re-organize my thoughts.

"He's there, Naomi, just trust him." Maria's voice was too close to be coming from over the cubicle wall.

I opened my eyes and she was standing right next to me. She handed me a cup of steaming hot coffee and smiled. She was on my side. I smiled back at her before I stood up to embrace her in a warm hug.

"Thank you, Maria," I said. "I really needed this."

The shrill ring of the telephone on Maria's desk interrupted the exchange between us. She cupped her warm hands over mine and shook them together lightly. She ran off to her desk and I stood there thinking for a few minutes. I guess Maria was a good person after all and I should probably get to know her a little better.

I sat back down at my desk and warmed my hands on the cup of coffee. My mouth watered and instinctively I raised the cup to my lips. I took a small sip and immediately spat it out. Images of Maria picking her nose appeared before me. I yanked open my desk and pulled out the sanitizer and slathered it all over my hands and face.

Maria walked past my cubicle and stopped. "Eww, smells like alcohol," she said and fanned.

"I know, I am such a germ-o-phobe," I said and smiled. "Thanks again for the coffee!"

She smiled and walked away.

I went back to work. It was going to be tough putting my hands on the fathers of the children, but I was ready to dig in. Paternal parents usually didn't care to take custody of their children. I knew in my heart that they didn't want them, but it was my job to at least ask.

Mona

I SLEPT FOR what seemed like forever. I didn't even have the energy to shower after I left that nasty police station—so I didn't. I was beginning to smell myself; the wild stench of my underarms mixed with my horrible breath filled my nose with a putrid whiff every time I moved. Still, I could not rise. I couldn't muster up enough energy to drag my drained body to bathe. My stomach had long since given up signaling for food. It had been two…maybe four days since I'd put anything in my mouth. The thought of food made me want to puke.

I don't think anyone understood that my kids were my life. Genesis was fourteen, no, she would be fourteen in three months. Yeah, for the first time in my adult life—I had no kids. They were my life and everything that I tried so hard to make it for. No one needed me, asked me for anything, or told me they loved me in five days. I doubled over in dry tears again.

"I want my babies!" It took everything in me to attempt to squeeze the words out of my mouth, which was just as dehydrated as my eyes. No verbal sound came. I was thirsty for water, but the kitchen seemed so far away. I doubted that I'd be able to make the twenty footsteps and one sharp right turn from the sofa to the kitchen. Instead, I picked up the huge bottle of Cuervo, leaned my head back and let the warm liquid quench my thirst. I'd had so much tequila to drink that it no longer burned my throat going down. I felt my body growing weaker and I decided to wait for death by loneliness to take me as I fired up another blunt.

My weed was the only thing that could calm my nerves. I rested the back of my head on the arm of the sofa and inhaled deeply. I held the smoke in as long as I could, swallowed it, and released the white cloud into the air through my nostrils. This was all I could do not to lose my mind—get high. It eased the reality of what I'd been through and washed out the echo of their voices— the bastards that did this to me.

"I don't think you'll be getting your kids back anytime soon, lady," the police officer that everyone called Shaw had said to me. He thought it was funny when he'd said it, too. It was more of a joke than a statement to him. "I guess you better get to looking for a J.O.B. 'cause there will be no layin' up on your ass, waiting on a check anymore." He chuckled as he pushed me into my cell and slammed it closed in my face. *Bastard*, I had a job. Probably not anymore. I'm sure the hospital where I worked as a nursing assistant on the pediatrics floor was gonna fire me over this latest load of shit to drop in my life.

Five days ago they took *my* babies. They called me unfit and everything. Five days ago, they told me not to try to contact my *own* kids; hell, they didn't even tell me where they were! They said I was unfit. The pain in my heart radiated like black heat inside my body and quickly festered into hatred. *And that uppity, freckled faced bitch had spit in my face.* I swore that I better not ever see that woman again as long as I was breathing.

From where I lay on the sofa, I could see her card on the coffee table in front of me. It's once crisp, white edges were now worn, twisted, and dingy from me picking it up a hundred times over the last few days. I squinted my eyes to make out the words but couldn't. The sun blazed through the window blinds and a bright ray hit the business card on the coffee table, illuminating the words and from this angle, they were illegible. It didn't matter anyway. I didn't care if I ripped that card into shreds because I had every single detail on that card memorized already. If I really wanted to, I could put my hands on her at any second. Name— Naomi Mitchell. Job title—CPS Investigator. Her email address; Naomi.Mitchell@cps.gov. Her telephone number and her cell phone number. And her office address—everything.

I dragged on my blunt again. Naomi Mitchell was gonna pay for turning my kids, or Xavier's dumb ass against me. Genesis knew better. Humph, I knew that I could always count on that girl. I don't know where I went wrong with Xavier. He was so much like his ignorant father, just pathetic and two faced. Even through my seething anger, I still wanted him back. I wished that I hadn't been so pissed that day or he wouldn't have gotten caught in the middle of some adult bullshit. I exhaled more smoke.

"Damn! Why did I let him go to school that day?" I hit myself on the head with a small pillow, knocking the blunt from between my lips. It fell on the sofa and I watched it as the glowing red embers burned through the fabric. I wondered how long it would have to burn in order to become a fire. I wanted to leave it, to let it rage into whatever it wanted to be—something that could take me away. An inferno. One so massive that it would consume me—consume my problems. Consume Naomi Mitchell—the source of my hatred.

The phone rang and I looked at it lazily. I refused to move just to pick it up. It could only be my mother. My kids were gone. My best friend Candice was gone. Sean's father was gone. I had no one left but her—lucky me. The ringing stopped. My cell phone vibrated against my keys in my purse on the kitchen table. It was my mother. The interesting jingle slash vibration stopped.

I picked up my fallen blunt and sucked on it some more while I put my finger on the smoldering fabric of the sofa. It scorched my thumb, but I held it there until it smothered out. The searing pain was the first thing I was able to physically feel since Naomi had slapped me. I touched my cheek and either my imagination was playing a spiteful trick on me or I was entirely too high, but it still felt hot from her hand. I puffed one more time and put the roach out on the edge of the coffee table when it hit me.

Sean's father! Shit, he was suing me for custody. I completely forgot about that court date. That bastard wanted my baby, too. When was it? He was not getting my baby. I had to get myself together. *Think Mona. Think. Think.* I willed myself. I was so drunk and high that I couldn't remember the details clearly. I did remember tacking the green notice to the fridge. I'd look when I got up, but right then, my eyelids were so very heavy. I had to close them. Yeah, after a little nap, I'd check it out. I had to stop him.

First, one more sip of tequila.

CƷ ƉƆ

I woke up in my own bed. I pulled the covers back and peeked at myself, I had on fresh pajamas. I smelled like my favorite soap and my damp hair was pulled back into a ponytail. I didn't remember getting up from the sofa or taking a bath. I must have been really drunk. I tried to think back over the last few days and only fragmented pieces came together.

Is that? Yeah, that's music playing downstairs. Panic set in because I didn't remember leaving any music on. In addition to the music, I heard someone moving around downstairs. Oh my God! Someone was in my house. I started to call out but decided to go down there and check for myself. I had a steel bat in the hall closet that I could grab on the way down.

I got up out of the bed and stood to my feet. I was so weak that I fell back onto the bed just as Candice walked into my bedroom carrying a plate of steaming food.

"My God, the dead has arisen," Candice said with a straight face.

It was one of our favorite lines from a movie that we'd watched together a million times.

"What are you doing here?" I asked, somewhat grateful that it was only Candice and not a thief. I didn't live in the worst neighborhood, but it wasn't the best. "How did you get in?"

"I still have a key."

"Oh, so you just let yourself up in here?" I questioned, while staring at the smoke piping upwards from the plate of grits, eggs, and bacon.

"Hey, if you want me to go, I will. Trust, I have much better things to do with my time, like take care of my own *kid.*" Candice placed emphasis on the word kid just to spite me.

I cringed at her intentional meanness. She rolled her eyes at me and walked back out the way she came in, taking the plate of food with her, her blonde hair swung in her annoyance. My hunger defied my pride. It reacted on a will of its own and let out a loud, painful growl that seemed to last for minutes. It must have been effective because Candice stopped before she reached the stairs and came back. She handed me the food. I hesitated to take it, trying to save the last bit of face that I had remaining.

"Take the damn food, girl," she said impatiently. "I didn't want to prepare it for you any more than you want to eat anything I cooked, so we should be even." She sounded irritated.

I wondered if she put something in it and crinkled my nose in response. She saw me and marched back out the room and down the stairs. My stomach whimpered in response. I threw my middle finger at her retreating back. I could make my own food. I didn't need that traitor doing me any favors anyway. Who the hell did she think she was just letting herself in my house. I pulled my legs up toward my chest and rested my head on my knees so I could pull some energy together to put her ass out.

"I know you think I put something in your food," Candice said as she entered the room again.

I glared at her silently and said nothing.

"You know, if it hadn't been for me, you woulda drowned in your own piss and shit."

I still said nothing. I was half embarrassed because I didn't know if she was telling the truth or not.

"No need to thank me."

Thank you? For what, helping to ruin my life. Although I knew that Xavier told on me, I was still mad at Candice for not helping me that day when those people came. She could have taken Sean or something. I heard her whistle when that woman slapped me. Humph, now she wanted some kind of merit badge. Not gonna happen.

"Your neighbor called me because she was tired of you screaming all night long. She said if I didn't come check on you, she'd call the police. That's when I found you laying on the sofa with that gash on your head and wet drawers." She smirked at the last part.

I instinctively touched my head to feel for a gash, but all I felt was the thin tape of the band-aid. She was telling the truth. I couldn't look Candice in the face.

"I had my husband come over here to help me get you up the stairs so I could give you a bath, and we put you in the bed. *And* I called your mother last night. She said she'd be over after church today because you hadn't been returning her phone calls." She paused. "Nope, no need to thank me."

"Thank you, Candice. I...I don't know what else to say to you." I spoke to the floor, too ashamed to make eye contact with her. My mouth felt like it was full of cotton balls, my tongue was so thick and my breath was rank. I hurried up and snapped my mouth closed.

Candice laughed. "Yeah, your breath is funky as hell. After washing your twat, I refused to brush your teeth, too. I just poured some mouthwash in there and I let you swallow it." She quickly erased her smile. "I want to be your friend, Mona, but I can't right now. You have to get some help first...My husband is very upset that I'm even here right now." She saw the hurt look on my face. "I'm just being honest. I meant what I said last week."

Candice walked in the bathroom and I heard the water run. She returned with a glass of water and two aspirin which she offered to me. My head was pounding so I took them in my wobbly hands and downed the whole glass of water so fast that I belched immediately. She filled the glass again and I drank the next just as fast as the first as I thought about her words.

"If that's how you want it to be. You just gone let a man come in between our friendship."

"Oh, no, Mona. Don't go there. This has nothing to do with him. It's you. You came in between our friendship. After you tried to fight me last week, yes, he said I better leave you alone because he thinks you are crazy. But only after that. You need to blame yourself for this mess. You can still fix—"

"Well," I said drawing a small amount of strength from the water coursing through my body. "I guess you better go ahead and leave now then. I'd hate for your husband to be worried about you."

"You aren't ever going to get it, Mona."

"No, you don't get it, Candice. If your plan was to come here and throw everything you did for me up in my face then point taken. Hell, it's not like I asked you to do anything for me anyway. You could've left me how you found me. I would have been fine."

"Oomph." Candice threw up both her hands in frustration. Her green eyes rolled with frustration. "You are impossible." She ran back down the stairs.

"Leave my key on the table, please!" My hoarse voice followed her down the stairs.

A few minutes later, the front door slammed closed. I tried to stand to my feet again. Good. I was up, my legs were shaky, but I was up. I went into the bathroom to get myself another drink of water before I dared the stairs. I decided to brush my teeth because I couldn't stand the smell of my own breath any longer. The bathroom was very clean. I made a mental note to thank Candice for that, too, since she wanted to keep score. I've helped that heifa many times before, and now that I was at my lowest, she wanted to get all preachy on me.

I checked myself out as I brushed my teeth. My appearance was shocking and that was me being nice to myself. I ran my hand through my limp hair. My skin was blotched and red. I must have hit my head pretty hard because the skinny little band aid barely covered the deep wound. I wondered how I did that. I was so out of it, it could have been anything.

I turned the water to hot and held my face over the faucet. I let the rising steam caress my skin for a few moments. My stomach grumbled. I shut off the water and headed downstairs in search for food. Candice had left the plate she cooked for me on the stove of my very clean kitchen. I was sure she would have thrown it away, but was grateful that she didn't. I was so hungry that I didn't wait to warm it back up. I snatched the paper towel off and ate it standing as I leaned against the kitchen counter. The grits were way too dry for my taste. Candice could clean but she was definitely no cook.

I opened the fridge and grabbed the orange juice. I went to reach for a cup when it hit me. I could drink straight out of the container. I was alone. The mouthful of grits making its way down my throat turned to stone as I realized that my children were gone. I opened the juice and took a huge sip to push down my sorrow. I slammed the door to the fridge a little too hard. Report cards, awards, and bills sprayed across the floor.

Custody Hearing for Sean Thomas: Monday, May 3rd at 1 o'clock. Shit. What's today? What's today? I scrambled to pick up the papers on the floor and found the calendar. Today was Tuesday, May 4th.

"No! No!" I bellowed out loud as I doubled over in pain. "Not my baby! No. God, please help me!"

"What!" My mother's voice came from nowhere. "What the hell is wrong with you, girl?" She rushed to my side, holding me up to keep me from falling to the floor. "What is it?"

"Mama. It's Sean, I missed his court date." My tears fell onto her shoulder.

"What? That's all? That's what you up in here carrying on for?" She pushed me off of her and wiped the residue from my tears off of her shoulder with her jeweled hand as though she was repulsed by them—by me.

"No, Mama, you don't understand. Sean's father was trying to take...to take him away from me," I said between hysterical sobs.

"Girl, look around. Do you see *any* kids here? How did he take Sean from *you*? You pretty much gave those bad-assed kids over to the state. Hell, if his daddy wanted him that bad, let that woman beater have him."

She walked over to the sink and wet her fingertips and proceeded to dampen the spot where I cried on her shoulder. "This suit is pure silk. You know your tears make their own saline solution which is mostly salt. And everyone knows that salt will leave a white residue on silk. Can't have that, can we?" she explained mostly to herself than to me.

"But, Mama, he's my baby." I tried to ignore her inconsideration because she'd always been like that.

"Your baby or not. That boy is going to live with his father." She took a piece of bacon off of my plate and shoved the entire strip in her mouth.

"How do you know? Maybe they couldn't let the case go on without me."

"Oh, someone from the state called me. Didn't they call you to notify you of the hearing and your rights?"

"Well..." I began to fidget. I hadn't answered the phone since I left jail. I had no intention of telling my mother about my week-long drunken stupor. Candice may have told her when she called, but I wasn't going to volunteer any extra information for her to judge me any more than necessary.

"Well, they called and asked if I wanted custody of Xavier and Genesis. Said that Sean would probably go live with his father."

"What did you say?"

I didn't know how I felt about my kids living with my parents. But at least I'd know where they were. Right now, I knew nothing at all and I was miserable for it. Shame moved in over me like a dark cloud as I realized that Sean's father also knew what happened. I played with a lock of my hair.

"What do you think I said?" she greedily swiped another piece of bacon.

"Uh, yes."

My heart filled with hope. I knew my mother wasn't too fond of children, especially small ones like Sean. She said they were too much work. That's why my father spent more time with me than my mother did when I was little. He said that she didn't have the mental sense or patience to raise kids. So he did everything himself because he didn't want to have to hurt her over me. But, if it was only the older two, maybe she'd do it.

"Yes!" She laughed out loud, exposing the contents of the mangled bacon in her mouth. "Girl, you crazy. I don't have time to take care of nobody else's kids." She laughed heartily like I told a joke or something, slapping her greasy hand on my shoulder like I should have been laughing with her. "Why do you think we only had you? I had my fair share of raising brats. Oh no, daughter, this one is on you."

"Mother! You said no! Please tell me you didn't say no. What did Daddy say?"

"I didn't even bother filling your father in regarding your foolishness. We did our job with you. Plus, you know he has a bad heart." She glanced down at her watch. "I don't have a lot of time. I have somewhere to be in an hour. But really, Mona, I can't help you."

"At least Genesis, Mother. Please. I know you can take her. She shouldn't be with strangers, she's a girl. Anything could happen to her," I pleaded.

"Your daughter looks like a grown woman, Mona. Acts like one, too. I can't have that hussy prancing around my hus—I mean, house like that." She looked me eye to eye. "I'm sorry, but

I told you not to have all those kids. I warned you."

"But they are your grandchildren. And it would only be until I can prove that I didn't do anything wrong and I can get my kids back." She hated crying so I held my tears in check this time.

"No!" She raised her voice as anger contorted her face. "Let me tell you something. Don't try to make me feel sorry for them or you with that *your* grandchildren talk. I told you to go to school. I told you how hard it was out here for a single parent. I told you that boy, that both of those boys you laid up with didn't love you. I told you that if you continued to put your hands on your kids like that and send them to school with black eyes and burned fingers, the state would take them from you. I told you all of this." She picked up her purse and keys from the floor where she dropped them when she rushed in. "But you know what? You didn't listen to anything I told you! Don't go looking for help from me now. This is your problem, dear daughter."

I was furious. We stood there for a moment, staring icicle-like daggers into each other's heart. I saw myself in her and that made me angrier. All the years of emotional and physical abuse that I suffered from that woman came back and punched me in the gut. I didn't get an abortion with Genesis because she threatened to put me out if I ever got pregnant. It was right up my alley because I was looking to get away from her anyway. I treated my kids the only way I knew how—like she treated me. I looked down at my own hands at the faint markings of cigarette burns on them.

"You know what you forgot to tell me, Mother?" I said with enough malice in my voice to kill her. "You forgot to tell me how to be a good mother. Can you tell me how to do that now? Do *you* know how? You forgot to tell me how to be a mother that doesn't abuse her kids. You forgot to tell me how to be a mother that wouldn't let her—"

"That's enough! I'm not going to stand here and be disrespected by you. You ain't even worth it. I don't know why your little friend called me over here. I have so much going on in my life right now and your pathetic little situation nauseates me." She turned her nose up and headed for the door.

"Wait, Mama," I said, coming back to my senses. She was all I had left. "I can't live without my children. Tell me what to do. Help me. Please Mama." The tears came then.

My mother stopped and turned around to face me. She came back into the kitchen grabbed me in a tight embrace and in it, I melted. She asked sweetly, "You don't think you can live without your kids, baby?"

"No, Mama. I can't." I cried, holding on to her with all that was within me. I couldn't remember the last time my mother touched me with so much warmth and it felt good. I never wanted to let her go.

She released me and turned all four burners to the ON position on the stove till they hissed and ticked loudly. Gas quickly permeated through the air and burned the inside of my nose. She opened the oven, and on her way out of the front door, she shouted one word over her shoulder and she was gone: "Don't!"

Naomi

BEFORE DAE GOT back from Vegas and tossed me off the Thomas family case completely, I managed to get Sean placed with his biological father. Actually, that was a situation already in the works. Imagine my surprise when I gave him a call and he had already filed for full custody of his son. From my desk, that was almost unheard of. We rushed through the process and he was able to take his son home within days. Mona never showed, so it was an easy deal.

What a man like Sean was doing with a woman like Mona was beyond me. I almost asked him how it happened. I'm sure she was a one night stand or they met on the Internet. Sean was gainfully employed, had his own place, and was an upstanding member of his church. His pastor, who was also his uncle, came to court with him to speak on his behalf, along with his mother and sister. The senior Sean and Mona—a strange combo.

I felt better knowing that Sean would be safe, protected and loved. Although I grappled with the fact that Xavier and Genesis didn't have a more permanent place to go, it was best for Sean.

He was very happy to see his father again but very distraught over leaving his siblings. Sean's father agreed to arrange frequent visits with the other children. I could only hope that he'd keep his word.

It wasn't that I didn't find the older kids' father. Actually, he was very easy to find being that he was in the military. Initially, I left a message with his wife. To my amazement, she knew absolutely nothing of her husband having fathered children outside of their marriage. She then adamantly denied the paternity as if she was there personally when the conception took place. I don't know how many times I've had to deal with the scorn of a wife in denial foolishly attempting to protect her man.

He eventually called me very upset that I had called his home. I explained the situation and what the state was looking for him to do. He immediately went into his financial situation and how it would not allow for him to take on any *more* children.

"Do you deny paternity? I asked.

"No. Well, I know Genesis is mine. Not too sure about Xavier."

I had his military photo in front of me, what a liar. Xavier looked just like him. Genesis looked more like Mona.

"Oh, so are you willing to take in *your daughter*, Genesis?" I was reaching at hope, obligation or humanity—something.

"I just can't do it. I can't put that additional burden on my wife. We already have three of our own children. And." He paused. "I just don't have the time."

"She said no, didn't she?"

"It's not only that. After all those kids have been through, who knows what issues they have? You know that Mona was always a real nutcase. She had a firecracker temper, which is why we broke up. Way too violent for my taste. She was just like her mother."

And you left your kids with her? I wanted to ask. He forgot to say a real piece of violent ass that bore him two babies which he abandoned her with.

"What about your parents? Do you think they'd be willing?"

"Look Miss, uh?"

"Mitchell."

"I gotta protect my other kids from that sort of element. I just can't go bringing anybody up in my house. You know how it is." He chuckled nervously ignoring my question about his parents.

"No. I don't know how it is," I said sternly. I couldn't talk to him anymore. "But you have a nice day, Mr. Johnson." I slammed down the phone as quickly as I could. I wanted the click to vibrate in his ear. What a loser! He didn't even bother with showing up to sign his children's birth certificates, why did I expect for him to show up to be the father they really needed. I wanted so much for him to do the right thing. Those kids deserved a break.

He sounded half decent, too. Like if he tried, he would be able to make a real difference in the lives of his children. He was self-ish though. He didn't want to interrupt the coziness of the fake life he had been living to make the lives of his own children better. I think I cared more about the welfare of his kids than he did and I just met them less than a week ago. I wrote *uninterested* in the file next to his name.

It's not like they didn't already know. Xavier had already explained to me that their father was not involved at all. He did say that if he was willing to take Genesis only, that he'd understand and was willing to remain in foster care alone.

Maria took over the case, so she handled the calls to the maternal side of the family, as well as to Mona. She said that she tried to contact Mona several times, but she never answered the telephone or returned any messages. I was surprised after that big show she put on in front of her house. Mona's mother flat out refused as well.

Maria told me the grandmother said that, although the events were very unfortunate, she didn't have the time to raise any more children and to please not contact her any further because her husband's health wasn't that good. Between Mona's mother and her choice in men, I could see why she was so screwed up in the head. I had to ask myself if I would have been just as crazy had I grown up in the same house as Nola my entire life. I think so.

In any case, there were no biological takers for Genesis and Xavier. It was final, they would stay in the care of Mrs. Fildhurst until the court said otherwise, or until they ran away, or heaven forbid, Mona got them back, which was highly unlikely as well.

Mona didn't even bother to show up for the court hearing to face the allegations of child abuse and the children became official wards of the court. Or in more understandable terms, the good ole state of Texas was from then on Xavier's and Genesis' parents. When no one showed up to fight for them on their behalf, they were declared abandoned. *Unclaimed.*

While I didn't fully regret slapping Mona that day, I regretted getting *unofficially* suspended from my job and being removed from the case which meant that I wouldn't get to spend any more time with Xavier. I think we developed a bond that I never had with any other child on my case load. Since he had my card, he often called me up just to say hello.

Genesis never warmed up to me, but she was a lot like her mother. I knew she would be a handful for Mrs. Fildhurst, so I told Maria to keep a good handle on her. I was thankful that the case didn't go too far from my desk. I would be able to check up on them by hovering over the cubicle wall for an instant update.

At the end of my last day in the office, I cleaned up my desk. I even gave it a really good wipe down with disinfectant wipes and put everything in its rightful place. All my case folders were properly labeled and filed. It was the cleanest it had been since I started working for the state.

I was the last one remaining in the office so I let my hair down and twirled huge chunks around my fingers as I looked around. The last time I was able to take any time off of work was for my wedding. I hoped Jake could stand me home all day for the next five days. It may have been a good thing though; we needed to spend some time together. Either he was at the shop or at church and I was always working, so we never had the opportunity to really talk—especially about what happened the evening I had that nightmare.

I was glad that it hadn't happened again. He tried once to get me to talk about it, but I clammed up. He was overly worried about me and refused to let me go to bed alone after that. The thought of all the attention I'd been receiving at home brought a gentle smile to my lips.

"Why do you look like the cat with two bowls of milk?" Dae asked, bringing me out of my revelry.

"No reason."

I wondered what she was doing at my desk. She'd been avoiding me ever since she came back from her conference in Vegas. I was still a little put off by her because she hung up in my face like I was a child or something. And when she came back, she was still not speaking to me.

"I know today is your last day in the office. Did you get everything squared away for your absence?

"My absence? You mean my suspension?"

"You know what I mean," Dae responded.

"Yeah, I'm ready, I guess. I've never been suspended before, not even from school when I was younger. This is a little weird for me."

"I can understand how you must feel."

"No, I don't think you can even imagine how I feel." The situation with Dae was strained and the atmosphere felt tense. I started gathering my things to leave.

She took the hint and said, "Well good bye, Naomi. Let me know if you need anything while you're away."

"Uh, okay."

Dae acted like this was a planned vacation for me. I walked out before anything else could be said. I felt her eyes bore into my back as I left. I wanted to turn around and hug my best friend. I wanted to tell her that I understood why I was getting suspended, but couldn't figure out why she barely spoke to me anymore. I didn't turn around to say anything though, I kept walking.

CȜ ȣↄ

Just as I figured it would be—it was odd being off work. By the end of the second day, I was bored restless. I didn't know what to do with myself and I felt pretty useless. Jake didn't need me and there was no child for me to rescue. I wanted to talk to Xavier terribly and it took everything in me not to pick up the phone to call him. Mrs. Fildhurst knew that I wouldn't be calling anymore. She was such a rat of an old woman that if I so happened to call she'd hang that over my head to use against me at her leisure. I resisted the urge.

After a couple of days of being cooped up in the house, I went out shopping for a new dress to wear to Jake's church for that special service they were having in honor of the new assistant pastor. A little retail therapy was every girl's prescription for the blues. I wasn't much of a shopper, one of the things Jake loved about me. I didn't toss our cash into the money pit he called the mall. But hey, every once in a while the woman in me came out.

I hit the mall with a vengeance. Almost everything I touched—I bought. I splurged on a new designer dress for me, with matching shoes and purse. I also hit up Kirkland's and that's where I did the most damage. You just can't go wrong with anything in that store, all the decorative items, clocks, and paintings. I bought so many of those little scented bags that my clothes and hair smelled like clean white linen.

I felt so guilty for buying so much for myself and the house that I went into a men's store and bought Jake a new suit with accessories to match my outfit. Of course it would need altering, I hated a man that wore an off the rack suit with sloppy sleeves that hung over the wrists. I made an appointment for Jake to go back to get his measurements taken. The tailor confirmed that the suit would be ready in enough time.

It was lunchtime, so I decided to pop in on Jake with lunch. All that shopping had my appetite going. I stopped at his favorite deli and picked up his favorite sandwich, extra banana peppers just like he liked it. I was on cloud nine when I pulled up to his job. I'd had an amazingly satisfying day and seeing my handsome husband was going to put me over the top. I just knew he'd be thrilled when he saw me.

I sat in the car a few extra minutes when I pulled up to his shop and applied lip-gloss and primped in the mirror. My hair looked frazzled, and I made a note to schedule an appointment to get something done to it. I had to look my best for that celebration at Jake's church. The piranhas would be out, looking their best and biting. I had to be on point. I never cared too much about how I looked, well, not that I didn't care. I was a more natural sister. It was those church women who had a way of looking at you like you were an extra piece to the puzzle that didn't belong when you weren't together just so. I hated that type of scrutiny.

I was getting out of the car when I saw Jake exit his building. *Naomi Mitchell, that's your husband, girl.* I smiled to myself at the thought. I loved him so much. I tiptoed up to him when he bent over to check the tire pressure on a car in front of the shop.

"Guess who?" I teased with my body pressed into his back and one hand over his eyes. "Uh…the gas company." He laughed. "No, from the perfume, I'm gonna guess it's the prettiest woman in the world. My wife."

"You know it. And I come bearing food," I held up our lunch.

"Oh…uh, for me. Lunch?" he asked, not sounding too excited.

"Yes, for lunch. Breakfast is long gone and dinner is hours away." I got a little defensive. "Do you have plans or something?"

"Well, sort of. You should have called first, honey."

"I didn't think I had to. You can change them," I said defiantly.

"It's not that easy, sweetness," he said, pulling me into his arms.

No sooner than I asked, "With who?" did Dae walk out of Jake's building. My mouth flew open.

"You ready—" she began until her eyes settled on me. "Naomi?"

"Hello to you too, Dae. What brings you to *my husband's* shop?" I asked coldly. Now, here was my best friend at my husband's job, ready for a lunchtime rendezvous, but she'd barely had a whole sentence to put together for me over the last week.

"Oh, she dropped her car off for an oil change and inspection." Jake interjected, "And I was going to take her back to the office." Jake had never been a very good liar and he was lying through his teeth.

"So where's her car?" I asked, looking around the parking lot for Dae's silver Honda.

"Inside," Jake responded. "Why all the questions, Naomi?"

"Excuse me. I just wanted to know what she was doing here. I didn't know it was against the law to ask questions. I just didn't expect to see *her* here. That's all. And I really wanted to have lunch with you today." I was probably overreacting, but something about their demeanor unnerved me. I knew that Jake was also Dae's mechanic, but still, something wasn't right and I wanted an explanation.

"I can grab something from the office cafeteria, Jake. If you could just give me a lift back to work that would be fine." Dae looked impatiently at her watch and never directly at me.

"Okay," he replied. "Go ahead and hop in my truck. I'll be right there."

Dae walked off without acknowledging me. We were all talking, but indirectly talking to each other. It wasn't like us.

"What's up with that, Jake? Is there anything I need to know?"

"Naomi! Don't be ridiculous. I've been friends with Dae as long as I've been married to you. Your imagination is really at it this time. I'm about to go drop Dae off and I'll be right back to have lunch with my lovely wife. Get inside and get it ready." Jake popped me on the behind and walked off. He hopped in the truck with Dae.

As the truck pulled out, I noticed Dae laughing. I twirled a lock of hair around my finger. Was I was the butt of their joke. I added Dae to the growing list of women to watch. Church women and best friends.

Dae and Jake? Together? No.

Xavier

"XAVIER, I CAN'T take living in this house anymore. I hate it here." Genesis groaned while we were sitting on the porch. "And if I tell you something else, you have to promise not to tell anyone. Not even Naomi."

"What is it? I promise," I said.

"I talked to Mona."

"You talked to Mona! When? You weren't supposed to do that, Sissy!"

"Shh," Genesis said. "I don't want that old lady coming out here getting all up in my business." She looked crossly at me from over the mirror she had in her hand and sucked her teeth.

I sat there absorbed in Sissy pulling her eyebrows out with a pair of tweezers. She had changed so much since we'd been in a foster home. She wore makeup and styled her hair like the rowdy girls she hung out with at our new school. People used to always tell us that we looked like twins because we were so close in age. Now, she looked like my older sister with all the short skirts and her hair down over her face.

Mrs. Fildhurst said that she didn't care what Genesis wore just as long as she understood that there would be no little babies up in her house. I cared and I was disappointed. I didn't like how the boys looked at her at school. I especially didn't like how she reacted to all the attention. Every day she showed a little more skin. Maybe being with Mona was best for Genesis because I didn't even know her anymore. She changed—a lot.

"Tell me, what did she say?" I asked.

"She wants us to come home."

"Why didn't she come to court then?"

"She said nobody told her when the court date was. That they wanted her to miss it so we could get lost in the system. She was crying, Xavier."

"That's not what Naomi said," I countered defensively.

"What? Naomi said she'd be here for you too, didn't she? What is it about her? You barely know that lady."

"I don't know, Sissy. I just kinda feel like she stood up for us that day in front of our house. Nobody ever did that."

"Yeah, look around. Where is she *now*?" Sissy smirked.

"I don't care, Sissy. She still saved us from living with Mona."

"Whatever. You ain't gonna ever see that lady again."

The smug look on Sissy's face was enough to shut me up. Sissy was right. Naomi said that she'd be here for me—for us. And that we'd stay together. Sean was gone to live with his father and we hadn't heard from him since. And Naomi dumped us off on someone else again. Some Hispanic lady named Maria was our new social worker. Maybe Sissy was right. None of it seemed worth it anymore. I was beginning to care less and less about everything and everybody.

"Hey, look, Xavier!" Jordan interrupted, pointing up at a small plane writing a message in the sky. Jordan was the little boy that was already living with Mrs. Fildhurst when we got here. Since Sean left, I had become pretty attached to him. He was my foster brother.

"Yeah, that's cool, Jordan," I replied.

We arched our necks and stared up in the sky. We didn't say a word. Even Genesis looked. By the time the plane was finished, the message was already beginning to dissipate. I could still make out the words. I didn't understand why someone would want to write that simple two-word message in the clouds. Trust God.

"What does it say, Jordan?" I asked.

"Trust God," he said.

Genesis sucked her teeth again and rolled her eyes.

"Do you believe in God, Xavier?" Jordan asked, ignoring Genesis. He could tell that she didn't like him very much. She almost never had anything to say to him, and when she did, it was always mean.

"Yeah, I guess so," I answered.

"My mother used to sing in the choir at church. She had a real pretty voice. Sometimes when she sang, I would cry. I don't know why, but I would feel so good inside and I'd just cry." A tear ran down his face as he thought about it. "My mother told me that the good feeling that made me cry was the Holy Spirit of God."

"Why did you say used to? Is your mom still alive?" It was the first time Jordan ever mentioned anything about his mother to us.

"No. She's not dead. She just doesn't want me anymore."

"How do you know that?" I asked.

"'Cause she asked me to understand that her life was different. And that I com...compli..."

"Complicated?"

"Yeah, I complicated it. She told me to never forget that she loved me, but she couldn't take care of me."

"Aww Jordan, that's sad, little man." I patted his shoulder.

"No. I'm not sad anymore. I know she loves me. My stepfather was a scary man. Uh, I'm gonna go play video games. Wanna play?" Jordan got up to go inside.

"No. It's too hot in there." I responded.

"Okay." Jordan shrugged his bony shoulders and went inside.

Genesis and I were left out on the porch with our thoughts of Jordan and our own mother. I could tell she was thinking about what he had said. We watched the Trust God message until it blended completely in the clouds.

"That sucks. At least Mona wanted us. She would have never let anybody do anything to hurt us." Genesis ended the somber silence first.

"Yeah, but *she* hurt us."

"It wasn't that bad, Xavier. You act like everything was bad about Mona all the time."

"You act like it was good most of the time, Sissy. Mona was getting worse. Remember what she did to me when Sean's father left. She put me out of the house. Then she beat me because I started walking away. She was bipolar."

"She wasn't bipolar!" Genesis got angry. "You don't even know what that means. That's why I hate talking to you about anything. I wish Sean was still here. Even little Sean said that Mona wasn't that bad and he wanted to go home."

"Sean said what?"

"Nothing! They should have just taken *you* from Mona. She's still my mother and I love her even if you don't anymore," Genesis snapped. "Even Jordan understands what his mother went through. And he still loves her."

"I never said that I didn't love Mona," I defended myself. I was sick and tired of fighting with Sissy about the same thing all the time.

"Well you never said that you did either. So, do you?"

"I don't have to say anything to prove it to you." I stood up to go in the house. I couldn't stand Genesis anymore. Every time we talked, it was always the same. We argued over Mona and whether or not, I loved her. Why? Why does it matter so much to you, anyway? Leave me alone about it!"

Genesis stood up, too, and got in my face. She was a little older than me, but I was taller than her already. She wanted to argue. I used to think my sister was so pretty, but the more I looked at her lately, the uglier she got with her squinted eyes and wrinkled forehead. The way she talked to me and treated Jordan she was just like Mona outside and inside—*hateful*.

"Humph, I knew you didn't love her." She sneered.

"Whatever." I slammed the door behind me.

ೞ ೲ

On the way to school the next morning, Genesis stopped before we reached the bus stop. I looked back at her thinking something was wrong.

"I left my homework. I'm gonna run back and get it," she said.

"Homework? You had homework over the weekend?" I asked. I tried to remember Sissy doing homework over the last couple of days.

"You don't know what I had to do," she snapped.

I just shrugged my shoulders and continued to walk. I wasn't going to start with her today.

"If I miss the bus, I'll get Mrs. Fildhurst to take me to school."

"Okay," I said without looking back.

Sissy took off trotting in the other direction. It was drizzling a little bit so I sped up. I knew she'd have to get a ride. We were already running late because Sissy took forever putting all that junk on her face and hogged the bathroom.

I barely made the school bus. I had to bang on the back of it for the driver to notice me. The bus passed the street we lived on, but I didn't see Genesis. There was no way she could have made it back that fast. I guess if she ran, which she probably did because the rain had really started coming down.

I looked out for her most of the day at school and never saw her. Usually, I'd catch a glimpse of her giggling in some boy's face between classes. When I didn't see her at the bus stop at the end of the day, I knew something was wrong. The bus barely pulled up to my stop and I was already impatiently waiting for the doors to open. It had rained off and on all day and the streets were flooded in the old neighborhood we lived in so it took the bus an extra twenty long minutes to get there. I was the only person to get off at my stop and I ran all the way to Mrs. Fildhurst's house.

"Is Genesis here?" I asked, panting, holding my side as I burst through the door. I was out of breath in the short amount of time it took me to run home. I got drenched in the downpour.

"Boy! What happened to you?" Mrs. Fildhurst asked.

"Sissy." My shoes squished and left muddy prints throughout the house as I looked for my sister. I opened the door to Sissy's room and peeked in. No sign of her. "Sissy." I went into the kitchen and opened all the cupboards leaving a trail of dirty water sprinkled all over the floor. I checked the bathroom and opened all of the cabinets there, too.

"Why are you opening the cabinets? Do you think she'd be in there?" Mrs. Fildhurst asked, following me around, puzzled at my actions. "What is going on?"

I know that I wasn't making any sense. I didn't know why I looked for her in the pantry. But I was getting frustrated. Although Sissy and I argued a lot more lately than we used to, she was all I had. I couldn't remember my life without Sissy. I loved my brother Sean with all my heart, but Sissy was…my everything. We had the same mother and father. We were less than a year apart. There was never a day in my entire life that I had been without her. I needed my sister!

"Xavier! What is going on here?" Mrs. Fildhurst was still following me, but she was closing cabinets and doors behind me. I didn't know what to say, so I avoided her questions. She didn't even realize that Sissy did not walk through the door with me.

My head started to hurt. Finding no sign of Genesis, I fell into a ratty old plastic covered armchair that smelled like cigar smoke. I put my head on my knees and cried like a girl. I was so glad that Jordan wasn't home from school yet so he wouldn't see me like this. I sobbed so hard that I started choking and gagged. I was more afraid than anything. I knew Sissy went to see Mona. I just knew it. No matter what Mona had done to me—to us. She still trusted her too much. She believed in her, she really believed Mona was a good mother. I knew that meant trouble for my sister. It was different when I was there because Mona hated me so much and took all her anger out on me. But I was here and I couldn't protect Sissy from Mona. I racked my brain thinking of how I was gonna get Sissy back.

"Why did she do it? Why? Why?" I murmured repeatedly.

"Xavier! That's enough. Come on, sweetheart." Mrs. Fildhurst stood next to me and rubbed my back gently.

The way she touched me, so tenderly messed me up even more. I began to holler even louder than before. All the anger that had been between me and Sissy lately. My sadness at Sean being gone. I felt wide open and the more Mrs. Fildhurst rubbed the more distraught I became about Mona. I felt like she was still messing with me. She was like a ghost, haunting me. I would never be able to get away from Mona. I wanted to be free from her for the rest of my life. I hated her. Why couldn't Genesis see Mona for who she really was—crazy? My body shook from loneliness and pain.

Mrs. Fildhurst pulled me to my feet and wrapped her huge, flabby, grandmotherly arms around my body as she whispered in my ear. "Let it out. That's okay. Just let it all out, sweetheart. Nothing is too big for God." She repeated over and over again as she continued to rub my back, stroking me up and down.

I was much taller than she was, but she seemed to cover every part of me. Mrs. Fildhurst's words had a calming effect. Mona's mother, our grandmother never hugged us. I couldn't think of the last time she even touched us. She almost never came to visit and when she did, she ignored us, and spent all her time yelling at Mona for having us. She only referred to us as those kids or Mona's kids. Never as her grandchildren, or sweetheart like Mrs. Fildhurst had just done.

"Mrs. Fildhurst?"

"Yes, baby?"

"Sissy's gone."

"I know. Let me worry about that."

"I'm alone."

"No, you're not. I'm here. Jordan's here. And more importantly, God's here."

"God? God doesn't care anything about me."

Mona

I RUSHED AROUND the house getting everything together. I ran out to the store and stocked the fridge. I even cooked, something I never did much of when I had my kids with me. I planned to do more of it in the future when I got them back. After that episode with my mother, I had made up my mind that I was going to get my kids back. I was going to be a better mother than that hypocrite of a Christian ever could be. She had called a few times, but I didn't even answer the phone. She only wanted to see if I did it. See if I had killed myself. If mother wanted to know then she would need to come see for herself.

That's why when Genesis called me I was so ecstatic. Hearing my baby girl's voice made my day. When she told me that she was going to come and visit me, I was overjoyed. She said that Xavier didn't want to come, so she would be alone. I thought it was strange that she was coming on a school day and by herself. Before I got the chance to ask any questions, she told me that she was ditching school to sneak over to my house. I knew then that it was a bad idea, but I wanted to see her so bad, I couldn't resist. I told her to just be careful.

I was so excited after Genesis called that I decided to give Big Sean a call and ask if I could talk to my son. I wondered excitedly if maybe he'd bring Sean over sometime. I dialed his cell number and my hopes were immediately dashed. Disconnected. I called his job and the receptionist said he no longer worked there before I could get his full name out of my mouth. *Liar.* I tried his mother's home and cell number, both were disconnected. A pang of regret shot through my heart. I cried for a while about it, but decided to focus on the one child that I had left. The only one that gave a real damn about me—my little girl, Genesis.

I was upstairs combing my hair when I heard a knock at the front door. I peeked out the window and saw Candice. I decided not to answer. I didn't want to get involved in any small talk with her; we still hadn't been speaking, so why start today. I had better things to do, like wait on my baby. Candice looked up and caught me looking out the window at her. She waved her hand as if to say forget it, and walked off. *Whatever.*

I heard another knock at the door, this time the back door. I rushed into Xavier and Sean's room which sat over the back door. I squinted my eyes to get a real good view. It couldn't be. Oh hell no, that was not Genesis down there with all that makeup on her face. What in the hell? She knew better. I raced down the stairs and snatched the door open with so much force Genesis gasped and jumped back.

"Hey, Mama! I mean Mona." Genesis screeched and threw her arms around my neck.

"Hi, Genesis." I never called her Sissy; that was Xavier's nickname for her. When he was little, he had a hard time saying Genesis, so he shortened it to Sissy. I wrapped my arms around her and decided I'd wait to have the conversation about the makeup later.

"Oh, I missed you so much." Genesis crooned. "You just don't know. I want to come home, Mona. Can I stay? Please? Please? Please let me stay?"

"Genesis, you know that won't be possible, especially not right now. I'm gonna have to get myself together first. Then I'm gonna get all of you back."

"Xavier too?"

"Yes, girl. Xavier too! I'm mad at him, but he's still my son."

We were still locked in an embrace in the doorway. I didn't want any of my nosey neighbors to walk past and catch Genesis there, so I moved into the kitchen and closed the door.

"Why'd you come to the back door?" I asked, trying to shake the image in front of me and focus on her just being there.

I leaned against the kitchen counter. I couldn't stop staring at the wildly painted palette that was supposed to be my baby's face. I couldn't take my eyes off of it. The black eyeliner and thick globs of mascara must have been applied by a blind person and especially the colorful array of eye shadow that she had doused over her lids. Her cheeks looked as though someone had stamped them with a huge, hot pink bingo marker and called it blush. There was so much of everything going wrong with her face that she looked like a smiling clown. It annoyed me.

"Because I was coming around to the front when I saw Candice knocking on the door. So I went around to the back and waited until I thought she was gone," Genesis said proudly.

My eyes finally found the will it took to move down and away from the rainbow on Genesis' face. I was even more appalled at the stripper pole ready costume that she had on her body. She had on a green plaid skirt that was closer to her cat than her knees. If she bent over, her entire ass would have been exposed. Her shirt barely covered...No, her shirt didn't even meet the hem of the top of the skirt. Her entire midriff was exposed. I know this damn girl did not show up at my door dressed like some floozy! I didn't recognize Genesis. Where did she get these clothes from?

I began to seethe inside. To get my mind off of my child's obvious poor taste of attire, I turned to the stove and stirred the smothered potatoes that I had cooked for our breakfast. I should have been hungry. I was before—not now. The seasoned aroma of the simmering food did nothing for my appetite. My daughter stood right behind me dressed like a ho. I was going to swallow a good ole unhealthy portion of pissed off for breakfast.

I barely heard a word she said as she chattered away non-stop about everything from Xavier, to Sean's leaving the foster home, and her new school. I couldn't focus on any of that at that moment. When Genesis opened the refrigerator, I was able to get a good view of her from behind. She had tied the bottom of her white blouse into a knot in the back and created that skank look by herself.

"Genesis! What the fuck do you think you're doing?" I barked. I couldn't hold it.

The tone of my voice scared her and she dropped a whole carton of milk on the floor. The white liquid poured into the cracks of the green tile and rushed in various directions.

"I'm sorry, Mona. I...didn't mean it." Genesis rushed to the sink and grabbed a towel.

"You are so damn clumsy, girl," I shouted at her as she bent over to clean up the mess.

"I'm sorry," she repeated.

Genesis got on her knees and began to wipe the floor. Her little skirt flirted back and forth, toying with the idea of exposing her panties. I thought I saw something on her upper legs as she reached to clean far underneath the fridge. There it was again. I was immediately concerned about what it could be.

"Get over here," I said.

Genesis took her time getting to her feet. She walked the couple of steps to where I stood as slow as she could.

"Turn around," I ordered.

Genesis turned around and watched me out of the corner of her eye. I moved my hand to raise the back of her skirt and she almost jumped out of her skin before I even touched her.

"Stop doing that," I growled. I hated when my kids did that. It hurt my heart when they flinched every time I tried to touch them. I remembered doing that to my own mother.

I reached for Genesis' skirt again and raised it. "What's this on your legs, girl?"

"Huh?" she asked me as she tried to crane her neck around to see what I was referring to.

"Go look in the mirror. There's some scratches on your legs."

Genesis rushed into the living room and stood in the full length mirror with me on her heels. I turned on the light so she could get a better view. Panic arrested my thoughts. What if someone had raped my baby? Hurt her? She hoisted her skirt and peered at the faded markings just under her behind.

"Who did that to you?" I quizzed.

Genesis dropped her skirt and sat on the arm of the sofa. She would have never done that before. I decided to let that go for the time being

"Who?" I demanded to know. "Tell me now, girl!"

"You, Mona." She buried her hands in her face. "That time you hit me with the telephone cord until my legs started to bleed. You did it."

"I don't remember that," I lied. I didn't want to remember.

"Remember when Xavier forgot to lock the door that one night when we went to bed. You got up in the middle of the night and checked. You whooped me and Xavier with the—"

"Girl, that was a long time ago. How am I supposed to remember that?" I didn't want to hear anymore. I was sorry I even asked.

"Well, I guess it took a long time to heal," Genesis said.

She walked back into the kitchen to finish cleaning up the spilled milk. I was left alone for a brief moment staring into the dusty mirror at myself. I still carried scars from my own parents. I walked up to the mirror and touched it. How did I become *her*?

Genesis and I enjoyed the breakfast I'd prepared for us. I guess neither of us wanted to ruin the little time we had. It was strained, but we made the best of it. I tried to push her appearance out of my head. It was hard. I wanted to beat her ass because of how she looked. It took everything in me not to touch her. Just when I wanted to thump her in her head because the eye paint on her face teased me, I got up and served myself another fried pork chop instead. I took a huge bite, so I could think and chew instead of fuss and cuss. I had to work on not being my mother. I hoped that I could do it.

"When did you start wearing makeup?" I slowly paced my words so that they would sound better coming out. Not so hostile—like I felt.

"Oh, my foster mother doesn't mind," Genesis said, touching her face lightly with her fingertips as though she forgot she even had it on.

"The clothes?" I kept asking questions. Someone else was raising my children, their way. I wanted to cry.

"Yeah, she doesn't care what we wear. Just as long as we go to school, do our homework, and don't give her any problems," Genesis said nonchalantly.

"Well, I care. That lady don't care nothing about you. I think you are too young for all of that makeup. And you are definitely too young for those clothes. You have no clue what you are opening yourself up to when you dress like that. I know. As your mother, not your *foster mother*, I also know that you are not ready for it."

Genesis hung her head and stared at her empty plate.

"Now, I need you to do two things. First, go upstairs and change your clothes. Then, go to the bathroom and wipe all that crap off your face."

Genesis didn't move. It was weird to me. My child was not jumping to do what I said. I felt my temperature shooting up and my anger rose right along with it.

"Now! Go now!" I yelled. She scrambled up from the table and stomped up the stairs.

Who had my daughter turned into? I hit my heels to run after her when the phone rang. I was waiting on a phone call from the human resources manager at work, so I picked it up. I really needed to get back to work. I hoped that I still had a job. It had been almost three weeks, and I was completely out of money.

"Hello," I said, hiding my irritation.

"Mona, it's good to hear your voice. It's Debra, from H.R."

"Yes, thank you for calling, Deb. I hope you have good news." I held my breath.

"I won't keep you too long with a lot of small talk, but we heard about what happened. We are so sorry."

"You did! From who? What?" I worried that they knew about the kids.

"Well, your sister, Candice, called and notified us that your grandmother had passed and that you took it really hard."

"Oh." Candice really was a friend. She thought of everything. I was instantly ashamed of the way I had treated her that morning.

"If you just let us know when you are ready to come back, we'll squeeze you into the schedule," Deb said.

"Monday, I can come back next Monday," I quickly replied. That would give me almost a week to get myself back together.

"Sure thing. Again, our condolences are with you and your family. Don't forget we offer bereavement leave. It won't cover the entire time you've been away, but it will help."

"No, that's fine, Deb." I was just happy I still had a job, considering everything that had taken place. I had a lot to be grateful for.

"Okay, we'll work out all the details when you come back. Take care," Deb said and hung up.

I kissed the telephone before I placed it back on its cradle. I was so freakin' happy! I wanted to have a smoke to celebrate. I went to my stash and rolled one up really fast. Then I heard Genesis sniffling upstairs. I almost forgot about her. I ran up the stairs to check on her and to tell her the good news.

She stood in the bathroom mirror sniffling as she attempted to remove the mounds of makeup from her face with a tissue.

"Oh, no, Genesis. You're gonna need soap and water for all that paint on your face, baby."

She completely ignored me and kept wiping with a dry paper towel. I got a washcloth out of the basket on the sink and wet it.

"Move your hand. Let me do it," I said.

Genesis reluctantly put her hand down to her side. She closed her eyes and allowed me to remove the makeup from her face. I got a chance to really look at her. My sweet daughter was growing up. I thought about when I was her age and played in my mother's makeup. I made a mess of myself and her makeup. She came home and caught me. She beat me so bad, my father made her keep me home from school for three days. I never wore makeup again until after I left her house.

Genesis finally had a sparkling face. "Go downstairs and bring me that junk you've been putting on your face."

Genesis ran down the stairs to do what I'd asked. She had changed into a pair of sweats and one of Xavier's black t-shirts that read, YOU DON'T WANT NONE OF THIS in bold neon green letters. My little girl was back. But not for long, I sighed. She was almost fifteen years old. That was about the time when I met her father. I shivered at the thought of Genesis having a baby. I wished I could tie her up and keep her locked in the house. But I couldn't. I couldn't do much of anything, especially when my kids were living under the rules of another woman's house. I really screwed up.

I pulled my makeup bag from underneath the sink. "Sit here." I pointed to the toilet and she nervously sat down.

She didn't even have a real makeup bag. She had blushes, liners, glosses, and shadows stuffed in the pocket of her back pack. It was a chaotic mess of cheap items. I started throwing things in the trash.

"Okay, I think you are too young to wear any of this stuff. But I will let you wear some of it. I know that you don't live with me anymore, and I won't be able to see you every day, but I'll trust you on this one. Deal?"

"Deal." Genesis' eyes showed the shock that she felt.

"Let me show you the right way to wear makeup. Put your head back and close your eyes."

I spent the next hour teaching my daughter how to apply mascara the right way. I gave her a brand new container of good mascara. I explained the importance of never wearing someone else's eye makeup, including mine. I told her to leave the eyeliner for extra special occasions, like prom, blush, too. She promised not to wear it anymore until then. I helped her pick out age appropriate colors to wear on her lids. We even traded glosses with each other. I took her dark colors and she ended up with the pale pinks and barely there tints. I even let her make up my face for practice. We talked about boys, love, first crushes, and everything in between.

"Did your mother show you how to put on makeup?" she asked, applying a hot pink lip-gloss to my lips that I would die before I ever wore in public.

"No," I said, quickly feeling tense. "So, tell me about the kinds of boys you like?" I asked. I changed the subject. She started giggling, so I knew there was a boy somewhere in the picture.

"Well, there's this one boy at my school. I think he is really cute."

"Go ahead." I urged. I figured I could talk about a few things with her, especially since I wasn't there to protect her from bad decisions. "You kiss him yet?"

"No!"

"Have you ever kissed a boy before?"

"Besides Xavier, just...just Grandpa."

I don't know why, but when she said my father's name, there was an uneasy twitch in my belly. I had never seen my father touch my children. I tried to tell myself that I was thinking irrationally.

"Have you ever done anything else? Like, has a boy ever touched you down there? On your cat?" I sat all the way up and opened my eyes to see her reaction.

Genesis giggled uneasily when I said the word cat. I had a hard time saying the word vagina. I was a grown woman with three kids and I still couldn't say that word with a straight face, so I smiled. She dusted gold shadow on the brush and flicked it across my lids. I was going to look like her when she walked in by the time she was done with me.

Genesis had giggled, but she never said no. I decided to ask again. "Has anyone ever touched you on your—vagina?"

I caught her hand as she was going for my other lid with the gold crusted brush. "Answer me." My voice cracked.

"Yes."

"Yes. Yes, what?" I felt the beginning signs of hysteria.

"Yes, somebody touched me there."

"Where?" My voice didn't sound like my own.

"Down there, where you said."

"Who?"

No answer.

"Who?" I shouted.

No answer.

"Who the fuck touched you down there?" I shouted again.

My mind instantly went to Big Sean. He was the only man that I had let in my house around my daughter. I started to think of all the ways that I was going to kill that bastard. I was going to put his shriveled up thing in a pickle jar. I was going to—.

"Grandpa Charles. When I was nine. You went to the hospital to have Sean and we stayed with them. He told me it was a game. He said that I was his princess. I told him that he hurt me and that I was gonna tell you. He said that I better not ever tell anyone. Grandma even walked in one time when he had his hand under my skirt and she whooped me for being fast. I'm sorry, Mama. I'm so sorry, Mama. I wanted to tell you all these years. I tried to stop him, I promise." After sucking in a long breath of air, Genesis broke down crying.

My mind was slow to register. Or maybe I didn't want it to. All I heard was Sean. I jumped up from my perch on the toilet and started pacing the bathroom floor. I flung all the makeup onto the floor. That bastard. I was going to make him pay.

"Sean, that son of a bitch!" I screamed. "You wait until I get my hands on him." I grabbed Genesis by the shoulders. "I'm going to kill him, don't worry, baby."

Genesis stopped crying and looked strangely at me. "Sean? No, Mama. Big Sean never touched me. I said Grandpa Charles."

I can't exactly say what happened next because I felt like I blacked out. I do remember swinging on Genesis, pummeling her with both of my fists and kicking her with the balls of my feet when she fell down while trying to run down the stairs and away from me. I remember yelling and screaming at her that she was lying on my father. I remember saying that her father never gave a damn about her or Xavier. That she came up in my house looking like a tramp that she probably hopped in the bed with him on her own. I told her that she was jealous because I was my father's princess, his only daughter. I chased her, yelling that she better not ever repeat that bullshit again as she ran out the door.

I tried really hard to stop myself from beating my only daughter. I couldn't help myself. I don't know what came over me. It's not that I really thought she was lying. I knew Genesis was telling the truth. I just didn't know what to do with what she had said, besides beat her quiet. If someone found out they would think I was a bad person and that I let it happen to her like it happened to me. That I was just like my mother.

Something in her words set an alarm to screaming in my head. It was a reminder of my tenth birthday. That was the day that my daddy told me it was time to grow up. It was time to teach me all the things a woman was supposed to know that only a father could teach. I was never quite sure, but I knew my mother was aware. She let it go on. She was always so conveniently gone when it happened or asleep in the middle of the day.

I tried to tell her once and she told me that it was better to confess my sins unto the Lord and did she look like the Lord? I never understood why she let that happen to me. Why didn't she protect me? How could she not know all of those years?

Damn, I couldn't do anything right. Maybe my children were better off without me. I couldn't protect them from myself or my parents; how I could I protect them from anyone else.

Xavier

SISSY CAME BACK later the same evening that she ran away. She knocked on the door while Mrs. Fildhurst, Jordan, and I were sitting at the kitchen table eating dinner. From where I sat at the table, I was the first to see her through the living room window. She walked past the house twice in both directions before she made her way up the walkway that led to the door.

I wanted to run right out the door and hug her close to me. I waited. I thought that I'd never see Sissy again. After everything she had put me through since we had gotten taken away from Mona, I wasn't sure if I wanted to see her. Mrs. Fildhurst told me that I couldn't take the blame anymore for anyone, including Sissy and Mona. She said that I needed to focus on what was left of my young life and live for me.

When Sissy knocked, I still didn't move. Jordan looked back at the door and then at me, then he looked at Mrs. Fildhurst. We both looked down at our plates and pretended to eat. Jordan got up and opened the door. He grabbed her around the waist and hugged her tightly. At first, she stood there as stiff as a cardboard with both of her arms pasted to her side, wearing one of my old shirts that I left at Mona's. Then like a flower opening up, Sissy put both of her arms around Jordan and embraced him. She held on to him as though he would disappear if she let him go.

Jordan pulled away first and reached up to wipe the tears falling from Sissy's eyes. In doing so, he left a greasy streak across her face with his little hand.

"Don't cry, Sissy, you're right on time for dinner," Jordan said. "Are you hungry?"

I waited for Genesis to start yelling at him for calling her Sissy. The first time he did it, she got so mad and told him that name was for family use only. She told him that just because we lived in the same house, he was not her family. I remembered how much it hurt his feelings. But this time she said nothing. She smiled and accepted his outstretched, oily hand. Jordan walked her to an empty place at the table and she sat down. She quietly began to serve herself a very small amount of food.

We all went back to eating. Sissy and I never made direct eye contact at the table. I was sure that we were all wondering about the bruises on Sissy's face. Because she was a little darker than me, they didn't show up so much, but you could see that they were there all the same.

Jordan took it upon himself to keep us all entertained at the table. He made us smile and relax until we had almost forgotten that Sissy had run away that day. Even through our uneasy laughter, we were all wondering who had beaten Sissy. I was sure that it was Mona. I knew that Sissy would only run away to be with her. I told her not to trust her. I silently fumed about it and taped a fake smile on my lips for Jordan.

After dinner, Mrs. Fildhurst said, "Jordan and Xavier, dishes. Sissy, you come with me," and they went into Sissy's room and closed the door.

Jordan and I were getting ready for bed by the time they both came out. I was in the bathroom brushing my teeth when Mrs. Fildhurst walked past the door. I was sure that Mrs. Fildhurst had told Sissy that she was going to tell the social worker about what happened. If that happened, then Sissy would have to leave. Mrs. Fildhurst told her that running away wouldn't be tolerated in her house the first time she tried to leave.

When Mrs. Fildhurst came out of the room, she stopped by the bathroom door. "Everything is going to be all right. If you don't mention today, then I won't," she said. She grinned at me, set the alarm, and went into her room.

Sissy came out next. "Oh, I didn't know you were in the bathroom. I'll wait."

"No, I'm almost done." I rinsed my mouth out one final time and wiped my lips on a paper towel.

"What's wrong with your eyes?" Sissy asked me.

I looked into the mirror; my eyes were almost swollen shut from crying all afternoon. They were so tight that it hurt to open them. "I was crying." I told the truth.

"What happened to yours?" I asked in return.

"Oh, I got into a fight, hanging out in the wrong part of town. I know better now." She lied, but she knew that I knew who she was referring to. Sissy gave me a hug as I stepped out of the bathroom to allow her in. "Goodnight, little brother."

"Goodnight, Sissy."

That was all that was said about Sissy running away. Nobody ever mentioned it again.

Naomi

JAKE CAME IN late from working at the church Saturday
night, but was full of energy. I knew he was excited about me
seeing all the changes that had been going on at the church. He
couldn't stop talking about it even while he was in the shower.

"Baby, did you pick up my new suit from the tailor? I forgot,"
Jake shouted, poking his head out of the shower.

If I didn't, wouldn't it be too late at this point? It was almost
Sunday morning already. I smiled, still lying in bed. My husband
seemed to forget everything. He'd forget his own hand if it wasn't
so securely attached to his wrist. I felt needed.

"Yes, it's hanging up in the closet."

I raised my head and looked toward the window at the lightning show outside. I was sure that it was going to rain—possibly
storm. It was going to be a murky and gloomy Sunday. I glanced
over at the clock and sighed—12:30 A.M. Jake was crazy, staying
out all night at that church. I put the pillow over my face to catch
a few snores while Jake finished his shower. It was sleep in late
weather, not fake and shout at church weather. I thought about

telling Jake that I didn't feel well, but I knew that particular Sunday meant so much to him.

He was so excited about the new associate pastor. I could tell that he really respected and admired her. He gushed non-stop about how great of a preacher she was while he showered. How much wisdom she would bring to the church. He almost giggled when he told me that the new pastor's husband would be relieving him of a few of his duties. Jake would only have to focus on the youth ministry, and that was it. He promised to spend more time with me after all of it was over, and that made me ecstatic because I planned to do the same thing.

After a week away from my job, I was able to put some things in perspective—especially my marriage. I was pretty much bored the entire time I was off. With no ringing cell phone, voicemails, or growing inbox of emails to return, I felt useless. I figured out that I didn't have a real life. My life consisted of my kids and Jake—that was it. I didn't have church activities like Jake had to fill the empty moments in my life. I barely had Jake because he was always at church—*according to his account.*

Most of the time that I was off, I cleaned. I cleaned the pantry, the kitchen junk drawer, and all the baseboards in our condo. I painted and redecorated our guest room. In no time at all, I had touched every room in the condo. While I cleaned, I realized that I had no friends; Dae was it. Since we weren't speaking, my cell phone hardly rang at all, except for Jake calling me, which was rare. I constantly worried about my relationship with Dae. Nothing in my life had ever lasted as long as our friendship. I knew Dae longer than I had known my own mother.

Whenever I became stressed, I also cooked. It was one of my creative outlets. In three days, I had cooked, labeled, and froze about six different dinner combinations. I even sent food over to the church with Jake for his best friend, Paul. On day four with nothing else to clean, cook, or organize, I decided to spend my last few free days at work with Jake to get his office at the shop in shape. Of course, I also wanted to keep an eye on him and my best friend. I felt that by rambling through his office, I could pick up some clues on his weird behavior. I didn't feel the need to tell him that I was going to be there. I just showed up one day, hoping that I wouldn't catch him doing anything. I found nothing at all, but I kept my eyes and ears wide open—just in case.

"Jake!" I screeched. "Why did you do that? Get your wet hands out of my hair. My hair, Jake! Do you know how long I spent in the salon?" Jake ran his dripping fingers through my hair snatching me out of my thoughts.

"Do I look like I care how long you were in the salon?" Jake roughly covered my mouth with his and drowned out my objections with a long sensual kiss. "I miss my wife."

I tried to push his soaking wet body off of mine until he grabbed my hands and held them over my head. He was too strong to fight and just a wee bit as irresistible. Every time he took his lips off of mine, I would try to protest again. He returned his lips to mine until all the fight in me turned to desire. It had been weeks since he last attempted to make love to me. My head told my body not to give in so easily and to fight the good feeling warming between my legs.

It didn't take long for my body to respond completely to his. He moved his lips from mine to the area just below my chin. When he let go of my hands, I instinctively rubbed them up then down the top of his head to the small crease in his back. I wanted to worry about the scars on my body. I was still afraid that he would change his mind about loving me if he got a good look at me out in the open. Jake felt me slipping away from the moment.

"No. No. Naomi. Don't shut me out." He kissed me again. "Just relax and let go."

"I'm trying," I whispered with his lips glued to mine.

I redirected my focus to how much I loved him. I thought about how good making love to my husband could feel if I just let go. The only thing that separated me from his growing manhood was a thin sheet and my short nightgown. . He maneuvered himself around and tussled with my nightgown until we were skin to skin with little resistance from me. He reached down and pulled the comforter up over us when I shivered from his wet body, making it very dark. It was like we were in a cocoon and I was glad. It was too dark for me to be ashamed in the light. I could barely see his eyes, but I felt his hands all over me, touching my face, cupping my breasts, and rubbing my arms.

He couldn't see me and I couldn't see him so I relaxed. He entered me easily and I let him guide me to ecstasy. "See, is this hard? Just let go," Jake said sweetly nibbling on my earlobe as he moved rhythmically over me.

My head was screaming no, but my body belonged to him. There was nothing I could do but go with it. I forgot about my hair and my scars and succumbed to the bliss of the moment. For the first time in so many months, I enjoyed making love.

Afterwards, Jake wrapped me in his arms and fell asleep with his head on my chest. I listened to him sleep in contentment for over an hour. I felt the rise and fall of his huge chest. He was so peaceful. I stroked his head and thought about everything that had happened over the last month.

I thought about my job, Dae, and especially Xavier. Part of me couldn't wait to get back to work so I could ask Maria about him. He was upset with me when I told him that Maria was taking over. I probably should have explained to him why it happened. Out of all the cases that I ever had, this one woke up something in my heart and I wanted to protect that particular little boy so much. I fell asleep dreaming about Xavier of all people.

C3 ∞ℂ

Jake's church had changed so much since the last time I'd been there, which was about six months ago, I think. Maybe more. Jake was in a great mood and touched me every chance he got in the car on the way over to the church. It was amazing at how one little rendezvous seemed to pull together the growing gap between us. As we pulled up, he proudly pointed out all the things he had done to the exterior of the building; the new beautiful landscaping, flowers in rich purples and vibrant hues of pink and yellow popped out in front of thick rich green shrubs which lined the driveway and framed the entrance.

A winding brick pathway curved around from the side of the church and stopped at a wooded circle of live oak trees. A single bench sat nearby. One giant tree towered over the rest. Its expansive branches seemed to stretch for miles overhead. The engorged roots of the tree bulged as though they were trying to wrestle free from underneath the earth. The roots looked like legs that had somewhere to go. It was the most beautiful tree I'd ever seen in my life.

Jake must have caught me eyeing the tree because he said, "We call that the tree of life. It's over two hundred years old. The kids love hanging out over there. I built the walkway because before when it rained, the old muddy path used to sink in with water. It was too dangerous. It's all safe now."

"I can't believe you did all this work. It's beautiful," I said in amazement.

"I can do a lot of things you don't know about," he said in a more serious tone.

"Good morning, Brother Jake." A group of kids surrounded us, singing greetings to Jake. "Good morning."

"Hey y'all. Who's ready for children's church?" he asked excitedly. "Today you're gonna find out how Jonah escaped from the belly of a whale."

"I am. Me. I want to know," they chanted. You could see the love in their exchanges. My heart ignited with love for Jake too.

One bold little boy stepped forward and tugged on the sleeve of my dress. "Are you Brother Jake's girlfriend?" All of the children broke out in a fit of giggles at the thought of Jake having a girlfriend.

"No silly. She's his wife," a little girl in a bright yellow dress with matching ribbons at the end of her ponytails said to the boy before turning to me. "My mama said Brother Jake went out and married a heathen. You don't look like a heathen, Miss Brother Jake's wife. I think you are pretty," the little girl smiled innocently.

"What's a heathen?" another child asked.

The girl in yellow huffed, "A heathen is somebody that don't love God. You don't know nothing."

Just as quickly as the children appeared, they ran off arguing over the true meaning of a heathen and if I was indeed one. I was embarrassed to say the least. If I could see my own face, I was sure that it was beet red. The one thing I loved about kids was that they'd say anything and to your face.

"You don't look like a heathen to me either," Jake said, grabbing my hand with a grin on his face. It took everything in him to hold in his own laughter. I slapped him on the back playfully.

"Go ahead, you can laugh. But remember, I'm the heathen that stole the finest man at The Tree of Life away from little miss yellow girl's mama. You are gonna have to point her out to me later so I can gloat." I smiled and reached up to kiss him right there in the parking lot.

The kids ran past us, giggling and pointing. Jake put his arm around my shoulder and led me into the building. The interior had undergone a complete facelift and was just as breathtaking as the outside. The church was about ten times the size as before.

"Paul…Pastor Paul has done an amazing job, Jake. And you too, honey." I still wasn't used to calling Jake's best friend, his number one boy—pastor. "I know how much revitalizing this church has meant to you both. I see why you were so busy. This was a huge undertaking."

"Told you! You thought we were over here playing in paint. This was a half-million dollar project. Membership has already almost doubled since the grand reopening of the building and growing every Sunday. Can you say room to harvest?" He beamed with pride. "We now have a nursery and our youth have their own separate wing. We also expanded on the south side of the building and added a gym, a family counseling and job training center."

"All that? A gym seems extravagant for a church, if you ask

me." I scrunched up my nose in disapproval. "Wouldn't all that money be better spent in the community?"

"This is the community, baby. This is a disenfranchised neighborhood. Do you know it has the highest crime rate in the whole city? Did you see any big name fitness centers anywhere around here? Our youth center has tutors, computer work stations; most of these kids don't even have Internet at home. And it's all either free or income based. Not to mention, we've created almost a hundred paying jobs right here." He waved his hand around for emphasis. We are putting our members to work." Jake stuck his chest out.

I'd never seen him so passionate about anything like he was about this church. I decided to keep my mouth closed. "I guess you're right, honey, don't listen to a heathen like me."

"Get thee behind me heathen…just kidding," a voice said, laughing from behind me.

I turned around to let someone have it, when I realized it was Jake's best friend, Paul. He grabbed me in his humongous arms, picking me up off of my feet. Truth be told, Paul, now Pastor Paul was a very handsome man. If I weren't standing in the church foyer, I'd bet all kinds of dough that he was the real reason membership had doubled in the recent months. His father had died and left Paul the church that he had built with his very own hands. Between Paul's short curly dark hair, deep mesmerizing voice, and smoky gray eyes, I just knew that the women were losing their minds up in here and calling it the spirit. Yeah, they were having an attack of the spirit all right, the spirit of desire because Pastor Paul was extremely pleasing to the eye.

"Naomi, you are looking exquisite, as usual. When are you gonna dump this chump and roll with me?" Pastor Paul chided, offering his arm.

"Thank you, Paul. You are so sweet. I hope you got the food I sent over for you. That's if Jake didn't eat it all." I took his muscular arm and planted a kiss on his cheek.

"Yes, I got it. It was much appreciated. See, that's what I'm talking about, beautiful, smart, and can burn," Pastor Paul said.

"Hey. Hey. Hey. Whoa partner. That's enough. You have to find your own Ruth, Boaz." Jake grabbed me around the waist and pulled me closer to him.

"Okay. Fair is fair. My brother here found you first." Pastor Paul punched Jake lightly on the arm. "You sure you don't have a sister hiding under a rock somewhere? A cousin...anybody. I'll even settle for ya grandma right about now. It's hard out here for a decent brother, like myself, these days. Today's good women— can't cook." We all burst out in laughter.

Pastor Paul went into business mode with Jake about the coming afternoon's induction ceremony. I looked on with pride at the two successful black men standing in front of me doing their thing and making a difference in so many lives. I really lucked up; Jake was a great catch.

For a second, I thought about hooking Dae up with Paul, but the women of this church would have a conniption if their beloved, eligible, fine as all get out bachelor pastor brought a Korean chick home to roost for them to call first lady. Even a heathen like me knew that. Thinking about it brought a smile to my face.

Dae's last boyfriend was from Pakistan. Her parents almost disowned her for that taboo slip up. It really hurt her to not have her parents' approval. I wasn't sure if Dae was up to dating a black man after that had happened. Well, besides my husband Jake. I sighed heavily inside because I still hadn't gotten to the bottom of that fiasco. Here I was thinking about hooking that home wrecker up with a great guy like Pastor Paul and she might be creeping in my bed.

"That's her. That's her, Mama. Brother Jake's wife—the one you said was a heathen."

I smiled and waved with my ring hand. My wedding ring twinkled as it caught the light from overhead. I stepped closer to Jake, appreciating the coordinating touch that I added to our outfits. We complemented each other very well. I was grateful that I took the time to gussy up a bit more than usual that day.

"That was rude. Girl, shut up!" the woman said as she smiled at me awkwardly. She was apparently mortified, considering that the pastor might have overheard.

"But you said that—" The little girl tried to explain while her mother yanked her arm and whisked her flowing yellow dress out of dodge before any further damage could be done.

"You ready to go in, honey?" Jake asked.

Pastor Paul kissed my cheek and waved us off as other members rushed to greet him.

"Naomi," Pastor Paul said.

"Yes?"

"It's good to see you here today."

Jake led me inside and down the aisle that seemed to last forever to the front of the newly remodeled state of the art sanctuary. Every few feet we had to stop for Jake to shake a hand or offer a hug. He knew everyone. There seemed to be hundreds of people pouring happily into the sanctuary.

The tiny little wooden pulpit was gone and an oversized stage with matching JumboTron flat screens on either side replaced it. Huge bright lights fell out of the ceiling and shone on the stage. Jake took the look of amazement in my eyes for approval and all but patted himself on the back. He squeezed my hand tightly in his.

Okay, so I got the gym and the youth center. But really, a stage that was more ready for a full on rock concert than a choir was doing way too much. As I had the thought, the choir started to fill the bleacher-like stands. They were all wearing jeans and loud fashionable tees in purple, gold, pink, and blue hues with a giant silhouette of a black tree printed on them.

"What happened to the robes?" I leaned over and asked Jake.

He shook his head and chuckled. "Choir robes are played."

I turned my attention back to the choir as the music cued up to a ridiculous level. I wasn't sure how God would find anyone, let alone hear their pleas at The Tree of Life. Loud and all, the music was good—really good.

"Better get ready for the show," I said aloud to myself.

"What?" Jake shouted, swaying to the music.

"I said this is a great row. Look at all these people."

I really didn't know what it was that made me so hesitant when it came to the Lord. I'd lived in several foster homes when I was a child. And in almost every last one of them, I was a regular church going member. It was pretty much mandatory in most of them. I had even enjoyed the services back then. When I went to college, it was up to me and I never went. I used the excuse that I was busy with my studies. That wasn't it and I really didn't know what it was that turned me away from God. Well, not that I knew Him like that anyway. It was more habit than anything else when I did go.

The service moved along like clockwork, as though choreographed. Pastor Paul stood up after about an hour and that was when I really settled in my seat. I had yet to hear him preach, so I was extremely curious. He started with a prayer and from that point on; I was captivated by sound of his voice. His words were weighted with so much power—and love, not to mention, compassion. I got lost in his sermon.

A sense of peace and stillness welled up within me as he preached about forgiving oneself for the wrongs done by others. I'd never thought about forgiving myself for what Nola and Uncle C had done to me. I'd never thought about forgiving them either, and I had absolutely no plans of ever doing the latter. But I did know that there were some things I had to let go of and accept. I had to let go of the past so that I could salvage my marriage. I looked over at Jake with tears in my eyes.

Pastor Paul was different than any other pastor I'd ever heard. He didn't jump around screaming and yelling about everybody going to hell for every little sin. He said that hell was a place that you damned yourself to. That hell could be the life you are living right this second if you made it that way with constant bad decisions. He said hell was living day by day allowing bad memories to haunt you, threaten you, and rule over your sanity. I squirmed in my seat and wondered how much Jake had told Paul about me because he was talking to me. I knew it wasn't just irony, it couldn't be. I fidgeted in my seat. I was so unnerved that I couldn't hold back my tears.

"You will be forever held in bondage. No, my friends, not the bondage of hell...in an afterlife that will take you after you leave this world. Oh no, hell will and can consume you right here. Your thoughts, your dreams will become nightmares that turn real and eat you alive. This will be your hell. Forgive yourself. Your marriage will become your hell. Forgive yourself. Your past will be your hell. Forgive yourself." I could have sworn he was looking directly at me.

I looked around the sanctuary to see if anyone else was as uncomfortable as I was. Or was it just me? My eyes scanned a few pews over on my left and stopped on a young woman that appeared to be staring in my direction. I looked to my right to see what she could possibly be looking at. Was it Jake? Maybe, but her eyes were focused on my every move and not his. Not seeing anything of interest beside me, I looked back at her. Yes, she was still staring at me and she looked awfully familiar. My brain did a quick mental inventory for facial recognition and stopped on one person. No. It couldn't be. Mona Thomas. *What the heck was she doing at this church?*

Pastor Paul began to wrap up his sermon and asked us to stand to our feet, take our neighbor's hand, and bow our heads with eyes closed. I grabbed Jake's hand then opened my eyes to find Mona again. But she was gone. I searched and searched, examining each pew. No sign of Mona. Maybe it was a figment of my imagination. Maybe she was one of the nightmares Pastor Paul talked about, haunting me. My body shook as I tried to contain a small laugh.

Jake must have thought that I was overcome with the spirit because he grabbed me in his arms and stroked my back until the prayer and altar call were over. *Poor thing*, he wanted me to find

God so bad. We sat back down and held hands as the announcements were presented. An image of a woman that looked a lot like Mona flashed across the giant screen. She must have been the person staring at me during the sermon. She was the woman being inducted as the associate pastor of the church that afternoon. The entire audience roared in applause, including Jake. They all must have thought very highly of her, so I smiled.

The screens went black and Pastor Paul stood before the congregation, holding the hand of the new associate pastor high in the air. He said a few words of praise about her, invited everyone out to the celebration service that afternoon. First things first, there was a catered dinner directly following service, *if* you purchased your ticket. The audience snickered. He passed the woman the microphone.

It was unreal how much that woman resembled Mona, except that she was quite polished. She was beautiful in a regal sort of way. I would have assumed that she was in her late thirties had her shining salt and pepper hair not defied her by telling her age. She smoothed a few wispy hairs away from her face and back into folds of her tight chignon as she smiled broadly before speaking. Her flawless smile sent a chill darting across the back of my neck. Something about this woman didn't quite sit right with me.

I looked over at Jake as he nodded eagerly, entranced by her every word. I tried unsuccessfully to read the look that was fixated on his face. Maybe it was her and not Dae that I should have been worried about. I barely listened to anything she had to say. I knew instantly that I didn't like her. I don't know why, but my gut told me not to. I watched as she caught a glimpse of Jake in the audience and she blew a kiss our way—his way. He caught it and held his hand over his heart. I didn't miss a thing. I knew that I had to watch this one for sure.

Mona

O F ALL THE people to run into, I had to run into that damn Naomi. I knew that I shouldn't have come here. I hadn't been to church in years, but my mother came by my house and pretty much bamboozled me into it. I kicked the trash can in the ladies' bathroom over and over again in frustration. Just seeing her made me so angry. I wanted to go out there and punch her in her damn face. I had done a great job the past week trying to forget, trying to put the past behind me and move on with my life.

After what happened with Genesis, I decided to let it all go. I spent days waiting for the police to come after me for hitting her. When nothing happened, I decided to listen to my mother and start my life all over. I would never be able to face my children again anyway. Genesis was sure to hate me now too so what was the use trying. I let it go and allowed my mother to let her attorney handle everything.

Once again, my mother came through as the only person that was there for me. When I called her pissed about what Genesis told me, she had come right over.

"She's lying. Your father never touched her," she defended my father.

"But Mother, I remember when Daddy tried to—"

"He tried to what?" she said, slow and deliberately.

She stepped to within inches of my face and raised her eyebrows daring me to say aloud that my father molested me when I was a little girl. I knew that she knew. My father was the only person in the world that my mother was afraid of. She could go toe to toe with the scariest and meanest of them. Not when it came to Daddy, she turned into a...a coward.

"Nothing, Mother," I said, defeated.

I backed down like I always did when it came to her. It was better to just agree. When you got on her bad side, she would make your life a living hell. I knew exactly what that pastor was talking about during his sermon.

"Good." My mother kissed my cheek. "Now run upstairs and get dressed. We are going shopping!" she sang. She reached in her purse and pulled out my father's black credit card and waved it under my nose. "On Daddy." She giggled like a little girl.

My father was a successful mortgage broker; he and my mother shared a financially rewarding life. They owned several small apartment communities on the south side of Houston, including the one I lived in. I never told anyone about that, including Candice. I never wanted people to know that my parents were wealthy. They had the money, not me. When I had Genesis, my father hardly passed a dime my way. He told me that I was no longer his responsibility after I laid down with another man. Anything that I got from *him*, came through Mother.

We headed straight for the Galleria. If there was one thing my mother had, it was great taste. She bought me an entirely new wardrobe, with shoes to match. There was so much stuff, that the department store manager, who was on a first name basis with my mother, agreed to have most of it delivered. All of it would have never fit in her little Jag. She told me that it was time I started enjoying the finer things in life. I had been loaded down with those unappreciative kids long enough and I needed to live.

My mother had planned the entire day. She took me to her favorite fancy exclusive salon and spa. She instructed her stylist how to cut and layer my hair. She even chose a new color for me. She picked a vibrant auburn with a few blonde highlights framing my face to bring out the amber flecks in my eyes. When the stylist spun the chair around, I was in awe of myself. I looked pretty good. My usually chipped nails were perfectly manicured and my makeup was flawless. I looked a little too much like my mother, but very nice all the same. I barely recognized myself in the mirror. My mother beamed with pride.

It wasn't until we returned to my place that evening that she dropped the church thing on me. She never actually told me what was going on today, but she told me that she *needed* me there. It was the first time that my mother ever said that she needed me for anything. After all that she had done for me that day, I eagerly agreed. Not to mention, it beat sitting in the house all day moping about the kids. She picked through the shopping bags sprawled over the living room floor and pulled out a beautiful green dress for me to wear. It was one of my favorites, too.

My parents picked me up for church, even after I insisted on meeting them. Mother wanted to go as a family. I knew that was a lie; my father hadn't stepped foot on my street in years. I knew the real reason was Mother didn't want me to embarrass them by driving up in my beat up SUV. She was fickle like that. Daddy probably didn't mind so much.

"You look really good, daughter." That was all he said to me.

"Good morning, Daddy."

I was more than a little disappointed that he never called to check on me or to see what was happening with the kids. Since Mother dropped a wad of his cash on me, I decided to let it go, especially about Genesis. I had mixed feelings about him but agreed with Mother to just let it all ride. I was grown now and there was no sense running back to the past.

I hopped in the backseat and Mother surprised me by sliding in right next to me. After we buckled up, she picked up my hand and toyed with my fingers. Daddy drove off.

Here we go, I thought. Something was up.

"Today is a very special day for your father and me," she started. "You know I completed seminary school a couple years ago and something amazing is coming out of all my hard work. God is good, ain't he?"

Yeah, she didn't even invite me and the kids to her graduation ceremony. I remember when she first announced that she was going to school to study religion. I fell out of my chair laughing. Hell, she only talked about God on Sundays or when it made her look good, so I never took the whole minister thing seriously.

"You are in for a big surprise. I mean huge." She could barely contain her excitement. "But..." She sandwiched my hand in between hers.

I should have known there was, a *but*, a catch. It wouldn't be like her to not have an ulterior motive. After everything she had done for me. I knew I owed her something. I nodded to let her know that I was listening.

"Sweetheart. Just for today, uh. Can you keep what's going on with you private?"

"What are you talking about? Keep what private?" I asked.

"I mean," she took a deep breath, "please don't mention that you have children. It's just that I wouldn't want *you* to have to explain where *they* are and what *you* did to them. That's all. If anyone asks if you have children, it will be better for you if you said no. You are going to meet some very important people today and—"

"No? That I don't have any children. I love my kids, Mother, I would never deny them!" I cut her off.

I caught my father's dead-pan eyes in the rear-view mirror. He reached over and increased the volume on the radio and looked back to the road ahead. I remembered when he used to love me. He used to talk to me and take up for me when it came to Mother. I wanted that love again—his love.

"Look, Mona. Be rational about this thing. Your kids are in a foster home. The state owns them, they are locked up in the system, and you will never get them back. My way will be easier for everyone, especially you. Trust me on this one," she pleaded.

Mother had a point. What she said made sense. If I ever had a chance to get them back, what I did to Genesis ruined that narrow margin. I knew that it was never going to happen. They were gone—forever. It was either choose to fight for them or choose Mother. That was her way.

"But if you want to tell people that you beat the crap out of your kids and the state came and snatched them away from you... be my guest," she said. Mother tossed my hand back into my lap as if I had a fungus growing on it.

She began to rustle around in her purse and pulled out a small bottle of sanitizer and slathered it all over her hands. I balled my hands up in my lap and stared out the window while I concentrated on keeping my tears at bay. Maybe she was right. I was going back to work the next day and what would I tell them. Actually, my plan was to get transferred to another department at the hospital where I worked. I wasn't going to be able to take them asking me questions about my kids every day either. I wished I had a blunt. I could have kicked myself for not taking a smoke before I left home that morning. It would have made for a much smoother ride. I would have agreed with anything she had to say without thinking or feeling.

"You're right, Mother. I won't say anything," I finally said. She won. Mother always got her way. I caught my father's eyes again and he nodded his approval that time.

"I told your father that you'd see it my way, honey." Mother smiled, showing off her perfect teeth. She offered me a squirt of her sanitizer. Then she held my hand again.

Then, after all that planning to keep the kids a secret, on the opposite side of town, in one of the largest cities in America, a city with two churches instead of liquor stores on every single corner, I ended up seeing Naomi Mitchell at this one.

"Shit! Shit! Shit!" I screeched, and kicked the trash can again.

An elderly woman walked out of one of the bathroom stalls and looked disapprovingly at me. She stopped in front of the mirror and adjusted the huge, flowery float that sat atop her shaky head and went straight out the door without washing her hands. *Just nasty.* If God heard me swear then I'm sure he saw her despicable action, too. That was a much worse offense than cursing in the church bathroom. I had to laugh at the way she looked at me.

I wet a napkin to cool my face. As I refreshed my makeup, I saw my mother looking back at me in the mirror. The older I got, the more I looked like her. I thought about what she would do if she were me and in this predicament. Humph, she would march right out there like she owned the place. She wasn't afraid of anyone. Neither was I. What was I worried about, there were hundreds of people out there. There was no way I'd run into Naomi Mitchell again.

My phone vibrated in my purse. It was my mother.

"Hello."

"Where are you? Your father said you went to the bathroom twenty minutes ago. Are you two years old or something? You can't hold your pee." She hissed into the phone. "Get out here now! We're waiting by the door. There are people you need to meet. Be presentable."

The phone went silent in my ear. I could *really* use a smoke right now I thought for the second time. I checked my appearance in the mirror once more. I held my head high, plastered one of Mother's fake smiles on my face and walked out ready for whatever.

"This is my daughter, Mona," Mother said proudly. "Mona, Pastor Paul."

"Hello, Mona," he said, gripping my hand firmly.

"Hi." I croaked out. I wanted to say something more intelligent like, nice to meet you, but the man was so damn fine that my voice got lost in a sea of gray that he called his eyes. I couldn't believe that he was a pastor.

"Pastor Lenora, you said you had a daughter, but you really should have told me how lovely she was. You two look more like sisters." He studied me carefully. He had yet to let my hand go. Not that I wanted him to.

Pastor? Did he just call my mother *pastor?* What the hell? I quickly forgot about the love god holding on to my hand. My eyes shot to my mother as she beamed with a huge smile on her red lips. That must have been the surprise she talked about in the car. My mother, Lenora Thomas—a pastor of *this* church? *Were these people crazy?* Maybe I did smoke something at home and was tripping

My thoughts must have been easily readable on my face because he finally let my hand go. "Why the surprised look, Mona? You seem as though you didn't know," he said, looking from my mother to me. I stood there with my mouth hanging open.

"Of course she knew, Pastor Paul. I think she's still getting used to people calling me Pastor," my mother quickly chimed in. "*I'm* still trying to get used to it."

"Yeah, I can relate. When my father passed away and I took over the church, I had the same problem. Folks would say Pastor and I'd look around for my father." He laughed a little.

I was glad my mother knew what to say. I was dumbfounded. Who the hell wanted *her* to lead them to God? I loved my mother, don't get me wrong, but I seriously doubted if she knew the way to anybody's heaven. I caught my mother's menacing look and closed my mouth. I inserted a replica of her fake smile in its place.

"What church do you attend, Mona?" Pastor Paul asked.

"The Fountain of Praise," my mother answered with a lie again.

"Oh, I know Pastor Wright. We're gonna have to steal you away from there. Well, Mona, I know you're staying for dinner and the celebration later." He placed his hand on my sleeveless shoulder, causing my arm to tingle from his touch. "I'll save you a seat next to me. Nice meeting you."

"It was nice meeting you as well, Pastor Paul," I said, finally speaking for myself.

He walked away and stopped to chat with some other people that stood nearby. Everyone was waiting on a chance to greet him. My eyes followed the pastor until he walked out of the door. I'd never seen such a handsome man in all of my life. I looked up toward the ceiling and asked God to forgive me for thinking all the sinful thoughts that I was having right at that moment about a man of the cloth. I could still smell his heavy cologne in the air, his scent rose from my skin where he had touched me; causing my knees to tremble a little.

"Well, looks like someone has a crush on you," Mother teased, snapping me back to reality.

"Who? Him? On me? Yeah right. Anyway, what I really want to know is why you didn't tell me that you were going to be a pastor?" I tried to recover. "Was that the surprise?"

"Yes, baby. All my dreams are coming true. I'm so happy." Mother spurted with joy.

I didn't want to appear thoughtless so I hugged her. "Congratulations, Mother. I'm very proud of you."

"Thank you, baby. Can you believe it? I'm going to be second in command of all this." She waved her hands around emphatically.

I knew it. It was all about looks and appearances for her. "No, I can't believe it. Where's Daddy?" I asked looking around.

"In the sanctuary talking to Brother Jake. Your father wants to take over the children's ministry."

My insides curdled at the word *children*. Mother and I both knew that Daddy had no business working with kids, namely little girls. I didn't want to be accused of ruining their moment as usual, so I kept my lips pursed and my opinion to myself.

"Enough about that. I think Pastor Paul likes you. You know he's single. He's one of the most eligible bachelors in Houston. All the single women are scrambling to be the first lady."

"Mother, I have enough going on right now. A man is not on my immediate to do list." I was feeling the young pastor just as much, but even I knew that he was way out of my league.

"Well, nothing like a good looking man to chase the blues away. If you catch this one, you'll be set for life. You won't find too many wealthy black men with no kids out there, especially one that wants you." She pulled me by the arm. "You better learn when you're on to something and play your hand. If I were you, I'd make a move. Let's go find your father, so we can go eat."

We quickly spotted my father walking through the thinning crowd with another handsome man. This place was filled to the brim with them. Maybe I did need to spend more time in church. This one was tall with a clean shaven head. He had a dark goatee displayed just right around his perfect lips.

My mother reached out both of her arms and embraced the man warmly. She turned him toward me. "And this is our daughter, Mona."

"Hello, Mona, it's a pleasure to meet you. I know you've heard this before, but you look just like your mother. My name is Jake."

Before I could open my mouth to reply, Naomi walked up and stood next to the man. I was livid. I stopped breathing as though all the air in the room had been sucked out with a vacuum. In an instant the temperature changed in the cool building to hot and extremely humid, worse than outside. I touched the now warming spot on my cheek.

He placed his arm around her waist and said proudly, "I'd love for all of you to finally meet the best part of me. This is my wife, Naomi."

Naomi

WE WERE ALL sitting at the head table having dinner when Pastor Lenora who sat on my right leaned over and asked, "Have we met before?"

"No, not that I can remember," I replied.

"What do you do?" she asked, apparently in my business.

Nosey church people I thought. "I work for Child Protective Services," I said loud enough for Mona to hear. I smirked when she looked over at me from directly across the large table. She immediately looked down at her plate.

"Well, you look familiar. I was just wondering," Pastor Lenora said, inching a forkful of potatoes into her mouth.

"So do you," I cut my eyes at Mona.

"Where did you get your name? Naomi is very uncommon these days," she asked attempting more small talk.

"I don't know, just born with it." I got a little uncomfortable. I hated getting into personal conversations with people. It always led to someone asking me about my parents, and that subject was off limits. It was always better to leave it out than to make up a lie.

"Well, it's from the bible, it's Hebrew and means pleasant and delightful. Did you know that?" she asked.

I assumed that she was being sarcastic because I was being especially rude. I wanted to ask—Did you know that your daughter is a child beater? But I didn't, I kept eating.

The new associate pastor had a child abuser for a daughter. I guess everybody has skeletons in their closet. I wondered if Jake knew. I doubted it. I bet Pastor Lenora would rather die before being exposed. She looked like the fake type. In my line of work, you really had to learn how to read people and fast. In this case, I could easily tell that the apple didn't fall too far from the tree. Pastor Lenora was very controlling and she had her grown daughter on a tight string.

The father was very quiet; he didn't say too much. He was a lot older than Pastor Lenora and they made an odd couple. She had a head full of dark hair and not a wrinkle in sight. Her husband had a sparse sprinkling of coarse graying hair and sagging jaws. I ignored him the entire dinner.

When I wasn't studying Lenora and Mona, Pastor Paul kept us all very amused with his jokes about being a pastor. I knew that he was funny, both he and Jake, but seeing the two of them together in their element had my side hurting from laughing too hard. He told us about the time they found a well-completed tithe envelope empty. The person had put zero for the amount of offering and dropped it in the basket. Paul had to stop Jake from mailing the empty envelope back to the person. The comfortable banter between Jake and Paul managed to lighten my mood a little.

I wondered how Mona managed to get the prized seat next to the pastor, of all people. I overheard Pastor Paul ask her if she was married and she simply said no. I folded my eyebrows in disgust. And if I wasn't mistaken, he was openly flirting with her. Her body language showed that she was also interested in him as well. He had no clue of the monster he was sitting next to. *Look at her sitting there with her pretty little fingers painted red after she had burned the skin off of her son's hands.*

"You all right, honey?" Jake leaned over Pastor Lenora and asked me for the third time. "You're awfully quiet down there."

How nice of him to notice that I was still sitting there. He had spent the last half hour chumming it up with the new associate pastor. She kept throwing her head back laughing at every little breath he took. I thought it was extremely rude of her to plop down in the only available seat next to my husband. He should have said something, defended my right to sit next to him. He knew that I didn't know anyone else at the church besides Paul.

"I'm fine," I said curtly. He knew what my tone meant so I left it at that.

I couldn't wait for that day to be over. I had been in Mona's presence far too long. I never took her for a preacher's kid. They say those are the worst ones anyway.

I glanced at my watch and frowned. The official induction ceremony would start in the next half hour. I wished that I had driven my own car because I would've conjured up a whopping headache and gone home. I couldn't stand to be in the presence of all that fakeness any longer.

"I'm so nervous about my sermon this evening," Pastor Lenora attempted to make more small talk with me again.

"Why? Haven't you preached before?" I asked dryly.

"Yes, of course. But I think everything happened so quickly for me. I never dreamed that I'd be the pastor at such a wonderful church," she gushed.

"Associate pastor." I felt the need to remind her like it was my church.

Jake looked at me again and raised his eyebrow in chastisement. Maybe my behavior was embarrassing, but he didn't know what I knew about these people.

"Yes, that's what I meant, Associate Pastor." She slowly sipped her water.

I may have judged Pastor Lenora based on Mona. True, I didn't know the details of their relationship. She seemed like a nice enough person. Seemed to be decent. I only wondered why she didn't take custody of her grandchildren. I tried to remember what Maria had said about it. I'd surely find out when I went back to work. For now, I would play nice for Jake.

I reached over and patted Pastor Lenora's hand and smiled. "You'll do just fine."

"Oh, thank you, sweetheart," she said. My words made her happy enough to smile. She had perfect teeth, like Mona.

For the next half hour, Pastor Lenora chatted on and on about any and everything. She talked so much I was barely able to get a word in edgewise, which was fine with me. She told me all about how the Lord had saved her and brought her out of a life filled with sin when Mona was a toddler.

"God gave me a second chance at life. I can still remember how useless I was to anyone around me," she closed her eyes lost in nostalgia. "I'm a living testimony of His grace," she sang.

"Amen to that," Jake said and raised his glass of lemonade.

"I want other hurting people to know that if I can make it, so can they," she said. "That's why we joined this ministry."

Mona said nothing as her mother poured out her testimony at the dinner table, while everyone else was enthralled by Pastor Lenora's enthusiasm. Her husband never said a word either. He didn't seem to be as excited about God as she was. I wondered what his exact role would be in the ministry. He needed to liven up a bit. He was as stiff as a log.

The only time Pastor Lenora stopped moving her lips was when an attractive female usher approached the table and whispered in Pastor Paul's ear. Pastor Lenora frowned and took another drink of water.

"If you all will excuse me, I need to go prepare before my sermon," Pastor Lenora said and got up from the table.

She motioned for her husband to follow. Mona rose to leave with them. *Good.* I was particularly sick of looking at her. Pastor Paul rushed to his feet, like a true gentleman. He helped Mona pull out her chair. I chuckled. That was no lady he was sitting next to. He grabbed her by the hand and spoke privately in Mona's ear.

He reached in his pocket and passed her his business card. She smiled at him and cast her light brown eyes my way before she scurried away to join her family. They were all a weird bunch if anyone wanted to know my opinion.

Jake and I sat very close to the front pew for the next service. I nodded off before it even started. I'd had a long day and wanted it to be over. I didn't understand how Jake spent hours doing this type of thing every Sunday. It always seemed to be something going on—Pastor's and church anniversaries, weddings, youth programs—something all the time.

"How long is this going to last?" I asked Jake the minute Pastor Lenora stood to speak.

"Naomi. Stop acting like a kid. What has gotten into you?" Jake turned his attention back to the stage.

Pastor Lenora was very gracious and thanked everyone for giving her such a wonderful opportunity to serve in The Tree of Life ministry. She began her sermon, something about faith, which I barely paid any mind to.

I closed my eyes as she spoke. The more I heard her talk the more she reminded me of someone. Yeah, she looked like Mona, but I couldn't figure out why she seemed even more familiar than that. In my line of work, abuse and neglect usually ran in families. We'd get reports on sisters, brothers, uncles, aunts, grandparents—the whole family tree. Families were cess pools reflecting generations of abuse. I planned to take a peek into the Thomas file and check their family history when I went back to work.

I almost jumped out of my seat with joy when the organist cued up music. It was almost over. I started packing up my things immediately. Jake had put his cell phone in my purse earlier and it began to vibrate. I took a quick peek. It was a text message from Dae: *Monday works for me. Call you in the A.M.* Okay, so what the hell was really going on with those two?

Jake looked at me and shook his head. He had some nerves. I couldn't wait to get him home. I tried to pay attention to the remainder of the service to get my mind off of the message from

Dae. Pastor Lenora asked her husband to come up and offer closing prayer, the lights dimmed. I closed my eyes, Jake grasped my
hand. I wasn't prepared for the voice that I heard next. I knew
that voice, even if it were lost in a sea of a thousand voices, I'd
know it. Although I didn't recognize his face, his tone sent the
tiny hairs on the nape of my neck jumping at attention.

No. No. No. It couldn't be. I convinced myself that I was
over reacting. Many men had that same bottomless, raspy voice.
I searched my heart for excuses. Maybe, seeing Mona had me
shook up. Yes, that was it. I let go of Jake's hand and held both
hands over my ears to drown out the baritone pitch of his voice.

"And they all said...Amen." He finished "See you all on
Wednesday night, right here at The Redeeming Tree of Life at
seven o'clock for bible study. God bless."

I opened my eyes just in time to see Pastor Lenora grab her
husband around the waist. He rubbed his hand across her hair
and smoothed away the flyaway strands of hair. It was him. No,
maybe not. My mind was definitely playing cruel tricks on me.

Jake pushed me from behind out into the aisle toward the front,
near the stage.

"Come on, honey. I want to go congratulate our new associate
pastor," Jake said.

"Umm, I'll wait right here for you. I'm a little tired and I suddenly have a migraine," I said.

"Come with me, it will only take a quick second and we can
just go out the side door." Jake urged me forward with his hand
pressed firmly in my back. He wasn't taking no for an answer. I
reluctantly let him lead me.

"Pastor Lenora. You did it! That was a wonderful sermon," Jake
put both of his arms around her.

Mona stood awkwardly next to me. I didn't have any energy to
pay her any mind. My legs felt like they wanted to give out. My
heart raced, I felt all the blood rushing from every part of my
body into my head. It was him. I knew it. I began to sweat. I felt
like a drum was thudding in my ear. I could not take my eyes off

of him. He was a lot older, gray hair, and less of it, but it was still him. I think.

"That is him," I whispered outloud to myself, straining my eyes, forcing myself to get a better—a clearer view of his face. I had sat next to him during dinner and paid so little attention to him. I wasn't sure.

"Excuse me?" Mona asked. "You say something to me?"

I just looked at her; my mouth was too chalky to move my lips. My ears were barely able to connect with her words. I shook my head from side to side to clear the drum beat.

"What's wrong with you?" she asked with a strange look on her face and moved away from me.

"Naomi, come get in the picture." Jake pulled me toward the photographer.

I was glad that he moved me. I thought for sure that my knees were locked in place and I'd never be able to move them on my own. I didn't feel well. Jake was so caught up in the festivities that he didn't notice my unsteady walk. He positioned me right next to Pastor Lenora. She grabbed my right hand. He put his arm around my waist on the left. I had no strength, they held me up. They had no clue as to how weak I was.

The music was still playing, the bass echoed loudly out of the speakers into the pit of my stomach. It seemed as though everyone had a camera pointed at me. Flashes with the intensity of lightning strikes electrocuted my pupils. I felt like I was in a moving tunnel. I was trapped in a kaleidoscope of people spinning—laughing, hugging, and touching, it was all spiraling out of control.

The lights blinded me. I couldn't see anyone at all, not clearly. I only heard empty voices ordering people to move around so that hungry camera lenses could eagerly seek out the perfect shot. My mind had a hard time processing the slow, mellow, bizarre sounding voices. Someone switched all the sound to chopped and screwed, like a record on slow. It was surreal.

"Smile everybody." *Flash.*

"Nola. Nooo-la. Is that you? I had to come up here to get a better look, but I knew it was you. It's me Ray." A man's voice said over my right shoulder. His voice broke through the chaos and filled my ear as he tried to speak discreetly to Lenora.

Did he say Nola? My heart dropped.

"Say Tree of Life." *Flash.*

"Nola...Barnes. I can't believe I'm looking at you after all these years. You have really changed for the better, but you still look just the same. I only want to say congratulations on everything. Praise the Lord."

Nola.

"You stand here." *Flash.*

"I see you and CT still hanging in there after all these years."

Uncle C?

"Turn to this side." *Flash.*

"Where's your daughter? Little mama was something else. So precious. Did you ever get her back?"

"Get in the picture, Brother Charles." *Flash.*

"I know she's all grown up now. Both of them, huh?"

I turned my head and looked behind me, right in the man's face.

"You too Sister Mona, get in next to your father." *Flash.*

"What was her name? Oh yeah. Naomi. Little Naomi. This is her, isn't it?" His eyes spanned over me. "I'd recognize those big ole light brown eyes anywhere. She's still pretty, looks just the same—just taller."

Me?

"Say cheese." *Flash.*

"The last time I saw you, y'all had baby. Another girl, Mona."

Mona?

"Where in the world have you been? I thought y'all went back to New Orleans. We have to catch up. Here's my number." He stuffed a small piece of paper in Lenora's free hand. "I know y'all real busy right now, but tell my boy CT to call me." The man named Ray, turned and walked away. He disappeared so quickly into the thinning crowd that it was as if he was never there, right beside me, whispering up years of bad memories.

The lights seemed to focus only on me—on us. I turned my head in slow motion to face Lenora, Nola, and the deep familiarity finally registered in my heart. The room opened and consumed everything in it, but me and her. The music, the people, the whole sanctuary vanished.

I took a good look at the woman standing right there next to me with her mouth hanging wide open. My hand was locked, tingling with identification in hers. I knew that hand. My heart began to thump irregularly. I knew this woman. She had haunted my dreams for years, faceless. I scrutinized every detail of her face now. I wanted to reach out my hand and touch her cheek, to dust the freckles that were just like mine from her face. That huge perfect smile that she got from her daddy. I knew that smile. The front tooth that was now whiter and brighter, more perfect than the rest because Uncle C had knocked it out. I knew those teeth.

She searched inside me, too. She opened and closed her eyes slowly as if willing me to be a mirage. Her nightmare. She shook her head as if to say no. No, it wasn't true. No, as if I were someone she could stand not to see—ever, and that if she flapped her long lashes one more time, I would certainly disappear. I felt her thoughts. She felt mine and let my hand go. I saw a reflection of myself in her evil, aged brown eyes. I knew those eyes. I knew everything about her. She was my mother—Nola Barnes.

"Nola." I finally got my mouth to work. *Flash.*

Her name pushed itself from my lips like bile thrusting from an ailing body. The room coughed and retched up all the loud, moving, smiling, happy people. Jake, my only tangible connection to the moment, let go of my waist.

My soul ran away from me.

Flash.

I passed out.

PART III
RUNNING INTO THE FUTURE

Naomi

"NAOMI! WHAT IN the world did you do to your hair?" Dae asked.

"What does it look like? I cut it." I snapped back.

"I don't know what to say. It's…It's." Dae rubbed her eyes as though she was forcing herself to believe what she was seeing. "What did Jake say?"

"Umm, you don't need to say anything. It's my hair and I did exactly what I wanted to do with it. And I don't need Jake's permission or yours for that matter." I moved away from the center of the walkway to allow Maria access to pass by.

Dae forced her head straight up to reinforce her authoritative position over me. "Oh…well, nice to have you back. When you get a chance, submit your vacation request for the extra time that you took off after your *suspension*."

I could tell that I hurt her feelings, but I didn't care. My feelings were hurt, too. I was tired of caring about everyone else and protocol. But, I had to admit that I missed Dae in my life. She would have been the only person that truly understood how I felt, that wouldn't have judged me. But, Dae had crossed me, too. She turned on her high black heels and quickly walked away. I stood there for a moment, watching her long black hair sway forcefully behind her as if tickled by an imaginary breeze. I wanted to take several thick strands of it and stuff them down her throat.

Out of habit, I put my hands up to my own hair. It was gone. All of it. I didn't know why I let it all go either. I walked into the nearest barber shop last weekend, sat in the first available chair, and ordered the barber to cut it off. All of it.

"Ma'am, you sure? It's a bunch of women out here that would kill to have all this hair," the barber had asked.

"Cut it," I repeated with more authority.

"Okay. How low?" he asked.

I held my finger up and used it to indicate how much, sat straight up in the chair, and closed my eyes. I heard the razor switch to on. The buzzing drowned out the voices in my head. I didn't realize that I was crying until I felt the barber pushing Kleenex into my balled hand. I threw it to the ground and let salty tears seep into the corners of my lips. I wanted everybody to see my pain. Usually I would have been too embarrassed to cry in a public place—not anymore. I couldn't fall apart at home. I had to do it somewhere.

Naomi *Barnes* Mitchell was no longer the together, got it all under control woman that I once was. Strangely enough, I felt myself falling apart, strand by strand just like the hair that once adorned my head. I felt hatred growing in me, by the second, like a cancerous disease called Nola. I couldn't control it. In one day my life changed drastically and Nola was back, with Uncle C and this time, they brought Mona. They escaped from the rigid confines of my nightmares. I wanted to scream.

"Let go, Naomi."

"Let go of what?" I said louder than I meant to.

Maria put her hands over mine and unbuckled my fingers, one by one, that clutched on to the inch of remaining hair on my head. As she did so, I realized that my teeth were also gnashed tightly together and tears were chasing themselves down my face as though in a race. I relaxed my jaw muscles. My teeth hurt. My head hurt.

She led me to my desk with her arm around my shoulders and helped me to sit down. I shouldn't have come back. Not yet. I wasn't ready for work with all that was happening in my personal life. Some of my nosey office mates took the long way around to wherever they were going just to pass my desk.

"Are you going to be okay, Naomi?" Maria asked with her thick rich accent.

"Yes. Yes, I'll be all right. I have a migraine, that's all," I said. It was only a partial lie.

The phone chirped into its usual song on Maria's desk. She looked at me then over toward her cubicle, unsure of which was more important. Even in my misery, I knew it was the kids.

"You better get that," I said.

"You sure? They will leave a message and I can just call them back."

"No, please I'm fine," I said. I took the aspirin out of my purse and popped three down my dry throat. That's what I'd been living on, aspirin, coffee, and wine for the last week—ever since Nola came back.

Maria stared at me with concern, and then rushed for the phone leaving me all alone. I heard her switch from English to Spanish. I was glad. I didn't want to overhear another sad story of abuse, or neglect—nothing. I powered up my computer, seventy-seven unread emails. I was instantly disheartened. The red light on my desk phone blinked nineteen. I had to start somewhere. I blew out a lung full of air as I pulled out a pen and pad; I chose to listen to the messages first.

I heard the single beep of my personal cell phone in my purse. I knew it was Jake, so I didn't answer. He had been so worried about me lately. Instead of making me feel good, it drove me crazy. It was the only reason that I went to work, to get as far away from him as possible. I reached in my purse and sure enough, it was him, and he had called six times. I left before he woke up that morning. It was so early that I drove around the entire 610 loop freeway and enjoyed the peace of the sleeping city of Houston, before I drove to the office. I was still first in the parking lot. The phone beeped again and I powered it completely off.

I had gone through all of the voicemails and was almost finished reading and responding to emails when Dae appeared at my desk.

"Do you think we can go to lunch today?" she asked.

"No, I'm busy," I responded. I didn't bother looking up from my computer.

There was a week old email from Mrs. Fildhurst. I sighed when I saw her name. I wondered how Xavier was doing. And Genesis, my niece. I hoped Sean was doing well with his father. I reminded myself to get an update on the Thomas kids from Maria. They were now *my* family. I had a niece and two nephews to add to my problems. I swallowed hard. The bitter aftertaste of the dry aspirin in my throat caused my stomach to churn.

"Please. I'd like to talk. A lot has been going on," Dae said. I had almost forgotten she was still standing there.

"I said no." This time I looked into her eyes as if I was staring through her and into space.

"Jake just called. He's been calling me. He's worried about you, Naomi. So am I."

"Oh so Jake has his other woman checking up on me now?" I said vehemently.

"What? What are you talking—you are crazy. Everything has to always be only about Naomi. You're not the only one having a hard time dealing with life."

"Get. The. Hell. Away. From. My. Desk. Before I forget where I am. I plan to deal with you later," I said between clenched teeth. *Where did that come from?* My level of anger even frightened me. The words had barely left my lips, and I already saw tears filling the rim of her dark eyes. Dae scurried away like a mouse that had gotten its tail caught in a trap. Dae and Jake could have each other. I felt nothing. I was absolutely void of feeling pity or anything else for anyone, including myself—anything except contempt.

I turned back to my desk to read Mrs. Fildhurst's email. It was strange to receive an email from her. I was sure she had told me that she wasn't in the least computer savvy. She was also fully aware that I was no longer the children's social worker, so why did she email me instead of Maria.

Dear Ms. Naomi,

I'm sorry 2 bother U. But Mrs. Fildhurst said that U wouldn't mind if I sent U an email. I know we have another lady in charge of us now, but I just wanted to say hi to U, We are doing okay here. Me and Sissy aren't mad at each other anymore. Maybe sometime U can come visit us like a friend or something when U have time.

Bye.

Xavier.

I read the email over and over again. The message was simple. They didn't have anyone. Mona, my sister, wasn't thinking about them. I knew what it felt like to be them. They were lost in a broken system, where nothing was constant or certain, especially social workers that came and went.

I looked down at the full page of notes from all the phone calls and emails I'd received. There were so many names…so many kids that were just like me. No matter how far I ran, how many I saved, there was always one more ready to take my place.

I thought about my job, my real job was to take kids from one miserable existence and plunge them into the unfamiliar of another. I had never felt as ineffective as I did right then. My hands were tied in knots when it came to those kids, my own blood.

I looked around my cubicle. I felt like a stranger in it. I knew that I didn't belong there anymore. I listened to the soundtrack of my life. I heard the sounds of my colleagues talking on the phone, the printers spit out paper, staplers clamped down, fingers tapped keyboards typing up unbelievable reports of abuse, and cell phones buzzed with emergencies. My life was one big trash can of procedures. I thought about my extended family as I punched my keyboard angrily.

Then there was Xavier. He never went away quietly like all the others. Why didn't he understand that I was not allowed to talk to him? Why did he want *me* so bad? From the beginning, he reached out to me. He was so persistent as though he knew there was a genetic connection between us. I hated Nola even more, if that were possible, for destroying his life and mine. It had been over thirty years since I had escaped her, gotten away physically at least and here she was again, haunting my present and theirs. Nola was a threat.

I was glad that Jake had been so caught up in celebrating that he missed the biggest news of the evening. He missed the discovery of my *supposedly* dead mother, Lenora Barnes Thomas. He was more worried about me passing out, which I had blamed on a migraine brought on by the stress of being suspended. He bought it enough, but he'd been pestering me to open up ever since. That was the main reason I was desperately trying to avoid him. I wasn't ready to talk about Nola or Uncle C. Not yet.

At first, I was on the edge of my seat, afraid that Nola...Pastor Lenora would say something to him before I got up the nerve to explain it all. When the phone calls started up again between the two of them, I knew he didn't have a clue. However, I also knew that I would only be able to keep my secret safely guarded for a limited amount of time. One nightmare was all it'd take to activate the ticking time bomb underneath the surface of my every action. It was coming though, like a fierce hurricane in the heart of September. The storm was named Nola and my life was about to wash ashore with yesterday's memories hanging on to it.

The phone on my desk interrupted my thoughts. I stuffed two more aspirin in my mouth, this time I chased it down with a swallow of the warm bottled water sitting on my desk. I looked at the phone and wished that I had never gotten the call that led me to Mona in the first place.

"Naomi Mitchell speaking."

"Naomi?"

"Yes."

"Baby! This is Pastor Lenora, your mother."

I slammed the telephone down as hard as I could. She felt that tremor resonate in her ear. How dare she call my job and announce herself as my mother. Nola was morbidly insane.

The phone rang again. I put my hand around the handle. Although I knew it was her calling back, I had to answer it. A small part of me wanted to talk to her. Longed to hear her voice even after everything she had done to me. I wanted to hear her side, if she had one. I wanted to hear something to make all those memories go away forever.

Then it hit me, I snatched back my hand as though the telephone was a melting chunk of searing hot coal. No. She didn't deserve to hear the sound of *my* voice. She didn't deserve to know that I was still alive and well. That I'd graduated in the top of my class from college. She didn't deserve to know that I was married to a man that was probably cheating on me with my best friend. It was none of her business that I had been trying to forget about her for the past thirty years.

All she *needed* to know, she already knew about me. I had survived the hell that she and Uncle C designed for me. I was a real jacked up piece of work. But I had survived. I'd be damned if I was going to let her back in my life.

The phone rang again. This time I picked it up on the first ring. I couldn't resist knowing.

"Naomi Mitchell speaking."

"Oh, please don't hang up." she sobbed. Her voice seemed to be filled with guilt. "If you hang up, I'll come to your office. I have to talk to you."

"I'm listening." I decided not to hang up. Not because I felt like I owed her anything, but because I was curious.

Xavier

"I WISH I was already grown," Genesis blurted out of nowhere. "I'd leave and go far away from here."

"You don't know anybody, any place else," I said to her.

"So, you think *anywhere* would be better than here."

Today was the last day of school. All the kids were excited about what they were going to do for the summer. Except me and Sissy. We started talking about what we were going to be when we grew up.

Genesis was reading a book about a boy named Santiago that was travelling all over the world looking for his life's purpose, and she was telling me about it.

"See, that's what I want to do. Start walking and end up where I end up," she said.

Leaving, running away, and disappearing forever was all she talked about ever since Mona beat her up. And then, Maria came over and said that Mona's lawyer advised her that Mona didn't want us anymore. Well, that's not exactly how she said it, but it didn't matter, it meant the same thing. She wanted to relinquish her rights—for good, like Jordan's mother had done. Genesis and I were looking at adoption. Mrs. Fildhurst said that our chances of getting adopted were virtually nonexistent, we were both too old. People wanted babies—not half grown teenagers.

"Would you take me with you?" I asked.

Whenever Genesis talked about leaving, she never mentioned me. We had been getting along better than before, but something was still different with us, and now Sissy had a boyfriend.

"Would you take your boyfriend with you?"

She didn't answer. She liked him more than she did me now. Sometimes, I walked with her to the mini mart a few blocks away so she could meet up with him. She would send me in the store while she hung outside kissing and hugging him. He seemed nice, but it was weird for my sister to have a boyfriend. I think I was a little jealous, that she talked to him more than she talked to me.

"He told me he loves me today," Sissy said, not answering my question.

She closed the book she was reading and closed her eyes. I don't know about her boyfriend being in love, but Sissy sure looked like she was.

"You just met him," I responded.

"What do you know about love, Xavier?"

"Well, I know that it takes longer than a couple weeks to happen."

"Says who? Not when two people are meant for each other. The way he looks at me and hugs me feels nice," she said to herself more than to me.

"That's nice, Sissy. He probably does love you."

"And I love him, too. I didn't tell him yet, but I'm going to."

Mrs. Fildhurst pulled into the driveway, ending our conversation. I was glad because I wanted to stop talking about love. I couldn't honestly say that I knew what love felt like. Mona said she loved me, but she beat me like a dog. Mrs. Fildhurst said Jesus loved me, but He was never around when I needed Him most. What's love?

"Sorry I kept y'all waiting today. It was a long line at the pharmacy," Mrs. Fildhurst said as she unlocked the front door. "I was all outta my blood pressure pills."

Mrs. Fildhurst had never given us a key to her house. So if she wasn't home when we got in from school, we had to wait outside in the heat, which was often. She said it wasn't that she didn't trust us, but that she'd had so many kids in and out of her house over the years that she just couldn't go around giving any and everybody a key. Plus, she didn't want nobody snooping around when she wasn't home, no offense.

We went inside and Sissy immediately went for the phone.

"Don't make no long distance calls on my phone, little girl," Mrs. Fildhurst said to Sissy as she grabbed the cordless and darted for her room.

Jordan wasn't home from school yet, so I went to my room and lay across the bed. My mind always went to Naomi. She never answered my email. The new lady, Maria was nice, but I didn't feel like I could talk to her like I could Naomi. Maria always seemed to be in a hurry. Genesis didn't care either way; she told me that I should leave Naomi alone.

Mrs. Fildhurst said that Naomi had a job to do and that her hands were tied in matters like these and that when I grew up, I would understand the politics of the system a little more. I didn't want to understand later, I wanted someone to explain it to me now. I wanted to know why she pretended to care so much then, if I was *only* a job to her.

I got up and asked if I could use the computer and checked the email to see if Naomi had responded. *Nothing.* My heart sank just a little. I guess I had already expected her not to answer. I was out of hope. I regretted trusting her. I felt stuck. I looked up at the ceiling and thought about God. I wondered how He could let people suffer, especially little kids.

I held out my hands in front of my face. I had never been sure if God was real, but the bruises on my hands sure were. No God in the world should let something like that happen to anybody.

"Who you think gonna care about you, take care of you, like me? I'm your mother. I'm the only person that gives a damn about you. Nobody is gonna love you like me." Mona's words screamed in my mind on repeat.

Maybe Mona was right. If she wasn't, it sure felt like it right now. Tears stung my eyes again. I fought them back. I had to laugh a little at myself. I had turned into a real cry baby lately.

A knock on the front door interrupted my moment. I put my hands to my eyes just to be sure that none of my tears escaped. Since I thought it was Jordan, I opened the door without asking. It was a boy that could have been about my age. He shoved a bright orange flyer in my face before I could even speak. An older man stood just at the end of the walkway waiting for the boy.

"VBS in two weeks," he said.

"VB what?" I asked. "What's that?"

"Vacation Bible School," he said like he couldn't believe that I didn't know what that was.

"Oh, okay," I said, not wanting to sound stupid.

"It's gonna be off the chain this year. You should really think about coming. They have a bus that will pick you up and everything," he said excitedly. He leaned close to me and lowered his voice so that the man wouldn't hear. "All the fine honeys go to The Tree of Life. You should come, dawg."

"Aiight. I'll check it out," I said trying to sound cool, waving the flyer in the air. I had no clue what the boy was talking about.

"All right then, I'll see you there," he said, holding out his fist to me.

I gave him dap and he went down the steps. I started to close the door when the boy turned around and looked at the house.

"Eh. Umm, Derek still live here?"

"Who?"

He gave me a strange look before he said, "Never mind," and walked off to the next house.

I stood in the doorway staring at the colorful flyer. It didn't seem like church stuff. The only thing churchy about it was a tiny little scripture in the corner, John 16:33. In all the pictures the kids seemed to be having a good time, shooting pool, playing video games, and basketball. I stared at their faces and started to get excited. I wanted to be happy like those kids. Maybe I could make some new friends to hang out with for the summer. The kid that came to the door seemed pretty cool. Hopefully, I would see him again.

Sissy walked up behind me and snatched the paper out of my hand. "What's this?"

"Some kid invited me to VBS," I said it like I really knew what it meant.

"Wait a minute!" she yelped. "This is my boyfriend's church. He asked me if I wanted to go to this thing."

"What did you say?"

"I told him no. That I don't do church," she said, studying the flyer in detail.

"Well, I'm going," I said proudly. "It looks like it will be cool."

"Oh." She handed the flyer back to me. "Have fun."

"I will."

I had to go to this VBS thing. I knew Sissy didn't think I'd go anywhere without her. I stuck the flyer on the fridge so I would remember to ask Mrs. Fildhurst. Since she wouldn't have to take me herself, I was sure she would say yes. That was another thing about her. Whenever we asked to go anywhere and do anything, she'd say it wasn't her responsibility. It was her job to feed us and send us to school and that was all the state paid her to do.

I went back to my room to wait for Jordan to come home so we could play video games. Jordan believed in God, so I knew he'd want to go. I felt better than I had all day. I finally had plans to do something.

Mona

I HAD NEVER met a man like him. He was so different, for once, my mother was right. A good man will make you forget about all of your troubles. The last couple of weeks were such a whirlwind that I made up my mind for good. I'd decided to move on and live my life, for me, from now on. And to think, I had Naomi to thank for it all. After that fool passed out at church, my parents had to help Jake carry her to the car. They were in such a hurry that they forgot and left me at the church.

Pastor Paul was gracious enough to give me a lift home. When he asked if I wanted to stop for coffee on the way to my place so we could talk a little more, I knew I had him. He was such a gentleman. He had said that it wouldn't be appropriate for him to come to my house so late at night and I hurriedly agreed with that. I had pictures of the kids *everywhere*. I had to clear all that stuff up before I could have him over. We chilled at an all-night diner not too far from my house and ended up staying there so long, we had breakfast.

We talked until seven in the morning about everything. He had already asked me earlier if I was married. I guess when I said no, he automatically assumed that I didn't have any children either, so technically I didn't lie about them like my mother said to do. I just didn't mention the fact that I had three. It didn't matter anyway. I'd enjoyed such a wonderful day that I'd made up my mind to let the state keep them—temporarily. I'm sure they were better off wherever they were, without me.

I deserved a break any way to get my mind right and get my stuff together. Pastor Paul was just the kind of break that I needed. I could picture myself with him for a long time. We became inseparable immediately. If we weren't texting like teenagers, we were sending emails. I would call him during my shift at the hospital when he was done working at the church. I even started reading my bible. Well, I bought a bible to read. If I was going to be a pastor's wife one day, I felt like I needed to be well versed in the scripture. *Amen.*

I had gone back to work and managed to get switched to another unit with better hours leaving me lots of time for Paul. We would meet up for an early breakfast in the morning and catch up again for a late dinner at night. Not having any kids had its share of perks. I was free to do whatever I wanted and whenever for the first time in my adult life. Things were looking up for me—the new improved Mona, and were only scheduled to get better. I was finally happy.

The best news of all came when I asked Paul about his friendship with Jake. It was obvious that the two were pretty tight. Paul said that Jake was his right hand man, but he had been worried about him lately. It seemed that Naomi wasn't up for the church goer of the year award and only showed up for special occasions, which was beginning to bother Jake—a lot. Paul left the conversation at that, but that was enough information for me. I knew then that I didn't have to worry about Naomi too much. If she said anything about my kids, anything at all, I would have that heifa's job. She hadn't opened her mouth so far. She knew not to play with me.

"Oh yes, God is good." I said under my breath.

"You say something, baby?" Paul asked, giving my hand a gentle squeeze.

"I said, God is good," and I squeezed his hand back.

We were about to go into a movie theatre on the far north side of town in The Woodlands to catch an early Saturday morning flick, followed by a bite to eat. He looked around nervously before he grabbed me in his arms and kissed me right in public. We never went to local venues because Paul was worried about someone from the church spotting us together, setting a rumor on fire. He said the fastest way for him to lose members would be for the pastor to be spotted with a girlfriend. Little did he know that I was worried about people finding out as well, for different reasons of course.

All I wanted was him, to be with him, to receive this wonderful treatment forever. Paul had already sent flowers to my job. Yesterday, I found a sweet little card stuffed in the outside pocket of my purse. On it he wrote, "Remember that I'm thinking about you today and every day. Love, your Boaz." He was the one.

"I'm sorry. I couldn't resist," he said.

"Oh, Pastor. You're a bad boy." I smacked his shoulder playfully.

"Can I do it again?"

Before I could respond, he already had me in his arms and his lips were parting mine all over again. If heaven was anything like this, like having a gorgeous, successful man take really good care of you, and kiss you until you forgot your own name, then somebody needed to sign my name on the roll, and quickly. The moment ended too fast and his lips moved away. I was left feeling so...open and vulnerable. I wanted him terribly.

I stared up into his deep gray eyes until I made myself dizzy. I laid my head on his solid chest and sighed louder than I anticipated. The man had me hypnotized. I was willing to give up everything for him. He made me so high naturally, that I hadn't smoked since the day I met him. I had to be completely crazy. I'd only known him a couple of weeks and he was the pastor of a huge and I mean huge church. *Me, a first lady?* What was I getting myself into?

"What's wrong, baby?" he asked.

"I've never met anyone like you before. You are so perfect and I'm so…so." I whined, not able to find the right words to express myself.

"I know I'm a great catch." He chuckled. "No really, I know how you feel. There's something different about you, Mona. I'm gonna tell you a secret. Yesterday, I was trying my last name on your name. I know it sounds crazy because we just met and all. But when you know you just…"

"But Paul…" I tried to interrupt

"No, let me finish, woman. I'm not saying I want to get married tomorrow or anything, but I have talked to God about you. So the judge is still out for now. You come from a good Christian family, you are beautiful, smart, and caring, just what I've been looking for all my life. What I'm looking for in a wife."

He raised my head up with both of his hands, my cheeks warmed instantly from the heat he created inside me. Every touch was like fire.

"Please don't let me being a pastor scare you. Most women don't want me, they only want the title. Heck, pastors need love, too."

He kissed me again and then quickly pulled away.

"There's only one deal breaker. There is one thing I cannot deal with. The thing that will make the judge hand down a 'not the one verdict.' I mean…"

"Just say it," I said about to burst with nervous anticipation. *What if he says kids?*

"Can you burn? I mean can Mona Thomas cook? Really cook? I'm not talking about warming up a little TV dinner either. I'm talking smothered pork chops, greens and cornbread—after the morning service type of cooking," he said with a serious expression on his face.

My insides sighed in relief because I thought it was going to be something I was already guilty of. "For a moment I thought it was going to be something hard. Of course I can cook. To prove it, how about dinner tonight, my place," I offered.

"How about you cook dinner at my place instead? I want to see how you look burning up my kitchen," he said, guiding me into the theatre.

"Even better," I said, relieved. Yep, life was definitely going in my direction for a change.

We walked into the theatre and I stood off to the side smiling like a school girl with her first crush while Paul purchased our tickets. I wandered around to check out the posters of upcoming movies and heard a child's voice that sounded all too familiar.

"Daddy, can I have my own popcorn?" the child begged.

"No, son, you're just going to waste it. We can share."

It was Sean. My baby, Sean and his father. I didn't see them though. I frantically searched the room with my eyes darting back and forth across the dimly lit entry. My eyes made contact with Paul who was next in line. I pointed in the direction of the bathroom and shot off as soon as he turned back around.

I was both terrified and excited at the same time. I hadn't seen Sean in almost two months, but I was with Paul, who didn't know I had children. My first thought was to go hide out in the bathroom, but I decided to follow the voice, just to see. I couldn't resist. I had to see my baby boy. I was only going to look and I planned not to say anything to them. I had to be careful because if Sean spotted me first he was bound to run up to me. My heart thudded so hard against my chest that I could feel it forcefully slamming into my body. I put my hand over it in an attempt to subdue the overwhelming feeling I was experiencing.

I saw them from behind walking away from the concession stand. I looked back at Paul who was still in line. I positioned myself just out of Paul's line of sight and whispered out Sean's name. Both of them looked at me. We stood there for a moment staring at each other, none of us moving or speaking. The moment was awkward. I still had my hand covering my heart so that it wouldn't leap from my body and run away.

Sean ran and jumped into my arms. It felt so good to hold my baby again. He had gotten taller and heavier. I could barely pick him up with the same ease that I had before. In so little time he had changed so much. I kissed him on the top of his head over and over again. His hair had been cut, gone were his huge curly locks that I used to twirl around my fingers. I looked up and Big Sean stood there, solid as stone, watching, shaking his head in disagreement.

"I miss him Sean," I said, about to cry.

He looked at me with pure hatred and shrugged his shoulders. I closed my eyes to avoid his. I knew that I wasn't supposed to see Sean, touch him, or hold him. I loved my son and I wanted Big Sean to understand that. His stoic stance said otherwise.

"Sean, son, come here. Come back over here with Daddy," Big Sean said sternly.

Sean refused to let me go. He shook his head which was buried so far into my chest that it felt as though he could physically touch my heart. He never looked up or mumbled one word as he held on to tightly to me.

"Sean! Get over here now!" Big Sean said again, this time with more force in his voice.

"Don't talk to him like that," I shouted.

"What's going on here?" I heard Paul ask.

Shit. I put Sean back down to the floor and slowly opened my arms to release him. I looked up and Paul was looking back and forth between me and Big Sean, his eyes finally came to rest on little Sean. I gave Sean a gentle push to nudge him back toward his father. He barely moved.

"Well?" Paul asked again. "Mona, what's up?"

Big Sean looked up at me and shook his head when I didn't respond. He walked over and pulled our son away by the shoulder.

"Come on, boy."

Little Sean started to cry, "I want my mama. I want my mama." I had to do something. I had to say something and fast. *Think Mona. Think like Lenora.* What would my mother do, I asked myself. I went and stood next to Paul and grabbed his hand. I made a choice.

"I didn't like the way he was talking to *his* son," I lied in a low voice. "The poor baby was crying for his mother and ran up to me asking me to help him find her. Then that guy got upset with him and me."

I dared Big Sean with my eyes not to say anything. My son's cries for me, his mother, grew more hysterical by the second. He sprawled out on the floor and popcorn flew everywhere. He reached up for me, screaming loudly. A few people gathered to see what was going on. I couldn't stand there for another second, my heart was breaking into tiny little pieces, but I refused to risk losing Paul at the same time. I was torn in half like a sheet of paper. The rip was audible.

"You just gone walk away, huh?" Big Sean asked. He was clearly undone by my actions. "You ain't shit." He bent over and picked our baby up and into his arms.

"Do you know them?" Paul asked, puzzled.

I looked back at my son one last time. Sean was rubbing his back as our child yelled for me. I pulled Paul's hand and quickly directed him away from the spectacle. I never looked back.

"Not anymore. Let's go. I don't want to miss our movie."

If Paul asked anymore questions, I'd just say that I used to date Sean. Problem solved.

Naomi

I SAT IN a corner booth at The Breakfast Klub on the outskirts of downtown Houston, in Fourth Ward, waiting for Nola to arrive. It was one of my favorite restaurants and I felt comfortable in the culturally enriched atmosphere. I'd already had two cups of coffee and the caffeine was kicking in hard on my empty stomach. I was so nervous that when Marcus, the restaurant owner, touched me on the shoulder, I nearly shot straight out of my seat.

"Are you okay?" He laughed.

"Yes, I'm fine. Too much coffee I think," I said, laughing at myself.

"Not good, let me get you some water."

He quickly returned with an ice cold glass of water. I hadn't realized how thirsty I was until he sat the glass in front of me.

"Not eating today, Naomi? I know you love the Katfish and Grits."

He was right, it was my favorite dish. However, at that moment, my stomach bubbled and fluttered in blind anticipation about my meeting with Nola. I dared to put one drop of food in my mouth.

"Not yet. I have a meeting, so it'll just be water for now," I said, raising my glass in appreciation.

"Okay, just let me know and I'll get you hooked up." He moved on to the next table.

The hospitality in the place was amazing, which was partly the reason I chose it. I felt safe. I had no clue of what to expect from Nola and I wanted to be among the familiar. If she was anything like I remember, her temperament could go from zero to a hundred in a matter of seconds. I was no longer afraid of her, but I didn't want to take any chances either. I didn't trust her one bit.

While I waited for Nola, I pulled out the notes that I'd taken from reading my old case file. I skimmed over the words again. I had always been too chicken to learn much about my own truth. I'd had access to my records for years, but I had convinced myself that Nola was dead just so I could put her behind me. So, I could sleep some nights.

From my file, I learned that Nola's real name was Lenora Barnes. She was born in New Orleans. Now it made perfect sense that people called her by the nickname, Nola, the initials of New Orleans, Louisiana.

The house I used to live in with Nola was only three blocks from Jake's church near Highway 288. I drove past it on my way to The Breakfast Klub. I could just see my young self sitting on the porch having a tea party with old Mrs. Frances. I don't think anyone had lived there for years. It was completely rundown and abandoned with vagrants loitering nearby.

Apparently, Nola was pregnant with Mona about the same time that I was taken away from her. By the time she gave birth to Mona, she was drug-free. I also read that Nola had made several unsuccessful attempts to get me back in the first couple of years that I was in foster care. While she had succeeded in getting clean—she had failed to rid her life of Charles Thomas, better known to me as, Uncle C. The courts refused to release me to her care because of him. After those two years, nothing more about

Nola was ever documented. During the court's yearly update of my case, Nola's whereabouts were listed as—Unknown.

I took another sip of water and waited. My seat faced the parking lot so I watched as she slithered out of her car. Out of curiosity, I looked to see what she drove. Humph, a Jag. Well, well, well, looks like Nola's doing pretty good for herself. She was also dressed impeccably in an expensive looking white, linen outfit. I immediately copped a serious attitude. It bothered me that she appeared to have a little money. I took another sip of water to cool the flames about to rage out of control inside me.

"My darling daughter," Nola said, rushing to my side with outstretched hands. "My MiMi," she paused as though waiting for me to get up from my chair and to greet her with as much enthusiasm.

Was she serious? Did she actually expect me to embrace her?

"Nola," I said without getting up from my seat. I was void of all feelings at that point.

Her smile faded and her hands fell to her sides. Not under the direst of circumstances would I call that woman Mama or Pastor Lenora ever again. She was an impostor. Just thinking about her standing behind the pulpit irritated me. She was faker than a three dollar bill.

"You called me. I'm here. What do you want?" I asked as straightforward as I could manage.

She pulled a strand of hair out of her bun and twirled it around her finger as she sat down. I was instantly glad that I didn't have enough hair on my head to wind around my fingers anymore, seeing I got that bad habit from her.

"Well. I wanted to talk about us of course. I'm so happy that I've finally found you."

I already felt the warning signs of annoyance. My forehead creased. "Found me? You didn't find me, you bumped into me."

"Same thing, daughter, it's—"

"Can you not call me that?" I asked.

"What?"

"Daughter. I am not your daughter. I was a ward of the court of the state until my eighteenth birthday. So technically, the great state of Texas was my mother. My father too."

She didn't respond immediately. She looked at her hands and fidgeted with her mammoth diamond ring for a minute. "Do you think you will ever be able to forgive me, MiMi?" she asked in a low voice.

"Forgive you. Forgive you for what?" Spit sputtered from my mouth as I spoke. "For letting Uncle C rape me? Or do you want me to forgive you for stomping me with your high-heeled shoes on? You must think I forgot about all that," I said with my eyes locked like a pit-bull on her ring. I wasn't jealous, but I would be paying student loans for the rest of my life and she was wearing a ring that should have paid for my college education. She didn't deserve anything that she had.

"I don't know why I came here. I should have known this was going to be useless," she said, attempting to rise from the table.

I was on a roll and not ready to stop. All the caffeine I'd ingested intensified the adrenaline racing throughout my body. "Sit down!" I said just loud enough for people to turn their heads and look our way. "I'm not finished saying what I have to say to you." I brought my voice down an octave.

Not wanting to be embarrassed any further, she quickly sat back down.

"You called *me*. You wanted to meet *me*. What did you expect? Huh, Nola? Hugs and kisses? A happy family reunion with mother and daughter finally back together again after thirty long years? You want me to call you Mama and love you like nothing ever happened? Do you realize that I didn't know your real name? You are crazier than I thought you'd be." I rolled my eyes.

"Look, Naomi. My intentions in meeting with you were to fix this thing between you and me. I want to have a relationship with you. If all you want to do is sit here and judge me and bad mouth me then I'm not going to tolerate that. I've been through enough. Times were hard for me back then. I needed help and I got it.

Glory to God and A.A. Now, I know you went through some rough spots of your own a long time ago too. You need to get over it. I already have."

I listened as the old Nola magically appeared in all her old splendor. Pastor Lenora disappeared and she was just as I remembered her being, cutting mean. I knew that church stuff was a charade. I focused my attention out of the window at the rain beating down on the parking lot so I wouldn't have to look at her face, but I still heard her voice bouncing off of my senses, which were all painfully aware of her presence.

Then, I looked at her. I mean, I really stared deep into her eyes, past my own hatred for a moment, and searched for a bond—a connection, even a little sympathy. *Nothing.* Lenora Thomas was absolutely oblivious to the extent of the damage she had done to my life or Mona's. Or, she did a great job pretending to be. Her voice echoed in my head. *Get over it.* As I listened to her speak, I realized how much Mona was just like her, how much she sounded like her. *Get over it.* Maybe I should have been grateful that I escaped Nola when I did. I could have easily been Mona. They were two hopeless generations and, by no choice of my own, I had escaped. I was lucky.

"You don't know my life. You don't know what I had to go through. I had you when I was thirteen years old, hell. I was just a kid my damn self. I did the best I could with you!" She pulled a few more strands of hair out of her bun and twirled them around her finger. "You think you're the only woman in the world that has had to give up her goodies too soon? Well wake up, honey. You're not and you won't be the last. You need to forget about all those old things that are passed away. Put them behind you and move on."

I was in a state of shock. I couldn't speak. I tried to force my lips to move, but they refused. My ears wanted to locate the OFF switch that controlled her voice. Nola was trying to rationalize. She came pretending to want forgiveness. But not once did she apologize for any of it, not for herself and not for Uncle C. After thirty years, she still wasn't sorry. I couldn't believe it, but I had to. When I didn't say anything because I couldn't open my mouth, she went for the jugular.

"Humph. It wasn't nothing but a little cat and you were gonna give it up one day anyway," she said sarcastically.

My voice came back and every word from my mouth pushed out as a scream: "You stupid bitch, I was five when you watched that bastard rape me. Every day he raped me whether you were high or not. And you knew. You were a worthless crackhead and you gave me away for a hit of that shit and some electricity. Then you turned around and married him after what he did to me. How could a woman do something like that to her little girl? I hate you so much. If there is a hell, I hope you bust the bottom out of it and it exploded with you in it." My entire body shook furiously, but not a tear.

She grabbed her purse and stood up. "You damn right I married him. After you left, I didn't have nothing and nobody but a new baby in my stomach to feed. And for what it's worth, it looks like I—*we* still ended up doing a whole lot better than you. Ha!" She smirked. "While you over here worried about my man, you need to be worried about your own and that Asian chick he's running around the church with." She laughed, counting on the reality that her final words had hurt me.

I picked my half empty cup of lukewarm coffee from the table and doused it in her face. She didn't even blink. I wished that it was still scorching hot. She grabbed my napkin from the table and gently dabbed at her face as the coffee dribbled down her chin and fell onto her white blouse, streaking it brown. She smiled showing all of her white teeth. I was back in the presence of evil.

"I really wanted you to forgive me, Naomi. But I'll let the Lord deal with your anger in His divine time," Nola said, bringing her alter ego, Pastor Lenora back. "I will pray for you."

"You have got to be kidding me. Do you even realize that you never apologized for anything? I deserve that, not your prayers." Like a broken dam, tears broke through the fragile dam of my eyes. "You really hurt me, Nola. It still hurts." To ease the ache, I touched the most tender part of my body—my heart.

"You always were a little cry baby. I see nothing has changed about you." She laughed at her own joke. "I don't owe you anything. God has forgiven me for my sins and that is enough. According to your husband—you could use a little Jesus. So, why don't you go find Him so you can finally get some peace in your life?" She turned away and walked out with her head high.

I watched from inside the window as Nola slithered out into the rain, back into her Jag, and drove away. My thoughts were on killing Jake, Dae, Nola, and Uncle C—anybody that looked shifty. I was so full of fury that I felt real strong.

"You okay?" Marcus walked up to me and put an arm around my shoulder.

"Yes, actually I am. You wanna know something, Marcus?

"What?"

"I find solace in knowing that karma is a real bitch!" I smiled.

"Well, the Lord said that vengeance is His."

"But did you hear what she said to me?" I countered.

"Did you hear what I said, Naomi? God will take care of her. You just be the best you that you can be."

Usually I would have been embarrassed by the things that Marcus and the other patrons heard from both Nola and me. But, I wasn't. She was wrong and embarrassment was her coat to wear, not mine. I walked out to my car in the rain. Again, I was happy about my short hair because I didn't need an umbrella. I let the rain pour on me.

∞ ∞

I saw Nola's Jag when I pulled into the church parking lot. Seeing it didn't bother me that time. I had nothing else to say to that *woman*—ever.

I was there for Jake. I wanted answers. Although it was still early afternoon, I knew he was there for vacation bible school. I hoped that I wouldn't have to search all over the church campus for him. I marched straight to his office, the wet leather of my pumps sloshed loudly down the corridor and up the stairs. I damn near knocked the door off of its hinges as I burst through it.

I was not prepared for what I saw and I paused for a second as my eyes attempted to take it all in. I even rubbed my eyes, hoping that it was a mirage before me and it would disappear. The moment lasted long enough for all the anger I had ever felt toward Nola and Uncle C to return to me—double. Anger swelled like a huge black cloud and swept me up into its center.

Jake, my husband that I loved with heart beats that I was willing to steal from someone else if I had to, sat at his desk with Dae leaning seductively over his shoulder pointing at something on the computer. Dae. Dae was all I had. She was the only person I could call family. She was like my sister. It was true and I had already felt it. Nola was right.

I wanted to break something. Do serious damage. Kill both of the people staring blankly at me, people that I truly loved and were supposed to love me, too. I willed my feet to turn around. I wanted to leave, to disappear for good. But they were stuck in place. *Move feet.* I willed my brain to order my feet to move. Everything was disconnected except my anger.

Dae's lips began to move, but the rage in my head was so loud that I heard nothing, but I read her scarlet painted thin lips.

"Naomi. What are *you* doing here?" she had the nerve to ask.

I lunged forward. Jake jumped in the middle to stop me just before I got to Dae. I reached out my hand and scraped my nails across his face, just short of his left eye. He screeched and covered his face. Dae tried to run around me, but I stood between her and the door. The only way around me was out the window and that tramp couldn't fly.

"No, don't try to run away now," I said calmly. "You should have been running before you came up here to steal my husband."

My voice…It was Nola's voice coming out of my mouth. I caught a handful of Dae's long, jet black silky hair and wrapped it around my left hand. She was a lot smaller than me, so it was nothing to overpower her. I held her face inches from mine, her neck stretched out of proportion looked as though it was going to break. Her short legs bent under my pressure. I could see the fear growing in her dark eyes and it excited me.

"Do you want to know what pain feels like?" I smiled as I raised my right hand to deliver a blow to her face. "Everybody just wants to take from me. My childhood. My body and now my husband. Is that what you want, Dae, to leave me with nothing?"

I wanted to close both of her eyes forever. The fear in her eyes became my target, the bull's eye my fist aimed for. I glanced up and caught sight of myself in the mirror above Jake's desk. *Was that me?* No. That was Nola. I looked behind me and dropped Dae to the floor in the process. I looked around for Nola.

"Mi—Mi, you're more like me than you think," I heard Nola whisper in my ear and I felt her kiss me on the cheek. "You're still mama's baby." She cooed.

"No I'm not," I whispered. "I'm nothing like you." I yelled out loud. Dae and Jake eyed me suspiciously. "Shh. It's Nola, did you hear her? She was just right here. You heard her, right, Jake?"

I turned in frenzied circles looking for her until I made myself dizzy in the small office. She was there, in that mirror, I knew that I saw her, I heard her, I felt her kiss me. Jake walked slowly toward me with pity filled eyes. Dae still on the floor stared wide-eyed up at me.

I opened my mouth and wailed. The unfathomable sound came from so deep inside me that I felt completely uprooted, outside of myself. I screamed and screamed. I screamed until I felt empty. I screamed out of utter rage, the pain, the anger and hatred. I screamed until there was nothing left but a dark empty space where my soul used to be. I screamed until my voice hid in fear from me. Underneath all the screaming, I heard Jake praying. *Didn't he know that no amount of praying would help me?* That I'd personally asked God so many years ago—and nothing. I was finished begging God for help.

When we first met, Jake once told me, "The soul longs for God's presence. No matter how you try to run *from* Him in search of human solace—your soul will find the way, and run back to the Lord on its own."

Jake was a smart man. Right then, my soul sought God. "Jake, can you help me?" I cried. "Tell me what to do?"

He tenderly touched my head, my lips, and my belly. He placed his hand just inside my inner thigh the one where the deepest of my wounds lay. He stared into my eyes with his hands on me, pleading with the Lord to fix me—to restore me.

"Talk to him, Naomi. You have to open your mouth and ask Him for help. Only He can heal this right here." Jake grabbed my scar, the one that ran in a jagged line from my crotch to my inner thigh. The scar he never asked me about and it pulsated underneath his touch. "He can restore you, baby. Just let go. You have to believe."

Restore me? How could people like me be restored? Tears covered Jake's face and mixed with his running nose.

Part of me wanted to believe that he didn't know what he was talking about. But the other part allowed his words to rain over me like warm honey until I felt like I was melting away. I began to sob profusely and doubled over in tears. I wanted to tell him how much it hurt—physically. But he knew. He pleaded with God to take the pain away. To take away the memories.

"They hurt me so bad."

"I know," Dae said softly.

I felt the heat of Dae's body come close behind me. I felt her head rest between the blades of my shoulders. I felt her body shake from crying. Her small hands intertwined with my fingers and lifted my hands. My pain screamed at me not to succumb to the trickling warmth running through my body. My anger tried to protect me and sent signals, warning that it was all a trick. *Hold on, my anger screamed.*

I wanted the warmth. I needed it to be whole. Years of hurt exploded in my spirit, "Please God!" I screamed, jumping up and down. "I'm tired. Help me. Please. I wanted to finally be complete for the first time in my life."

For a split second, the warmth cleared my mind so I screamed again. "Please God."

Silence. Then, somewhere in my mind, I heard a calm voice not belonging to Jake or Dae, say, *let go. Just let go, Naomi.* And I did—finally.

There was a God. He said my name. I suddenly felt His love. He was real. The warmth turned into a tickle and I began to giggle, then laughed, and finally I cried some more. God heard me and He loved me. And I felt it.

The dull ache that had been blocking love from reaching my heart—was gone. I felt Jake and Dae's love and adoration surround me, like armor. They were like two extensions of God. A rush of peace swept through me and a warm tingle spread throughout my body from the top of my head to the soles of my feet. I felt lifted.

The rain outside pelted against the window. The sound was refreshing. Jake's voice floated back into focus and his prayers were like a calming song filling my ears. It was amazing. I felt like I was hearing his voice for the very first time.

Everything felt so new. I knew that was it, the Holy Spirit. I had often asked Jake what it felt like. He could never describe it, now I understood. I wanted to tell him that I knew, but I was so in awe that I didn't want to speak and ruin the experience. I wanted to stay in that place forever. Later, I would tell him later that the Holy Spirit felt like pure, unfiltered—love—pouring all over you.

⋘ ⋙

"I just cannot believe that after all these years your mother turned up and at Jake's church of all places."

"You? Me either," I exclaimed as Dae and I sat inside her car.

"You look exhausted. We'll talk more after you get some rest, okay? I want to explain what I was doing here."

"You don't need to explain. It's okay," I said.

"No, I want you to know. We've been planning *how* to bring it up to you."

"Bring up what?" I was still a little bit curious.

"First of all, I want you to know that I didn't tell Jake anything about your past. I thought that was for you to do. I only agreed to help him get *you* to talk openly with him, and possibly talk someone. Like a—a therapist."

"A therapist? That was it?"

The pieces of the picture came together and I was ashamed for thinking what I had been thinking about the two of them. Guilt washed my good feeling away. I should have known better. I had so much to sort out in my mind. The day had been unreal. I decided right then that I *needed* to talk to someone.

"Now, I know how you feel about therapy, Naomi, but Dr. Dalton *is* the best." Dae grabbed my hands, "I think you would really like her and—"

"I'll talk to him," I cut Dae off. "And Dr. Dalton."

"Pinky swear?" Dae held out her hand. We were still cool.

"Pinky swear," I sighed.

"Well, I better get going, I have to go back to the office. And it looks like it's going to storm."

Dae leaned over and hugged me. I exhaled and held on to her for a few more seconds. My friendship remained intact and that meant the world to me. I was glad that I never got the chance to actually hit Dae. I would not have been able to live with that.

"Do you believe in God, Dae?" I asked out of curiosity as I got out of her car.

"Yes."

"How? When?"

Dae and I had never talked about God or anything that sounded like religion. I didn't recall her parents being deeply religious.

"Today, with you," she said.

I watched Dae drive away. I loved her so much.

I then began to wonder what was taking Jake so long to come

out. He was supposed to only tell Paul that he needed to leave early today and that was it. Knowing my husband, I had about another hour to wait for him. I climbed in his truck.

I leaned my head back on the seat and thought about how I was going to tell Jake that my supposedly dead mother, Nola, was Pastor Lenora. I couldn't put it off any longer. I had to tell him everything. I stared out of the car window and watched the dark clouds move across the sky. It was so dark that it looked a lot later than four o'clock. The thunder rumbled and sounded more like an approaching earthquake than an occurrence in the sky. The truck windows trembled.

From where I sat, I could see the giant tree that I had been fascinated by the last time I was at the church. Its long branches seemed to wave, beckoning me to come over for a closer look. I hopped out of Jake's truck and started walking toward it. *Maybe I'll sit on the bench for a few minutes and clear my head.* It had rained so much that I was careful to stick to the path that led to the wooded area. The tree's overgrown branches blocked out any meager amount of light that attempted to escape from the clouds.

I made a mental note to tell Jake that he needed to put some lights out here. I held my hands out in front of me so that I could feel my way. My feet sunk in the mud after the path ran out. A squirrel ran past my feet and I almost passed out. Trepidation began to creep up inside me. When the hair on my arms stood on end, I decided to turn around. I'd come out to the tree another time to bask in its beauty when there was more light. With all the rain, it was a soggy mess once the brick path ended.

Just before I made it back to the bricked path, I heard something. A faint whimper then it went quiet again. I didn't know much, but I knew that squirrels didn't whimper. I bet some little girl was out there being freaky under the tree of life with her boo.

There it was again, that time a moan. Unless squirrels moaned someone was out there doing the dirty. How low could you get. I remember telling Jake that these kids weren't as innocent as he made them out to be. I turned to go back to the truck so I could call Jake on my cell. He would be better suited to handle these fast kids and he needed to bring a flashlight. They were so busted.

I crept away on my tiptoes. Then, I ran.

Mona

HOW I ENDED up shooting pool and throwing water balloons at a bunch of teenagers, I'll never understand. That man could talk me into almost anything. It was fun though. It made me a little sad that I never enjoyed my own kids like that. It seemed easier to play with other kids and have a good time with them than it was to play with my own.

Paul had asked me to facilitate a small group session for girls. I was to talk to them about putting God in real life situations. It was something I had never done before, but I ended up enjoying them. Of course, at first I didn't know what to say, but they started asking me questions and we were off. When the whistle blew for them to go into the main hall of the youth center, a few of the girls ran up and hugged me. They were so thankful that someone had taken the time to talk and not yell at them.

They were so sweet. I gave a few of them my telephone number to call me when vacation bible school ended so we could keep in touch. Paul walked in just as I finished writing my number down. After all the girls left, he closed the door and kissed me.

I began to have those sinful thoughts again as soon as our lips connected. I was digging that man so much that I'd do anything for him. And anything to keep him.

Well, I already knew that it wasn't going to be any of *that*. He already made some things perfectly clear. Absolutely no sex until we were married, which we talked about every day. I was sure that by this time next year, I'd be the first lady of The Redeeming Tree of Life Church, one of the fastest growing churches on the southwest side of Houston. *First Lady Mona.*

"Baby, you did good with the girls," Paul said with his fingers tangled up in my hair. "They loved you."

"You really think so? I was so nervous. I'm usually not that good with kids."

"If you say so. We need you over here in our youth ministry, but first you need to move your membership from The Fountain. You can't play between churches. I can't have my wife-to-be paying her tithes and using her talents somewhere else and getting all this good word over here. Not to mention this good love." He kissed me again and held me close. Paul was a magnet and I was completely drawn to him.

Jake stepped through the door just as we pulled apart. We both jumped like a couple of teenagers. "Oh excuse me," Jake said, snickering. "I didn't realize that we had two love birds hiding out in here. One of the kids said they saw you come in here, Pastor."

Paul looked sheepishly at his feet. I couldn't even look Jake in the eye. I know we were both adults, but Paul *was* a Pastor. I was glad that it was Jake and not one of the other nosey workers.

"Well, how did it go with you today, Mona?" Jake asked.

"Oh, it was fine," I said.

"Good. We hope to see more of you then." He turned to Paul. "Can I talk to you for a minute, Pastor?"

It seemed like they had official business to discuss, so I stepped away to give them a little privacy. I also didn't like being around Jake too much. I'd seen him around a few times since I'd been seeing Paul. I was always guarded with him, unsure of how much he knew about me. I saw Mother earlier that afternoon and she said that I wouldn't have to deal with Naomi much longer. She said Naomi and Jake were on the road to a divorce. Mother and Jake had become really close since they started working together, but I wondered why he felt comfortable telling her. Church people tell their business way too much for me. When I became first lady, I would keep my mouth zipped tight.

I pulled one of the chairs over to the window and sat down. The sun was completely covered by the overcast and the gray clouds had turned the sky almost black despite it being early afternoon. It was going to pour later; maybe Paul and I could grab a movie and hang out at his place instead of going out.

I looked back, and Paul and Jake were totally engrossed in a very serious conversation. I instantly became worried. I wondered if they were talking about me. Had Naomi told Jake about my kids and the child abuse allegations? I stood and put my forehead against the cool glass and closed my eyes for a second.

Jake's voice became increasingly louder the more he spoke. I tried not to look, but I strained my ears in an attempt to figure out what they were talking about. When it came to Jake, I was extremely paranoid. I heard Naomi's name a couple of times and something about her being hysterical and looking for her mother. *She was a crazy fool.* I exhaled a sigh of relief; it was about her, and not me. I went back to minding my own business.

I opened my eyes and saw Genesis right outside of the window. She was walking with some skinny, young boy. He was leading her toward the other side of the building. I could tell that she was a little hesitant, but she was still following him. All of the kids were supposed to be inside the main hall for the afternoon service. What in the world were they doing out alone? Out of instinct I tapped on the window as they passed. They didn't hear me.

Where was she going? Worse than that, what in the world was she doing here? It seemed as though every time I turned around my past tripped me up. Sean at the movies and now Genesis. All I needed was for Xavier to show up and we'd have a family reunion.

I tapped harder and without realizing it and called out her name, just above a whisper, "Genesis."

"You say something?" Paul asked.

"No, I was just reciting the books of the bible," I said.

I knew it was a lame excuse, but it was all I had time to come up with at the moment. He didn't respond and continued talking to Jake. Whatever it was they were talking about must have been deep. Paul placed his hands on Jake's shoulders and prayed for him. Right there, in front of me. I don't think I'd ever had a friend pray for me. They'd say that I was *in* their prayers, but never actually did it while I was standing there and could hear them.

I turned away. I couldn't watch because the moment seemed so private. I slumped into the chair and stared out of the window again. I was no longer able to see Genesis. I wanted to march outside to find her and drag her little hot tail right back in the building by her hair. She didn't have on any makeup, but her shorts were very inappropriate, especially for church. Nothing I taught her seemed to register in her mind. She couldn't say that I didn't try to warn her. Whatever, she was somebody else's problem now. I just wanted those kids to go away so I could move on with my life with Paul.

Jake and Paul had sat down in a couple of the chairs. They were going to be awhile. I started to get antsy. If Genesis was here, then I bet Xavier was somewhere not too far. Those two never went anywhere without each other. I didn't want to run into either of them, especially Xavier. I had gotten over my anger with him for putting us in this position, but I wasn't ready to see him and especially not here at Paul's church. They were much older than Sean; they understood what was going on and were sure to bust me out.

I pulled my cell out of my purse. I needed my mother's advice. Although Paul wanted me here, I couldn't risk it. I sent my mother a text alerting her that I'd seen Genesis outside and I wasn't sure if Xavier was at the church too.

She immediately messaged me back that she'd be on the lookout for them and that I better come up with a reason to go home. She also added just to rub it in my face, *I told you those kids were going to be your downfall. You should have listened to me.* I didn't respond to her message. It was all too much—the hiding from everyone. *Naomi, Paul, Mother, and the kids.*

I threw my bag over my shoulder and stood off to the side so that Paul would know I wanted his attention. I waved at him when I caught his eye. He waved back. I hurriedly slipped out the door. I know he thought that I was going to wait outside, or at the youth service.

I walked along the back of the main hall where all the kids were seated. A few kids were on the small stage rapping as the audience went crazy over the performance. I kept my eyes straight ahead and on the red exit sign. I wanted to blend into the wall I was so nervous. I wished that I'd been more familiar with the church layout, but I only knew one way out.

I pushed the swinging door open hard and exhaled all the air I had pent up in my lungs. I made it out of the main hall and into the foyer. *Safe.* I felt a thud and heard a thump from the other side of the door. I had hit someone with it. I pushed it closed behind me to check out the victim. *Xavier.*

He was holding his head. I got a clear view of the burns on his fingers. The discolored skin was basically nonexistent. His hands were a mixture of brown and white where the skin would most likely never heal. He had on one of the bright orange TRUST GOD tees that we passed out to the kids earlier that day. He had to be at VBS the entire week to get one of those. I also had on one. He stuffed his hands in his front pockets and looked up at me. We stared at each other before I started to walk away. What else was I supposed to do?

"Mona." He called out to me.

I kept walking. The last thing I needed was a guilt trip. I had to go before Paul appeared. I didn't want a repeat of Sean.

"Mona," he said again, louder.

I stopped but didn't turn around. His voice was choked up. I didn't want to look at him again. I wanted to hop in my car and drive far away so that I could cry. I wanted to disappear—forever. No, I wanted to take off and just run. I wanted to run away as far as I could until I was free from everything.

"I saw you earlier today and. I...umm...I just wanted to say that I umm,,,I'm sorry. I think I messed up. I wanted...I don't know. I'm sorry, Mona, for telling on you I know you think I hate you, but I don't—not anymore."

The image of his scorched hands burned into my heart. A neon sign like the one that hung over the pool hall near my house blinked *Guilty—Child Abuser—Liar* in bold red and blue neon. I felt so bad for doing that to him. For doing what I did to all of them. I knew I was wrong, but I couldn't stop myself. I put burning hot blunts to his knuckles and dared him to scream or move. I did it so many times and just thinking about what I'd done tormented me. Xavier's hands were the evidence that I was a monster. I beat my kids. I beat them like my mother beat me.

Now, there I was, at church wearing a TRUST GOD t-shirt and treating other folks' kids better than I had ever treated my own. Him apologizing to *me* for it really touched me. I thought about one of Paul's sermons when he'd said, "Watch out. Hate will make you become the very thing you hate in life. Watch out." I hadn't watched out and I was just like Mother. I slowly turned around. *Maybe I should—.*

"You should be sorry, you little bastard," my mother hissed. "Y'all bad asses done put my daughter through enough. She went to jail because of you like she was some lowlife criminal or something. I paid a lot of money for that attorney to make all of that and *you* go away. I told her not to have y'all anyway. She should have listened to me. If it were up to me, you woulda been locked up in some foster home a long time ago."

I could tell that her teeth were clenched from the tight sound her voice made. She must have been walking down the hallway behind me. This church had far too many pass throughs and connecting wings. She brushed abruptly past me and got in Xavier's face.

"Go ahead and leave, Mona. You don't want Paul to see you with them. I'll put the garbage out," she said over her shoulder. "Go now!"

I didn't move. I couldn't. I wanted to say something, but Mother looked so angry like she did when I was younger. I felt like a child again and I was afraid to confront her. I wanted to hug my son and tell him that I was sorry, too. I wanted to ask for another chance. I thought about how I left Sean at the theatre screaming for me. How I beat Genesis because *my* father molested her. I had done so many things wrong and couldn't figure out how to do anything right. I blamed her. It was supposed to be her job to teach me how to love, and all she taught me was how to hate, kick, and scream. How to fight everything and everybody except her and Daddy.

I thought about Paul, too. I loved him so much already, but I knew that everything he saw in me was a lie. I didn't know who to choose, Paul or my kids? If I left, perhaps Mother could fix everything like she always did. If I stayed, everything would surely crumble. I stood there bonded to the moment and waited for whatever magnetic pull that held me hostage to the very spot I stood on to release me.

"Where's your sister?" Mother asked. "It's time for the both of you to leave. And I better not ever catch you around here again. I've had enough of you two." She grabbed Xavier by the chest, bunching up the TRUST GOD letters into a wrinkled ball in her fist. She slapped him with her free hand and sliced his skin with her ring. A thin strip of blood exposed itself to the light.

I cringed when I saw her strike my child. Xavier stood his ground.

"Don't ever hit me again. *Nobody* will ever hit me again," Xavier said with so much authority that I was shocked.

"What the hell did you say, boy? You just don't get it, do you? We want you to go away! Do you understand that?"

She raised her hand to hit my child again. Her apparent distaste for him made her words, as sharp as razors. I looked away. Was that me? Did I sound like that?

"No. It's time for *you* to leave," Paul said.

Humph I knew this was going to happen. I heard the resentment trembling over the bass in his voice and felt his raging presence right behind me. He was so close that I felt the heat of his words blow harshly against the back of my neck. All of the blood in my body rushed to my head. The silence of betrayal attacked the room and froze us all in place. It was quiet. I wanted someone to talk, to say something. I knew it wasn't going to be me. I looked at my mother and she looked at me or past me at Paul, I wasn't sure. I heard a cell phone vibrate, interrupting the hostile moment in the room.

"Hey man, I think I'll let you handle this. Naomi just sent me a text message and we got some kids trying to hook up out by the tree of life." I heard Jake's voice. "I'm about to grab a flashlight and go check it out."

Naomi was here, too. I bet she brought them to the church. Things were headed from bad to worst. Out of the corner of my eye, I watched Jake go out the enormous front door of the youth center, allowing in for a brief moment, a sliver of dark gray light from outside. I wanted to run for that tiny beam into my freedom. The door creaked open again. I thought it was Jake coming back. Instead, in walked the boy I had seen Genesis hanging onto earlier. I waited for him to hold the door open for my daughter. He didn't and the door closed with a thud behind him. If he was here, where was Genesis?

My stomach dropped with dread as I thought about Jake's words. I watched the boy cross the foyer. Something wasn't right. He glanced at all of us standing there, like statues, shrugged his shoulders and pushed the swinging door to the youth hall open. I knew once that door closed answers would have to be given. I didn't have any answers that I was ready to admit publicly. Mother's face flushed white as a ghost; her gig was up and she knew it.

Deep inside it made me feel good—relieved even.

The voice of the youth minister speaking floated into the foyer and settled in my ear: "If you Trust God, your path will be filled with light."

The quiet settled once again as the door closed shut. I ran out the front door, racing for the gray light.

Xavier

I WATCHED HER playing with all those other kids all day. I wondered why she never played with us. I thought she saw me earlier when everyone was outside throwing water balloons before it started to rain. I even got close enough to her to hit her with a big blue water balloon from behind and it broke on her cheek. Sissy thought that was so funny and she rolled on the green grass laughing until she caught a cramp in her side. She picked up a balloon and tried to hit her too, but she missed.

I don't think I ever saw Mona look so happy. She looked really young, too. I never realized how pretty she was. I guess her real beauty was hard to see when she was being so evil. When we lived with her, she was either at work, mad at something, getting high, or on the phone. Today, before the clouds came and covered the sky, I saw her laughing in the sunlight for the first time in my life. She looked happier without us. She dressed different. Her hair was shorter and had a different color. I liked the way it made her eyes look alive. They were a beautiful light brown that I could see even from a distance. I always thought she had coal black eyes.

I followed her around most of the day. I was going to talk to her when I saw the pastor go in the small group room with her and close the door. Sissy was supposed to be in her group but she didn't go; she went for a walk with her boyfriend instead. I knew it was wrong, but I held my head against the door and listened. I heard them kissing. Mona was going to marry the pastor of this big church. I heard him tell her. I wondered what he saw in her because he seemed really nice. She seemed really nice now, too. I hadn't talked to him at all, but I could tell he was a good person. Look at what he did to her—he changed her. Mona sounded really happy to be with him. Maybe she wasn't bipolar anymore and we could all go home and live with both of them one day.

Brother Jake walked up and caught me with my ear to the door. He told me that it wasn't polite to eavesdrop and it really wasn't a good look on a man to be nosey. He sent me back to the main hall for the sermon. I listened to him because I really liked him. He had been really cool the entire week I'd been at VBS. He gave me a ride home on the first day because I missed my bus. I was having too much fun and didn't want to leave.

"What happened to your hands?" he asked me in the car.

"Burned," I said.

"How?"

"Don't want to talk about it."

He left it at that. When we got to Mrs. Fildhurst's house, she was sitting out on the porch talking to Sissy.

"Is that your mother?" he asked.

"No," I said quickly. "She's too old."

He laughed. "Sorry. Your grandma?"

"Nope."

I opened the door to get out of the car. He was asking too many uncomfortable questions. I hadn't figured out how to answer them yet. It was better to say that Mrs. Fildhurst was my grandmother because I didn't want everyone to know that I was in a foster home, but I didn't want to lie to Jake. I never knew that leaving Mona would be so complicated. At least she was my real mother and the only thing I had to explain were the bruises.

Jordan walked out of the house. I knew he would be waiting for me when I got back. He didn't want to go to VBS either. I don't think anybody thought I'd go by myself. I smiled at my own independence.

Brother Jake grabbed my arm. "Xavier, you in a foster home?"

"Why you ask that?"

"Because I know *that* little kid is not your brother," he said, pointing at Jordan.

"Why? 'Cause he's white?" I asked, laughing.

"That was a clue. Plus my wife works for CPS. I know these types of things."

Brother Jake gave me his telephone number and told me that I could call him whenever. He asked if I'd like to hang out with him sometime even when VBS was over to play basketball or something like that. I was so excited. I hopped out of the truck and ran up the steps. Somebody wanted to spend time with *me*.

He leaned over in his truck and yelled out of the window. "I better see all of y'all at VBS tomorrow or I'll come get you myself."

The next day, my sister agreed to go. Sissy really went to see her boyfriend. Jordan didn't want to. I asked if it was because we were black.

"Kinda," he said.

"Don't worry about that, Jordan. You just my brother from another color mother, that's all. I feel like we're real brothers anyway. Plus, I saw some white kids there, too."

Jordan refused. I understood how he felt. It was hard explaining this life to people that had never lived it. We were kinda like a drawer of mismatched socks. I didn't push him. I went anyway. I wanted to hang out with Brother Jake again. On the last day of VBS after all the fun I'd had all week, I saw Mona. The only reason she hit me with the door was because I positioned myself in her path—on purpose.

I thought because she was so happy that I should take a chance and talk to her. Sissy told me not to. She said that I should go my way and let Mona go hers. It was the last day and not to ruin it for everybody. I couldn't help myself. Seeing the new Mona made me miss her. I wanted to get to know the Mona that threw water balloons with kids, wore nice clothes, and flipped her nice hair. Now that I saw the fun Mona, I knew she existed. It was unfair for other kids to know my mother in that way and not me. I guess that was the one time that I should have listened to Sissy.

I felt the blood trickling down my face as I watched Mona run out the door. She had never been able to stand up to Grandma Lenora. I snatched my shirt loose from her hand and backed away from her. She wasn't paying any attention to me anymore. She smoothed her hair back and faced Pastor Paul.

"Pastor, I was just—"

"No need to explain, *Sister* Lenora. I saw what you were doing and like I said, it's time for you to leave."

"But Pastor. Really, I had nothing to do with this. He tried to..."

"I heard enough to figure out the truth. Trust me. This sick picture is painfully clear. I don't have the desire to hear why I walked in here and you were putting your hands on this child— *your* grandchild." His voice rose in anger. "Now, if I have to tell you to leave my church one more time, I will have security escort you out of here. No, I take that back, I will toss you up out of here myself."

Pastor Paul walked up and stood beside me. She knew then that she was defeated. She gave me one final look of hatred before she straightened her jacket and smoothed her hair back again. Grandma Lenora turned and walked stiffly away. Maybe it was just me, but her walk, all of a sudden made her look a lot older.

"Don't forget to take your husband and *your daughter* with you," he said to her retreating back.

He turned me toward him. When I saw him earlier, he was different—happy. His face was sad now, like mine. I understood how he felt deep down inside where no one else would ever be able to see. Mona had hurt me too, just like that.

"What's your name?" Pastor Paul took a handkerchief out of his pocket and passed it to me.

"Xavier Thomas."

"Mona, is that your mother?"

I shook my head yes.

"I figured that," he said. "How many of you are there?"

"Three."

"Do you have a little brother about four years old?" he asked. He held his hand over the floor to Sean's approximate height.

"Yes, His name is Sean. He lives with his dad now. My sister's name is Genesis and she's here at VBS, too."

He didn't know we existed. Mona planned on marrying him and he didn't even know she had us. We were nobody, we were less than nothing. That's why Grandma Lenora was so angry when she saw me. Because I was here and because I had been born. I wanted to hate her, too. I willed myself to do it—hate. I didn't have enough energy left to do it.

I thought about something Mrs. Fildhurst had said when Sissy ran away. She told me the best revenge was to survive. She told me if I wanted to beat the system, then I had to force myself to really live. I had to use all the hate festering inside me as fuel to create the best me possible. That was good advice, except for some reason I wasn't angry enough to generate any fuel. I was really, really sad. I felt sorry for Mona for having the worst mother in the world. I was glad that I got away from her. I didn't care where I might end up, just as long as it wasn't with her. I knew that I would never trust Mona again.

Pastor Paul's phone rang, interrupting our conversation. Brother Jake yelled into the phone so loud that he seemed to be standing in the room with us.

"Get out here to the tree of life, NOW!" The phone went dead.

Pastor Paul took off without saying another word to me. He snatched the heavy door open and before it could close, I ran through it after him. I didn't know what I was running for, I just did.

Naomi

I HEARD A faint stifled scream from inside that mesh of trees, but it had gotten really dark and I was afraid to go in. I stood next to Jake's pickup, checking my phone for a response every few seconds. *Come on, Jake, hurry.* Something was going on. The air even felt solemn. I looked around and saw Nola run out from the side of the building and hop in her Jag, her tires screeched against the pavement as she sped off.

"No. Please No!" A girl's voice was clear that time as it wafted across the dimly lit parking lot.

I had to go in there. It was extremely dark and I was afraid; I could feel danger covering the air like a shroud. I walked toward the big tree slowly. I was trying to wait for Jake to catch up so that he could go in the brush of trees with me. I reached the clearing faster than I expected and the thicket of trees was only a few dark feet away. It was either go in or wait for Jake. I didn't hear any more screams, so I thought twice about entering, and then I heard moans of pleasure again.

I almost turned around. I was so irritated at the game these kids were playing that I marched straight through the trees. I forcefully pushed my way through the low hanging branches of the old tree. I didn't even try to be quiet as I huffed my way closer to the sounds. I wanted those bad kids to know that I was coming, perhaps give them a little time to make themselves decent. I wanted to bust them, but I didn't want to actually see anything.

The closer I got to the moans, the farther away they seemed, as though they were running from me. I used the tiny light from my cell phone to see. I was so furious that I cursed under my breath. I heard a thump and then there was silence. I knew they probably heard me coming.

Something reached out from the black cloak of the shady trees and pulled me, yanking my feet off the ground. My cell phone flew from my hand. I lay there for a moment, immersed in the muddy earth, dazed. That *was* a hand that grabbed me, wasn't it? I questioned whether I had really felt a hand wrap around my wrist or if I had tripped. I didn't hear the moans or screams anymore. It was quiet except for the sound of my breathing. Maybe I was imagining and my nerves were playing a trick on me.

I felt pressure fall on top of my body and that was when I attempted to scream, but a hand clamped down hard, covering my open mouth, smothering my howl. I bit at the fingers hard as I tried to push the mass off of me. I felt a smack to the left side of my face. My cheek burned from the sting, but I kept fighting and clawing.

"Stop it, girl. It's me. It's me," a man's voice said as he held my hands pressed down in the mud over my head."

My body froze. I stopped fighting and tried to force my eyes to adjust to the darkness, but the branches overhead blocked out whatever light the cloudy sky purposed for me.

"Yeah, that's it. Lay back and relax. It's Daddy," he said again.

My mouth felt as though it were full of peanut butter doused thick with fear. Had he moved his hand away from my trembling lips, I still wouldn't have been able to open my mouth.

"Mother told me to take care of Genesis," he said. "And I did." His rank breath fell on my face. He kissed my forehead.

"I took real good care of her and she's right over there taking a little nap. Just like you used to do after I loved on you." He kissed my forehead again. "You know, baby, I forgot how beautiful you were. You were always my number one princess. I don't know why you had to go and get pregnant by that dog. And what did he do? Huh?" He smacked me again. "He left your dumb ass. After that boy touched you for the first time, I knew it. I felt it in the way you made love to me after that. That's why Daddy didn't love you no more. You violated *our* bond with another man. I don't know why you did that to us. I would have given you anything." He hit me again—harder. "I loved you."

Uncle C thought that I was Mona, and I immediately felt sick and sorry for her at the same time. I felt his body tighten up over mine. I didn't want to speak. I didn't want him to know that I was Naomi and not Mona.

"I shouldn't have been surprised. Lenora did the same thing. I had been in love with her since she was a little girl when I babysat her every summer. She was so pretty back then, just like you were when you were little. When I came back home from college and she had your sister, Naomi." His grip on my hands tightened as his rage at Lenora elevated.

"By another man, another lowlife that didn't give a shit about her either—just like you. Oh, wait, you didn't even know you had a sister, did you?" He chuckled. "You look just like her, too."

He forced my legs open with his and rolled over on his side, releasing the pressure of his obese body off of mine. I was finally able to gasp for air. He didn't have any clothes on. I felt his manhood growing on my leg, and I was instantly repulsed and began to gag in between bouts of trying to inhale air into my lungs. He was so lost in his own world that he didn't notice because his hand continued to cover my mouth.

"I never understood how she could do that to me. We were like family. She said she was trying to get away from me, same as you did. Genesis almost got away, but I caught her just in time with that boy today. I stopped them." He snorted in laughter. "See, smell how sweet she is." He put his free hand over my nose so I could smell the essence of *my* young niece.

Although I was pinned underneath Uncle C, still I knew one thing for sure. If I got loose from him, I was going to kill him. *Period.* I closed my eyes and prayed that God would let me do it with my own hands. I envisioned the many ways I could slaughter the rabid dog—he was ready to be put down. I wanted to watch his heart stop beating. He needed to die, he deserved it. I planned to help him get to hell—first class. I convinced myself that it would be God's will if this fiend never breathed again.

Vengeance is the Lord's and I'm the executioner.

He yanked my arms. I inhaled the pain as he stretched them as far above my body as possible. He pinned them with one hand. He grabbed at my slacks with his free hand and pulled on the button until it popped free. I didn't fight him at all. I waited for my chance to wipe the bottom of my foot with his miserable existence. If I had to let him enter me, defile me, one more time, I would. I was so calm that I frightened myself; there were no tears or hysterics. I waited patiently because I knew that before I went to sleep that night, the bogeyman would be a sleeping legend—a ghost. I almost smiled at the peace in knowing that I finally had the perfect plan to rid myself of my demon.

He flicked his nasty tongue across my face. The residue of his saliva felt like a sticky paste spread across my cheek—wet and heavy. "Do you miss Daddy, Mona?" he asked snatching my thin shirt until the silky material shredded in his hands.

I moaned as if I enjoyed his aggression. I thrust my hips in mock anticipation. My mind only plotted out one detail of the plan at a time. First, I had to get him to relax and put his guards down. He was a lot older than me. However, he was stronger and he was still a man. I had to keep my wits together if I was going to finally slay...

"Oh, you like that, huh?" He slapped me again.

I thrust my hips up harder. I was completely numb inside, so I felt nothing.

"I've been waiting on this for so long, baby. Tell Daddy you missed him and I'll forgive you for everything you've done. Daddy will love you again. Tell me," he whispered harshly, climbing back on top of me, crushing my air supply again.

His penis thumped at my inner thigh in about the same spot where he had sliced me open with a shard of glass when I was six years old. He wanted to prove to me that he could really hurt me if he wanted to. *Bastard.*

"I loved you, Daddy." I heard Mona, but Uncle C didn't.

Mona screeched like a feral animal and her weight dropped on top of Uncle C's. His taut grip released my hands and I took that as my last opportunity to fight back. We clawed and kicked. Mona and I managed to strike each other as the darkness seemed to protect its master from our rambunctious blows. I yanked at her hair and she scratched my shoulder.

Somehow, Mona and I got tangled up in a heap still struggling with each other. Uncle C had disappeared and my mind sent constant reminder signals to kill him. I tasted blood on my tongue and I wanted it to be his.

Suddenly, the heavens opened up and the trees parted as the rain pounded on the already water logged earth. I finagled my way to my feet and reached out my hand to drag my sister up along with me. Two bright lights closed in on us and we were able to see the outline of Uncle C's naked body a few yards ahead of us. He was on his knees crawling through the dense mud. I took off after him, torn shirt, shoeless and all. I was going to kill him. I stumbled on a rock and picked it up.

I had my weapon and I moved quickly as the rock weighed heavily in my hand, itching, thirsty for blood—for revenge. Even the rock wanted me to bash Uncle C's head open. Mona was right by my side.

I heard Jake yell, "Get out here to the tree of life, NOW!"

That's where I was. What was he talking about? Delirious, and in position to rid myself and my new family of Uncle C forever, and I wasn't going to allow Jake to deter me.

"No, Naomi! Baby, come here." Jake's voice closed in on me.

Uncle C was in my sight. "No Jake, I'm okay. I'm going to kill that bastard, tonight," I yelled. "I need you to go find Genesis. She's out here somewhere, too."

Mona caught up to Uncle C first and suddenly he stood straight up and yelped as though in excruciating pain. He clutched his heart and fell down, hitting the ground with a thud, shaking violently.

Jake caught me and dragged me back to his truck, which he had driven straight through the cluster of trees and brush. His touch seemed to calm my thirst to kill—a little.

"At least go find Genesis," I shouted. "Please."

Pastor Paul and Xavier ran up just as Mona's squeals filled the air.

"Help us. Snakes. Snakes. They're on me. Help me. They're on Daddy." Mona danced in an eerie frenzy as though in a mad performance. She pulled her hair and snatched at her clothes. Her mind was gone, even in the dark, you could clearly see it.

Paul and Jake slipped and skidded through the thick mud until they were able to pull both Mona and Uncle C toward the truck. Mona kept screaming about snakes as she jumped and twitched, rubbed and touched herself.

Jake called the police on his cell phone and threw Paul his flashlight to help Xavier look around for Genesis. I crawled over to where Uncle C's naked body lay. I still had the rock in my hand. He jerked and grasped his heart and looked up helplessly at me.

I dropped the rock by his head, close enough for him to feel it. I knelt next to him. I leaned in close, hovering over his disgusting body and whispered in his ear, "Uncle C, I hope you can hear me. It's me, Naomi. I know you remember me and everything you did to me, so I won't talk about it now. You look like you are in pain, Uncle C. I was *going* to bust your head open with this rock." I nudged him on the side of his face with it.

"I'm so glad I changed my mind. Watching you squirm like this is much more fun." I laughed. "Now, do me a favor and go ahead and die right here—tonight. Don't try to fight the throbbing stirring in your body, let it take you. You see, if you don't allow yourself the privilege to die right now, I will make sure that you get screwed every day for the rest of your pitiful life in prison. It's your choice. You won't have to mess with little girls anymore. Oh, no. I will make it my business to make sure that you become somebody's prized bitch. I promise."

He wasn't able to answer, his lazy left eye jumped around frantically in his head. He grunted in pain as he stared up at me. I smiled as I watched him.

☙ ❧

"Well, was it a snake?" I asked.

"Yep, they found a bed of Texas Corals in a mucky hole," Jake said, looking at me. "The rain washed 'em up. They had a bunch of eggs they were trying to protect. They said he had about five bites on him. That's not what killed him though. He had a massive heart attack." Jake studied my face for a reaction.

I smirked. "What? Don't look at me like that, Jake." I raised my right hand. "I didn't do anything to that man. God said vengeance is mine."

"Look at you quoting the bible now." Jake laughed.

I stopped smiling. "And where is, umm? You know." I didn't want to taste her name on my lips.

"Lenora?" Jake hunched his shoulders and frowned. His face was full of disappointment. "Doesn't even matter right now. We have more important people to worry about." Jake squeezed my shoulder and I rested my head on his chest.

"Did you say it was a Texas Coral, Uncle Jake?" Xavier asked.

"Yeah. Why? You know something about them? Jake asked.

"Sissy does. She loves snakes. She told me once that those were poisonous." Xavier grasped his sister's hand tightly in his. "When will she be able to get out of here?"

"Soon, baby."

"What's gonna happen to Mona?" Xavier asked.

"Boy, you are full of questions." I tried to smile at him. "They admitted her to the state mental institution. She will get the kind of help she needs in there."

He sighed and stared at his sister. He touched the IV that slowly dripped pain medication into her body. They had sedated her to ease the trauma; she was hysterical when they brought her in. I knew she would be okay in time, physically. It was the emotional scarring I was more worried about.

"I'm really alone now," Xavier said sadly.

"Oh really, so me and your uncle Jake are invisible? I already told you that you have us now. We're your family. Can you believe it?" I walked over to him and gave him a big hug. "I love you, Xavier. I loved you the first day I laid my eyes on you."

He smiled warily but didn't say anything. It was too much for even me to believe.

He squeezed Genesis' hand again. "I miss her. Do you want to know what else she told me about Texas Corals?" he changed the subject.

"What?" I was willing to be patient. I knew that teaching someone *how* to accept love wasn't going to be easy. Jake and I had already talked about it, we were up for it.

"You will always be able to tell if a snake is poisonous like a Texas Coral by remembering this rhyme, red touch yellow—"

Genesis blinked her eyes open and said softly, "Kill a fellow."

"Why did you think Dae and Jake would betray you that way?"

"I don't know. Like I told you before, nobody ever loved me. I must have deceived myself into seeing what wasn't really there. I think that I was somehow always waiting for them to hurt me— like everybody else in my life that said they loved me did. I forced myself to believe my negative thoughts."

"Naomi, love is something you must accept in order to have."

I smiled when she said that.

"Why are you smiling?" she asked.

I didn't know how to explain to Dr. Dalton that it had taken all of that to happen for me to finally get it. Somehow telling her everything helped me put my life in the right perspective—made my life seem much clearer. So clear in fact that I could now feel the sun reach down from the heavens and kiss my face even on the cloudiest day. I was ready to see life and truly experience everything it had to offer. I was no longer running from anything, especially not my past. I was really living for a change.

"Because you're right. Thank you for today, Dr. Dalton." I sat up on the sofa and glanced at my watch. "Look at the time. I have to go. My family is waiting for me."

"Oh, Naomi. One more thing before we wrap up. I'd like to give you a little something to think about for our next session. Tell me, how will you handle Nola, if she wants back in your life? What if she wants to be a part of your new family?"

"Wow, that's a really good question, Doctor. I'll give it a little thought. See you next time."

AFTERWORD

EVELYN L. POLK, LMFT

"Hurt People Hurt People"…is an old adage many of us have heard repeatedly over the years. However, the true implications of this statement often go unacknowledged, buried underneath a semblance of normalcy until fatal tragedy strikes. I am currently a licensed Marriage, Family and Child Therapist, and I have worked in the field of Child Welfare and Foster Care for more than 30 years. It is apparent to me that just as a forensic investigator might detect blood, and follows the cold trail to/from the scene of a crime; it is much the same with invisible wounds of the heart. When one encounters a person who from all human perspective, seems heartless, I challenge you to look closely long enough and you will usually find pieces and trails of a bleeding heart(s) protruding and decay from a very dark place lost within the inner child.

Looking at the characters vividly portrayed in this book by Ms. Laushaul who boldly and shockingly speak and act out their truths, realities, it is easy to dislike, even hate, judge and wish harm and eternal damnation to these perpetrators of abuse, (both self and to others). However, it sometimes also goes unsuspected and unrevealed that harm is usually what initially brought the abuser into the place of a living hell before becoming the demons of demise themselves.

As you read the intertwined stories of the characters in Running from Solace, you may have found yourself experiencing very real and intense emotions of shock, disgust, protectiveness, fear, vengeance, relief, laughter, familiarity, and discomfort, to name a few; and even some physical reactions in your body e.g., uneasiness in the pit of your stomach, a lump or tightness in your throat or chest, among other responses. Did you find your feelings and perceptions of the different characters changing as their stories unfolded? Did you hear yourself talking to, yelling at, comforting, or praying for the characters? Did you want to explain certain things to/for them? If you experienced any of the above, your response to the broken hearted inner child explanation still could possibly be, "Well, so what! Everybody has a story!" And you're absolutely right! Everyone on this earth is living their *life story*. However, we ALL play a role as either participatory or non-participatory characters in the lives of those whose journeys we cross. I hope through this book you have been incited to pay a more in-depth attention to the faces and hearts underneath the masks and behaviors of your inner child, and the real life stories of those who are targets, survivors, perpetrators, or protectors of abuse, of which you are a part. Make a bold declaration to consciously choose to direct your actions in a participatory manner towards bringing yourself and others through awareness, boundary setting, intercession and forgiveness, to a place of spiritual, mental, and emotional reconciliation and solace.

Hearts & Blessings!
Evelyn Polk, LMFT Founder, For A Child's H.E.A.R.T., Inc.
Author, It's Heart Work: Being The Village That Raises A Child

"Do Something Special For A Child's Heart"
www.forachildsheart.org

ACKNOWLEDGMENTS

Lord, you activated the *write now* button in me and gave my life more meaning, more purpose, more depth, more everything than I ever imagined. I thought that I was destined to be ordinary and You spoke Jeremiah 1:29 over my life, my hands, my mind, and my heart. Thank you Lord. I won't disappoint You.

My beautiful son, Jovante Tunon. I am the envy of all the mommies in Mommyland. Raising you is my true pleasure. Everybody wants a J like mine. You have cooked for me, washed my clothes, put me to bed, and encouraged me with kisses as I sat glued to my desk for countless hours writing, thinking, crying, and hoping without letting nary a complaint fall from your lips. My success is ours. You know how we do it. Mom loves you.

Austin, Savannah, Dakota, Brandon, Jazzi (a special, THANK YOU for all of your encouragement. All those nights you rushed me off to write because you needed to know what was going to happen next gave me fuel. Bet you thought I'd forget—never!), Greg, Jaison, Jayvier & Jackie, you all live in my heart.

Now, how do I acknowledge someone that never grows weary of me? Who are you? My brother? My father? You are everywhere in my life and become a blur, my dear cousin, Maurice Hawkins. Brooke Hawkins, my number one fan, my sister and friend, my first reader and cheerleader. Okay, I have to stop this list or it will go on forever. You are a blessing. Grandma Ethel & Rita Rushing, *keeping it real?* I learned how by watching you.

The Pack: Dev Isemeyer, Susan Espree, & Isa Neuenhaus, thank you for all you do. Arnette Zimmerman, my BFF and fan from the beginning, love you. Mary & Eric Grant, it's showtime again.

Tonja Watkins, you told me and I am ready. Adria Carter, always there! Women of Strength, keep praying for me. Monica Bates, my how we've grown together. Nikea Moffett, you have been so helpful to this project. You are every writer's dream reader—thank you for being there for me, sister. Angela Thomas, every time I call with this book stuff—you say yes—my ego thanks you. Patrice & Jerome Simmons, what would I do without you? Todd Needom (Kliktastik), I cherish your assistance, opinion, friendship, and I got mad respect for your talent! Kayla Perez (Pixel Parties), now you know this cover is all that— right? Amanda Canales, thank you for letting me use our cutie, Lucinda Canales, picture perfect! Ms. E (For A Child's Heart), your passion is a blessing to many, including me. James Z. Smith, *my* B.U.D.D.Y. and Geoffrey Ball for always coming through for ya girl.

Ella Curry, your advice and encouragement—I ate it all up and used it. To my editors, Shonell Bacon and D'edra Armstrong, thank you! You are priceless. Get ready to do it again and again and again.

My literary family, it's nothing but love for *all* of you. Monique D. Mensah (Inside Rain), we're back like the Terminator. Cherlisa Richardson, my ear whenever I need it (tag 2X—come on girl). Marguerite Benjamin Parker (Where Credit Is Due), you believed in me from day one. C. Mikki (Men & Sex), "put yo big girl panties on and keep it movin." My all night writers, Kimberly Bibbs, Sheretta Edwards, & Faynetta Burrle, you ladies kept me going, high on encouragement. Patricia Haley, you know just when to come in, thank you! Tia Ross, what can I say about you? You inspire me. Is there anything you can't do? Here's another one for Team BWRC! Thank you.

A special thank you to ALL the readers that take the time to shoot me an email, you inspire me! And of course, a proper and useful acknowledgment just wouldn't be right if I didn't miss somebody. You know the routine, put your name right here _____, cause YOU know that I that didn't mean to forget about YOU, with your extra special self.

NOTE FROM THE AUTHOR

That's it, for now. I hope you enjoyed reading Running from Solace as much as I enjoyed writing it. It took me a long time to pen this story and write the truths of this particular set of characters, so let me know what you think. Visit my website for Running from Solace discussion questions. Also, please check out my other title, The Truth As I See It: In Poetry & Prose.

I'm currently working on another novel, Do You Know Daisy McCloud? So keep an eye out for it. For now, hold tight, I'm always in the literary lab dreaming up new and exciting story-lines for your reading pleasure. Well, when I'm not shuttling my teenage son around Houston, Texas, where we currently live.

In the meantime, come and rant it up with me online. Check out my blog! Random Rants of Truth of a Social Butterfly: http://nakialaushaul.blogspot.com and visit my web site for new happenings at www.nakiarlaushaul.com.

Until next time,
Nakia R. Laushaul

CPSIA information can be obtained at www.ICGtesting.com
Printed in the USA
LVOW061506190612

286815LV00003B/5/P

10